Judy Astley was frequ[...]
dreaming at her drearily [...]
found it to be the ideal training for becoming a
writer. There were several false starts to her career:
secretary at an all-male Oxford college (sacked for
undisclosable reasons), at an airline (decided, after
a crash and a hijacking, that she was safer elsewhere) and as a dress designer (quit before anyone
noticed that she was adapting *Vogue* patterns). She
spent some years as a parent and as a painter before
sensing that the day was approaching when she'd
have to go out and get a Proper Job. With a nagging
certainty that she was temperamentally unemploy-
able, and desperate to avoid office coffee, having to
wear tights every day and missing out on sunny
days on Cornish beaches with her daughters, she
wrote her first novel, *Just for the Summer*. She has
now had eight novels published by Black Swan.

www.booksattransworld.co.uk

THE RIGHT THING

Judy Astley

BLACK SWAN

THE RIGHT THING
A BLACK SWAN BOOK : 0 552 99768 4

First publication in Great Britain

PRINTING HISTORY
Black Swan edition published 1999

5 7 9 10 8 6

Copyright © Judy Astley 1999

Set in 11pt Melior by
County Typesetters, Margate, Kent.

Black Swan Books are published by Transworld Publishers,
61-63 Uxbridge Road, London W5 5SA,
a division of The Random House Group Ltd,
in Australia by Random House Australia (Pty) Ltd,
20 Alfred Street, Milsons Point, Sydney, NSW 2061, Australia,
in New Zealand by Random House New Zealand Ltd,
18 Poland Road, Glenfield, Auckland 10, New Zealand
and in South Africa by Random House (Pty) Ltd,
Endulini, 5a Jubilee Road, Parktown 2193, South Africa.

Penguin Random House is committed to a sustainable future for
our business, our readers and our planet. This book is made from
Forest Stewardship Council® certified paper.

Printed and bound in Great Britain by Clays Ltd, St Ives plc

For Annie, my dancing friend

Chapter One

Large Antonia must have slimmed down a huge
amount to fit into her coffin. Instead of the four-
square mahogany box the size of a grandmother's
wardrobe that Kitty had been expecting, the casket
was a narrow, elegant pale oak number, reminding
her of the flooring she'd almost chosen for the sitting-
room. She was glad now that she'd gone for the beech
instead. The last thing she wanted, as she trod
between the front door and the kitchen for the next
however many years, was to be reminded of the tall
fat frightened girl she and Julia Taggart and others
had so brutally bullied at school all that time ago.

'Upside down in the Range Rover, three hours to
cut her out . . .' a woman was murmuring in the pew
behind her. Julia Taggart, next to Kitty, turned her
ferrety head and her eyes swivelled sideways to see
who was speaking. Kitty nudged her, embarrassed.
Julia had always been shamelessly nosy, progressing
from early trawling for scandal with her ear to the
school staffroom door to taking on the running of
the Hartsvale Old Girls newsletter. No-one she'd ever
come across in her whole life could marry, give birth,
get divorced, ennobled, imprisoned or die without
the information somehow finding its way past Julia
first.

The small village church was full and its chill

stony air was moist with so much unaccustomed collective breath. Some people were even standing at the back, and as the congregation rose to sing 'Jerusalem' Kitty wondered how many of them, like her, were simply there through chance rather than a heartfelt wish to pay their last respects to Antonia.

'Oh *do* come with me, it's only a couple of miles from you. I'll come to you, stay the night, and we can go together,' Julia had persuaded over the phone, assuming as all people from London did that Devon-and-Cornwall formed just a teeny village peninsula tacked prettily on to the end of England. 'After all, funerals aren't like weddings are they, you don't need invitations. No-one will ever know you weren't her very closest friend. They'll just assume you kept up with her through the HOGS, like I did.'

'*Except* her very closest friends, not to mention her family, her neighbours, all that. And I haven't even set eyes on her since the final speech day,' Kitty had protested, picturing Large Antonia at fourteen, green eyes wild for mercy as Kitty, Julia, Rosemary-Jane Pigott and the rest of their vicious circle had hoisted her up high in the cloakroom and made her swing from the hot-water pipes till she shrieked with pain. What a cruel, exaggerated fuss they'd made about the weight of her, stamping and circling the great dangling body with rhythmic chants of '*Large! Large!*' and falling to the floor in mock-faint as if they'd just captured an elephant and hauled it up a tree.

'And it's not just a couple of miles, either, Julia,' Kitty had added, 'it's at least fifty from down here and the far side of Bodmin.'

'Yes but,' and Julia pulled out the clincher, 'you just *must* see her house, it's to die for, truly.' Not perhaps the best choice of words in the circumstances, Kitty now thought as she mouthed her way through what had been their school hymn. She doubted it would have been Antonia's favourite. There could hardly have been happy abiding memories of her time at their dull Home Counties girls' school where the casual spite of the pupils was equalled by a bitter streak of sarcasm among disappointed teaching staff envying the careless youth of their charges. It was possible she'd never spoken of those days since, either walling up the hurt from the awful years or even shrugging them off with no apparent effort. Either of those would be just as well, if Kitty and Julia were to offer convincing sympathy to Antonia's widower in the polite funeral aftermath out in the churchyard. How awful, but how justified, if he chose that moment to accuse loudly, 'Oh, so *you're* two of those bullying bitches she talked about . . .'

The house *was* worth the trip, though. It took pride of place on the edge of the village, just tantalizingly visible from the road. Driving past its ornate iron gates on their way to the church, Kitty could only admit that Julia had been quite right, it wasn't often you got a close look at one as grand as that without paying folding money on the door first. Antonia, against any odds Ladbrokes would have dreamt of offering, had married more than well and lived in mellow Georgian splendour in the depths of personal parkland just out of view of the farm her husband's family had run for several generations. It was owed to her, Kitty granted guiltily, after that appalling teenagehood. Some sort of compensating karma must have been operating the day Large Antonia met the supremely eligible man she was soon to marry. Kitty, coming in with well-remembered precision on the beat for '"*Bring* me my bow of burning gold . . ."' wondered why the fickle gods had then so callously changed their minds, claiming Antonia back soon after her forty-first birthday. They must have loved her. Wasn't that what they said, that those the gods loved died young, like Princess Diana, Marilyn Monroe and Jimi Hendrix? They wouldn't love me, Kitty admitted to herself, eyes meekly towards the floor during the Lord's Prayer, I'm just a run-of-the-mill not-bad-not-good person who doesn't deserve any special deal. She saw herself condemned to a stickily overripe old age, mouldering in a plastic-covered chair in front of daytime TV, wondering if Lily and Petroc (teenagers now, but they'd be sulky pensioners themselves by then) were ever going to visit.

The coffin was being lifted and carried back along the aisle and Kitty thought of her children. Not so much the two who thrived and prospered in lazy comfort at home, but the absent one from before their time that she'd called Madeleine and given away to strangers. She might be dead too, perhaps years ago or yesterday, Kitty couldn't know. Her mind skipped through a variety of possible coffins, starting with a tragically tiny one, white, posy-decked and carried lovingly in the arms of a grey-faced, weeping man. Next she thought of a box like Antonia's, narrow and pale but shorter – a child who'd dashed out into the road after a puppy, or, heart-churningly, a dark wood-land murder victim, half rotten from months in a shallow grave. Kitty felt in her pocket for a tissue and dabbed at her eyes as Antonia's mortal remains were borne past the end of her pew. No-one would guess it wasn't a lost schoolfriend she was grieving for, but a misplaced baby.

'We'll go back to the house. There'll be drinks,' Julia hissed in Kitty's ear a little later as they lurked politely at the back of the crowd by the graveside.

'I'd rather just go home,' Kitty murmured. It was cold; March darkness was starting to sneak up on the afternoon sky and she longed for her big snug kitchen and the soft constant breath of the sea out beyond the window.

'Well *I'd* rather just go home too, but what would it look like, and besides . . .' Julia was looking round rather wildly as if she was seeking out someone in particular. Her pointed nose jabbed at the air as she searched through the backs of the assembled heads. The rector was doing 'ashes to ashes . . .' and Kitty tried not to hear him throwing the first terrible clod of earth down onto poor Antonia's casket.

'Besides what?' she whispered.

'Oh, just *besides*. You never know who's here do you?'

'Well we won't know any of them anyway, so what's the difference?' Kitty's feet, in too-delicate black suede boots, felt as if they were turning to stone.

Julia's face moved close enough to Kitty's for her to scent the pre-funeral sherry. She whispered, 'Oh you'd be surprised. You'll never guess who rang and said she'd be coming . . .' A tall broad man in front of them turned and glared and Kitty, feeling small and told-off, stared at the ground, mortified. She shifted her feet in an effort to see if her toes still moved without cracking and tried to concentrate on how awful the whole day was. Antonia had children, three of them, evenly spaced in size like Russian dolls from mid-teens or so down to about ten, welded together at the grave-edge in their grief, clinging and weeping quietly, their distraught faces every bit as scarlet as Antonia's had habitually been through her tortured schooldays. She might well have wept daily, too, either after or before school hours, perhaps both. Probably the salt tears had worn her skin to that rough red rawness that so astoundingly clashed with her crazy tangerine hair. Poor girl, if only she hadn't looked so *exactly* like a victim. She'd been

11

irresistible bully-fodder, a devil-sent target. No counselling had existed to help her then, no Childline, no comfortable teacher-pupil committees where sweet moral reason prevailed, no drama work-shops on the evils of pupil malice, with role-play and group hugs. Fair play had been something to do with netball, complaining about classmates was snitching and intolerance of the odd hard knock (mental or physical) was drippily spineless. Most of the stiff-backed schoolmistresses had worked their way through a world war and considered a good dose of being hard-done-by to be character-building, so there'd been no point seeking sympathy there.

'I am sorry, Antonia,' Kitty whispered under her breath. The man in front flicked his head slightly again and she shuffled guiltily backwards away from the crowd to where a looming churchyard yew pro-vided shelter from the bitter breeze. Around her chilled feet fat bright spikes that would become blue-bells were pushing their determined way through the earth, and she marvelled at their ability to thrive so well in the shade of this ancient, almost black, tree.

'Kit Cochrane! I *thought* it was you! Saw you in the church with old J. Taggart. After so long one can't be sure, can one?' The voice, a sort of piercing hiss like a cross cat, seemed to be coming from inside the tree and Kitty peered through the branches to where she could just make out a glow from a cigarette and a long thin shape swathed in layers of pale grey wool. 'I mean, we could all have been only steps away from each other on any number of occasions and not known about it. School fêtes, Sainsbury's, airport check-ins, all that.'

The garrulous body stepped forward into the light and Kitty gasped. 'Good grief, Rosemary-Jane Pigott!' she squawked.

'Ssh! They're still at it over there!' Rosemary-Jane

giggled. 'And it's just Rose now, and Ruthermere, by way of Madison, not Pigott any more, but then you knew that, didn't you? All years ago, of course.'

'No I didn't know actually. Julia insists on sending me the HOGS newsletters even though I don't subscribe, but she can't force me to read them.' Kitty laughed. She didn't much feel like laughing. No less than three of poor Antonia's childhood tormentors turning up at her funeral was no joke to anyone.

'So. Come to make sure poor old Large is really dead?' Rose grinned, her teeth huge and menacing. Gums receding, Kitty noted, certain that Rosemary-Jane's pretty little egg-shaped face at seventeen had been nothing like as wolfish.

'I was dragged along by Julia, actually,' Kitty confessed. 'She's always trying to round me up for some Old Girls' function or other and insisted that this particular event was "in your area, sweetie". She even came down into deepest Cornwall and stayed the night with us, just to make sure I couldn't back out. I wish I had. This is awful isn't it. Poor Antonia. And those children . . .' Kitty felt glum and shivery. She wanted very much to ask Rose exactly which Ruthermere she'd married, just so she could be reassured that it wasn't Ben. Of course it wouldn't be. Clever Rose had gone off to Oxford straight from school, then married someone glamorous on the fringes of motor racing. She could have come across dozens of people with Ben's particular surname. Whoever would slink back to their home town with a dazzling degree and one flighty marriage behind her and marry some underpowered local? Even the question would sound dismally parochial.

'Oh, so you two found each other.' Julia looked disappointed, discovering Rose and Kitty together by the yew, thwarted by the two of them managing this small reunion all by themselves. The graveside gathering was dispersing. Groups of mourners hovered near their cars, giving each other gentle hugs of comfort and chatting quietly. An impatient groundsman smoked against the side wall of the chapel, leaning on his spade and wishing them all away so he could get on with the filling-in that nobody liked to see and go home.

'We must all go together, back to Antonia's place for the knees-up,' Rose suggested brightly, striding off across the grass without waiting for a reply.

'Is it really such a good idea?' Kitty hesitated. 'I mean, Antonia might well have talked about us at home, you know, to her family about how her school-days were . . .'

Rose turned and looked at her, puzzled. She pulled the blanket-like grey coat around her, folding her arms across her long angled body. Kitty recalled their games mistress, keen on deportment, commenting that Rosemary-Jane always looked as if she was lounging against a gatepost that no-one else could see. 'Whatever do you mean?' she now asked Kitty, head on one side like a confused dog. 'We were her *very best* friends!'

'Absolutely,' Julia agreed, sliding her arm through Kitty's and pulling her towards the cars. 'I mean, if she'd had that bad a time, she wouldn't have kept up with the Old Girls, now would she?'

Kitty thought about being warm, about a smoked-salmon sandwich, just the one small creamy sherry and perhaps a log fire to thaw her bones. 'OK. Just for half an hour and then I must get going,' she conceded.

Rose and Julia, one each side, smiled at her, smart women in early middle age who were wearing more than well enough and were pleased with themselves.

'There you are, you see, not so difficult is it?' Julia

said, satisfied at having got her own way. 'Now isn't this nice, the three of us all together again?'

Antonia's widower greeted his guests with unnerving gratitude, welcoming Kitty, Julia and Rose into a suitably subdued library — all treacle-dark shelves and murky book-spines. A large buffet was laid out on a table beneath rows of ancient volumes that were probably being secretly munched away by paper-mites, and trays of what looked like the traditional post-death sherry were being offered round. Kitty was rather disappointed. There weren't many houses like this one that hadn't been fossilized by the National Trust and were actually properly lived in and still evolving. She'd been looking forward to inspecting a grand pale-panelled drawing-room, overlooking the terraced formal gardens she'd glimpsed from the drive, and having a look at what she assumed would be terrifically good heirloom paintings. Perhaps the family hadn't wanted to blight future enjoyment of such a room with sad memories of this funeral feast. And maybe Antonia's broken body had been brought to lie in state in here and after today the room would be locked and left with romantic poignancy to the dust.

'Tom Goodrich, so sweet of you to come.' Antonia's husband shook Kitty's hand briefly but with strength. His hand was hard and dry, an outdoor hand. He was tall, broad but not fat and with that lucky handsomeness that some men have when the lines on their face deepen in all the right places with age. Lamentably tempted, Kitty looked him straight in the eye and hoped he couldn't tell she was trying hard to imagine him naked aboard the schoolgirl Large Antonia that she remembered. Somehow she could only summon up a ludicrous cubist tableau of a tanned muscly slab balanced precariously on a mottled red and white jelly. 'Er, Kitty Harding um . . . old friend of Antonia's. So sorry . . .' she mumbled, feeling ridiculous and ashamed. How could she claim to be 'so sorry' about someone she hadn't actually seen for more than twenty years? And 'so sorry' was such a pathetically limp phrase of general pity for untimely death. Anyone's.

Rose, with no such compunctions and a boldness that Kitty well recalled, was kissing Tom on each cheek, carefully as if deliberately choosing for her lips the most tender spot. Her face was a picture of barely-contained profound grief and Kitty marvelled at her temerity. This, after all, was the woman who had once, in a moment of after-hockey 'helpfulness', threaded a big dead goldfish from the biology lab tank into his late wife's untidy carroty plait. Hours later in Maths Antonia's shrieks had made the windows quake. Julia waited behind for her handshake, watching Rose closely, a small knowing smile hovering on her lips, which she banished quickly as her turn came and she made her own obsequious mutterings.

'I take it back. It *is* just like a wedding reception,' Julia whispered to Kitty over the sandwiches. 'Only needs a string of cute bridesmaids and Antonia's mother in a hat. I wonder whatever happened to her, by the way. I *should* know, come to think of it.' She looked intensely thoughtful, mentally thumbing through back numbers of the Old Hartsvale newsletters.

'Fizzled out quietly in a nursing home, couple of years back,' Rose chimed in, her impatient fingers playing with an unlit cigarette. Her eyes scanned the room for a fellow-smoker, squinting slightly. At school Kitty remembered she'd possessed glasses but only worn them for games, to make sure she wasn't called upon to do anything too strenuous.

'How do you know that? You really *did* keep up with Antonia then?' Kitty asked. After the way Antonia had been treated, Kitty could hardly imagine she'd have been thrilled to chat with Rose over a diet lunch, or ring up to swop intimate gigglings on pregnancy problems.

Rose grinned, those huge teeth glinting. 'Well you know, sort of. Here and there. More Tom really, I suppose. To do with work, of course. My company makes garden programmes for TV. We came down here and did this one. It's gorgeous out there, you should just see. I was *amazed* of course, you can imagine, to find out who Tom had married. I suppose I've run into him in London once or twice since.' The hand with the cigarette was gesturing airily and her voice had a peculiar over-casual drawl to it, Kitty thought, as if she was saying something she'd rehearsed. It left a sense of information omitted.

Kitty felt slightly nauseous after guzzling three deceptively delicate cucumber and cream cheese sandwiches far too fast, and wandered off in search of fresh air. She squeezed past guests who, loosened by drink and relieved to be neither dead nor outside in the cold, had progressed to general discussion of schools, racing and the price of land. The children were not in the room and Kitty imagined the younger ones in a vast basement kitchen, cuddling up to a rotund cook and being allowed to dip their fingers into bowls of chocolate cake-mix. If the teenager was anything like Lily – and he'd looked about fifteen – he would be skulking in his room, submerging his grief in loud music and wishing all these sociably mingling guests to hell.

She headed towards the back of the house, hoping to find the elaborate conservatory she'd spotted from the driveway and draw breath among cool greenery, away from the cocktail-party atmosphere in the library.

'Looking for the loo? There's one just round that corner on the left.' Tom emerged from a brightly lit corridor, presumably leading from the kitchen (not in a basement then, and probably with a hostile au pair, not a cook) carrying several bottles of wine.

'Oh er, yes. Good idea.' Kitty felt awkward, wary. Tom might haul her into a corner and cross-examine her on her relationship with his wife. She bit her lip.

'You OK?' Tom hesitated, waiting for her to follow his directions.

'As much as one can be at these things,' she replied with a smile that she hoped looked sympathetic enough. The English simply weren't good at grief, she thought, they were just too fearful of emotion. Tom might have wanted to collapse onto a bed, clutching Antonia's oldest nightie, and simply howl like a lonely spaniel. Instead he had to top up glasses and look pleased to have guests.

A collection of framed family photos hung on the lavatory walls. As in Kitty's own home, they were just informal holiday and home shots, people having fun together, children at various stages of growth in gardens, on horses, on beaches, skiing. Kitty had a good look at them, noting with some surprise how Antonia had, as her own mother would have put it, 'grown into' her looks. As a girl she'd been constantly out of place, appearance-wise. Always cumbersome and red. On school photos she'd had to be the one at the end of the row, sticking up too far to be placed in a line, found space for after the neat symmetrical ones with manageable hair and clothes that fitted properly had filed in. She'd been the one, on the school ski trip (oh brave Antonia) who'd been too big for the hire company that had supplied all their ski-wear and had had to be equipped with a man's

18

salopettes and jacket. As an adult, Kitty could see, she'd found her niche, her man and her role. She hadn't found Weight Watchers though, that was also clear from the photos.

Looking at the pictures of this robust and jolly woman with a proud cloud of auburn hair, Kitty shuddered at the dreadful casual suddenness with which such a strong, vibrant life could be snuffed out. The world was full of frail, skinny people who, as they said, looked as if a puff of wind would knock them down, as if the slightest chill could be the edge of pneumonia. But really there was no difference when the cat-like gods chose to play with the mouse-like mortals: size and vulnerability just weren't linked. She flushed the loo and had a last look at the photos, sad for the young, laughing children whose childhood had been blighted the day their mother drove her car up an oak tree. The baby Madeleine's adoptive mother might be dead too, she suddenly thought. But surely, if that had happened, she'd come looking for her, there were ways of doing that now, unless she'd never been told she was adopted. Quickly she rinsed her hands under the green-mottled brass tap. She was taking too long, thinking too morosely and outside the door she could hear people waiting, murmuring.

'Of course it wasn't exactly an accident, you know.' Kitty's hands froze on the towel and her ears tingled with the effort to listen.

'Everybody knows that. Doesn't even need saying.'

'Broken heart.'

'Bastard. They all are. Who'd kill themselves over a man?' A sharp inhalation of cigarette followed.

Kitty opened the door and a trio of women smiled politely, assuring each other of nothing untoward heard or said. So that's how Antonia got thin, Kitty decided. Some cheated-on women hit the fridge, cramming food into their faces double-handed: left-over chicken, taramasalata scooped with their fingers and chunks of hard cheese wolfed down too fast to notice the irony. Presumably Antonia had been one of the other sort, the starvers and fretters and the takers to the vodka. In a rush of fondness for Glyn, who'd be wondering where she'd got to, Kitty thought of hearth and home. On reaching the library again she looked round for Julia.

'If you still want a lift to Bodmin Parkway we have to go now,' she told her. 'I promised I wouldn't be back too late. I've got this out-of-season prize-winning author checking in tomorrow and loads to do.'

'I forgot you're a *landlady*.' Julia's small mouth pursed up as much as it was able, reminding Kitty of a cat's bottom.

'Usually only in the summer. In the winter I'm still a painter. When you specialize in local scenic views it's a lot easier when the tourists aren't cluttering up the horizon.'

'Oh yes, I remember you were arty at school. I called you a creep for volunteering to paint the scenery for the play. A landlady though . . .' Julia mused. Kitty could see exactly the picture Julia was conjuring up.

'Hey, I don't wear fluffy high-heeled mules and charge for use of cruet you know, and they're all writers, there for either their own projects or a work-shop session so they're pretty much self-contained,' Kitty reminded her patiently. 'So are you coming, or shall I make my goodbyes and disappear?'

Julia peered past Kitty and gazed around the room. 'Oh look, there's Rose, still here, must just say bye-bye to her. She's got a lot of nerve, I'll say that for her,' Julia murmured, gazing at her oldest friend with admiration. Kitty waited, holding her breath. Rose was standing by a small and delicate walnut desk, her hand resting carelessly among silver-framed photos. Kitty guessed they must be more family shots. She looked like a cat toying idly with treasures in a room from which it was normally banned. As if she was listening to her thoughts, Rose shifted slightly and smiled across at Kitty over the shoulder of the man she was talking to, Tom.

'She's got a perfectly good husband of her own at home. Her second one of course, but then women like Rose rarely stop at one,' Julia confided through discreetly gritted teeth. 'But of course you knew that, didn't you?' This was the second time that afternoon that this assumption had been made. Kitty felt even more in the dark than before. 'Old boyfriend of yours from the sixth form, *you* know the one, just before your little bit of trouble.' Kitty felt a horrible urge to put her hands over her ears to make it not true but it was too late. 'Ben Ruthermere.' Julia's wide eyes were slightly bloodshot. 'Don't tell me you don't remember. She ran into him in Paris, oh, five years back. Coincidence or what?'

Kitty couldn't tell her she didn't remember Ben so she didn't reply. Julia was looking mildly triumphant. 'You should have read all those HOGS newsletters, you see, instead of shredding them up for your organic compost heap or whatever.'

Kitty looked across at Rosemary-Jane who was still eye to eye with Large Antonia's husband. Ben Ruthermere, fresh out of the sixth form, sexual novice and all-round ordinary boy, had never known he was Madeleine's father. So he'd married Rosemary-Jane Pigott who could hardly be better cast as a wicked stepmother. Or just simply as wicked.

Chapter Two

Kitty fought her way up from a dream in which her father, towering huge through candlelight, was thumping the edge of the pulpit and denting the wood like dough, leaving a caving imprint of his pudgy hand. His bulk loomed bigger than a Disney monster's shadow and he leaned hard with the palms of his hands so the wood bulged forward, out like a ship's prow. Beneath it in the congregation were hundreds of identical grey crocheted hats on heads that cowered and keened and wailed into white twitching hankies with hand-embroidered corner initials in pink. Kitty's eyes flickered open with relief that this wasn't how she would ever again have to spend a Sunday morning. Her father had been a vicar with a keen eye for promotion and a congregation of adoring old ladies squabbling over the church-hall tea urn and flower rota, just like characters in a Barbara Pym novel. Humble, penitent and pious during his fiery services, the faithful would emerge from his church shaking off their sins in the sunlight like dogs fresh out of a river. Thus purged, they'd go straight back to claim-staking over the post-service biscuit provision and whose turn it was to tidy away the vestments. 'Worth your weight,' he used to smarm and charm at them, though weight in what he never specified. In manky old tea-leaves, Kitty used to think whenever she found furtive pairs of these women hunkered down on the vicarage sitting-room floor, picking through bags of jumble like rooks on a run-over squirrel.

Kitty's waking mind found its way back to the present and she thought about Julia, the day before, referring to her 'little bit of trouble'. It was just the sort of dust-under-the-carpet euphemism her parents had favoured. Julia enjoyed the phrase because it hinted at the privilege of knowing a secret; her mother liked it because it avoided uncomfortable truth. 'Trouble' was what Kitty had 'got herself into', as if no-one else could possibly be involved and she'd done it out of spite. With a father who feared his bishop far more than he feared God, this Trouble had to be got out of the house and away from sight as fast as possible. The right thing had to be done.

The trouble hadn't felt so little at the time, either. *She* hadn't felt so little. Her grossly pregnant eighteen-year-old body, skin distended to near-translucency by a baby that must have been meant for a much bigger and more grown-up mother, had felt like a dragged sack of swedes. She'd felt as if between her legs some precarious collapsing bulge was threatening to thrust its way to her knees. Each day for the last four pregnant months, banished to one of the nation's last mother-and-baby homes, she'd spent eight hours perched in cramped agony on a hard chair, sure that only the seat's unyielding wood was forcing this parasitic growth to stay inside her as she sat with the other inmates addressing envelopes and stuffing them with flyers for cut-price garden equipment. 'Anyone who wants a cheap tool can have my ex,' one of the girls had giggled.

Kitty remembered they'd all sworn to keep in touch, friends for life linked by their months of exile,

23

but no-one really did. One by one, they peeled off to the hospital to give birth and were sent back to the home to be safely segregated in the baby-care wing, where they couldn't contaminate those who still had the births to get through with any tricky and emotional changing of mind over adoptions. Arrangements had been made – any girl who made a fuss and insisted on leaving with instead of without her child was deemed thoroughly selfish, having no concern for the dashed hopes of the deserving childless. Leaving that place must have been like coming out of prison, she'd thought at the time, you didn't want to be reminded, you just rushed to get on to the next thing and of course no-one outside wanted to talk about it in case you got embarrassingly upset or told them difficult truths.

Baby Madeleine had been handed over to the social worker in a tiny night-blue dress, embroidered with silver stars and with the name that was unlikely to stay hers in gold thread at the hem. Kitty's mother had watched her carefully handstitching it, her eyes full of fear that she might yet change her mind and bring home the child inside the dress. 'It's what comes of being artistic,' had been said more than once in the house before Kitty was sent away, though whether her parents meant the pregnancy or the starry little outfit, Kitty was beyond calculating.

Madeleine's adoptive parents had probably binned it the moment they got her home, Kitty assumed, eagerly wrapping their own identities round their chosen child with maybe a lovingly crocheted pink shawl, traditional Viyella nighties and a different name they'd had waiting, perhaps something from the Bible or fiction. She imagined, trusted for her baby's sake, that they, childless and longing, might well have had a long-treasured store of locked-away baby clothes, hoarded against the hope that one day

24

there'd be some reason to get them out of the case on top of the wardrobe.

She closed her eyes again and sniffed gently, inhaling the remembered smell of a newborn's downy scalp. Madeleine, heading for twenty-five, could well be a mother herself by now, incredulous from those first seconds after birth that anyone could ever, ever consider giving away their child.

'You awake?' Glyn rolled heavily out of bed and twitched a curtain aside to look at the day and decide what to wear. Kitty didn't need to look out at the weather, she could hear from the sea what the day would be like. The tide was high and close but the water was calm and whispering, promising a much-needed spell of gentleness at this end of a long bleak winter. There was no surf, so Lily would at least go to school instead of pleading a headache which would clear up magically when she slipped out of the kitchen door and down into the sea with her surfboard. When she opened her eyes again Glyn was moving around the room, large and loud and shadowy like a hopeless burglar. She could smell his showered cleanness, sense the traces of dampness on his body and realized she must have dozed into an extra ten minutes of sleep. There would be droplets of water between his shoulder-blades and a dewy sparkle left in the fold of his arm.

'Bloody socks,' he said, staring down into an opened drawer. 'Does everyone else's dryer eat them or what?'

'Everyone's does. Didn't you know it's one of life's great mysteries? You should just buy dozens of identical ones then you wouldn't notice if the odd one went missing,' she suggested from the depths of the duvet. She glanced at the clock on the blue wicker table beside her, pulled herself up in the bed and looked at him properly in the half-light. He

25

cared about clothes, pointlessly for an early-retired ex-head teacher who lived in such country depths and spent so much time digging vegetables. He made sure that trips to London coincided with the smartest sales, scorning clothes shops outside the capital as fit only for those whose spiritual home was a golf-club bar. Calvin Klein was etched in the elastic round Glyn's middle, reminding her of an over-large schoolboy whose mummy still went in for name-tapes.

'You can't just have all the same socks.' Glyn looked almost shocked at the idea, pulling back the curtain and using what early light there was to check his colour-matching skills. He held the socks at arm's length by the window, the way he did when trying to do the crossword without his reading glasses. 'What about ones for tennis and for skiing and winter walks and gardening? And silk ones for formal stuff and weddings and proper cotton in case of athlete's foot?'

Kitty groaned and laughed and sank back under the duvet. She didn't care about socks. No-one could. Glyn shouldn't – he wasn't much over fifty but with no school to run, like a prime minister suddenly deposed, hadn't enough to think about. She dreaded to think with how many trivial obsessions he might start filling those intellectual gaps. 'The sky wouldn't fall in if you wore odd ones. Or none,' she told him. She'd just remembered Rosemary-Jane Pigott – *Ruthermere* – air-kissing goodbye and saying, 'Now we've all met up again, we must keep in touch. Ben *adores* Cornwall . . .'

So Ben Ruthermere adored Cornwall. Since when? she wondered now. And would she have recognized him if he'd been nearby, this summer, say, crewing in the Falmouth Classics or browsing among the artistry at the Penwith Gallery? She tried to picture him:

26

portly, perhaps by now balding, scrabbling at his inside pocket for *his* reading glasses. He'd been what her mother had disparagingly called Remarkably Average: medium build, neutral colouring and average height. 'They don't age well,' her mother had forewarned as if, for one moment, there'd been any likelihood that Ben Ruthermere, if told of the results of his sexual carelessness, would be prepared to do the decent thing by her pregnant daughter and submit to a hasty wedding. It was such an unlikely and unwished-for outcome that Kitty hadn't thought there was any point telling him. Besides, he'd gone off to do VSO in Ethiopia before Cambridge and had parents so burstingly proud of him that even the conscience of Kitty's fire-and-brimstone father quailed at the thought of destroying their delight. 'What is the point in putting *two* sets of parents through all this?' he'd said with a profound sigh of Christian resignation. Madeleine had Ben's brown-haired, hazel-eyed genes mingled with Kitty's own slim, blond and brown-eyed ones – she could look like absolutely anybody.

'So how did it go yesterday? You didn't say much last night.' Now that Glyn had clothes on he was ready to be conversational.

Kitty hauled herself out of bed and went to the window to look at the sea. It had a bright and menacing cold sparkle. 'No, well, I was just so tired. That last bit from Truro, it's so familiar I got scared I really was driving with my eyes shut.'

'Dangerous. People die driving too tired.'

Kitty shivered and reached for her velvet dressing-gown over the back of the small shabby sofa that they'd had too long to be able to throw out.

'Poor old Antonia was killed driving her car up a tree. On their own land too, which makes it worse somehow.'

Glyn looked puzzled. 'How could it be worse? Dead's dead. An absolute, *the* absolute.'

'Yes I know, but don't you think, and I know it's not logical, that you should somehow feel safe on home ground? You should be able to trust it, feel secure, the same way you should be able to trust the people you live with.' Struck by sudden childish irreverence she went on, 'When we were young and horrible but should have known better, Julia and the rest of us would have laughed and said that in any contest between Antonia and a two-hundred-year-old oak, the tree would be the one to cop it. There wasn't much to laugh at yesterday though.'

'No. Well, there wouldn't be.' Glyn looked solemn but at a loss, Kitty thought. She could see his face searching for something encouraging to say, just as he would have done to a downhearted pupil. Eventually he came up with, 'Nice to see old school pals again though.' He waited for her to look cheered.

'Well, strange anyway. Nice doesn't describe it. Nice *couldn't* describe Rosemary-Jane Pigott actually, you should meet her.'

Glyn considered this more seriously than she had meant him to.

'Well perhaps we could . . .'

'No! Please, I didn't mean it. Don't even think of it!' Kitty laughed. 'If we'd wanted to keep in touch properly, I'm sure we'd have done it before now. It's been over twenty years.' Glyn looked doubtful. He still had a cohort of old school chums, people who'd bonded at fourteen in the post-rugby bath and still met up for drinks, weddings (quieter, second or third ones these days of course), blokeish support and Test Match outings. They swopped snippets of legal and educational advice or edged round medical matters, carefully editing out fallen income or flagging sexual potency.

'Besides,' she said, drifting through to the bath-room, 'you'll only look at her and me and decide I maybe haven't worn as well as I might. I'm not giving you the chance to do that.'

From the bathroom window Kitty could see Lily already down on the beach with Russell the cat. Lily kicked moodily at the sand and slung pebbles into the water. No surf, no fun, no excuse to dump the coursework. The orange and white striped cat picked its way along the sand and shingle behind Lily at a safe distance, stopping every now and then to investigate bits of seaweed and washed-up coloured twine. It would have followed Lily on to the school bus if she'd let it but instead it waited around at the end of the lane every afternoon, nonchalantly washing its feet on top of a gatepost as if it just hap-pened to be there at home-coming time. Kitty, testing the bath water with her toe, wondered suddenly if Madeleine was a dog person or a cat one. If she was alive that is, if she was allowed pets at all. She thought of a mean strict family, an aging mother over-keen on hygiene who thought furry four-footed creatures harboured germs and fleas and things that threatened the perfection of a scoured kitchen floor. 'Poor kid,' Kitty said to herself as if she'd conjured up a real-life picture.

Petroc Harding, who worried that he might still be growing, ate four slices of toast and honey and wished he had the kind of mother who fussed in the mornings and concocted huge, grease-strewn, man-building breakfasts. Mornings had never felt right, not since he'd realized at the age of about six that unfairness was possible and that grown-ups got away with it. It was to do with being the son of a head teacher. He felt that as a pupil, right from being very small, teachers had always looked at him in an odd way as if they expected him of all people to sympathize with what they were trying to achieve for their charges, and not give them any disruption and trouble while they did it.

'I didn't expect that from *you*,' Ms Warren had said when at the age of seven he'd thrown Sam Tremayne's wellington boot into the stream where they were pond-dipping. Sam had yelled a bit but hadn't really minded much – his boots had already been filled with water and emptied out a couple of times simply because they were better for catching tadpoles than a torn net on a stick. Sam had looked from Ms Warren to Petroc and back again as if there was something weird that he wasn't being told. Petroc had known immediately what it was about and had stared sullenly at the ground, pretending to refuse to acknowledge his position of being half on the inside when it came to teachers.

There weren't that many schools in the area. Parental choice with regard to secondary schools, his mother had complained, was an item for dinner-party discussion only where there *was* choice. Places like Surrey or Greater Manchester perhaps. Here, you got the school bus on the far side of the main road for one town or the near side for the other, or you fell off the edge of the world to boarding-school and never quite joined in again. At the age of ten it had slowly dawned on him that his next headmaster, the one his swanky know-it-all classmates with older siblings already referred to as Old Hard-on, was going to be the man he called Dad.

He blamed his father one hundred per cent for the five years of being called Rock-Hard when he'd been planning to be known as Pete, and found it difficult to forgive him for waiting till the very year Petroc himself was to leave the school for the sixth-form college to take up an offer of early retirement, due to the money-saving merger of his school with another. Now, more mature and uneasily pretending he didn't feel he was being shadowed, he affected a casual tolerance of his father's presence two days a week at this same college, banging the essentials of the English language into the slow heads of reluctant GCSE retakers.

'Are you going to college?' Lily brought in the fishy scent of the beach with her and a blast of cold damp air.

Petroc scowled. 'You want a lift to the bus stop? 'Cos if you do you've got less than ten minutes.'

Lily shrugged. Petroc worried about how pathetically thin her shoulders were. The shrug looked like a wire coat-hanger twitching beneath her school sweatshirt. Even her long fair hair looked underfed and lank. It was as if, aspiring to be a poet, she was keen to take a good old-fashioned share of Keatsian consumption and demise as well.

'Have you had any breakfast?' he asked her, keeping his voice casual and barely interested so she wouldn't think he was having a go. It was hard to get it right with Lily, one wrong word and she flounced off, furious. She could flounce for Britain, but then his mum said any girl of fifteen could: it was what they did. He pushed his plate across the table towards her. She gave it a look, turned her nose up and he grinned. 'Yeah I know. Not much of an offer, cold toast.'

'Cold toast with a bite out of it.' She pointed a pale skinny finger at it, not quite touching as if it was something nasty the cat had found on the sand. Her nails were almost blue, as if they'd taken on the cold of the outside air and kept it stored.

'So *did* you have any breakfast?' he persisted. Lily sighed and started twiddling a strand of hair.

'Cereal. Bran flakes. Six fluid ounces of milk, one

31

cup of lukewarm coffee – two sugars – oh and half a soggy custard-cream biscuit – last one in the packet.' She smiled. 'Is that enough?'

'Not in this weather. This is fry-up weather,' he grumbled, getting up and shoving his plate into the dishwasher.

'You can get me a Bounty bar at the Spar then,' she countered, picking up her school bag. 'Where's the parents?'

'Abluting. Dressing. Planning a red-carpet welcome for the Great Author arriving today.' Lily smiled, her eyes brightening at the thought of at last having on home ground a fellow writer who wasn't just one of the usual holiday-break amateurs. To him she would confide her poems, let him read her soul. Better still, he'd know a publisher or two.

Petroc's Mini had a rimy coating of cold drops, each one a perfect, separate, shimmering blob. It would rot, he was told by friends, being kept so close to the sea. The salt would eat under its sky-blue paintwork. The tyres would perish and the chrome on the bumpers would soon rust and flake. Envious people liked to say that sort of thing, liked to pile on the bad-luck curses. He patted its back corner, feeling as ever that it was like the rump of a dumpy young girl left looking lost at a party when her tall, gorgeous friends have been claimed for the night.

'Why do you bother to lock it? Who'd want it?' Lily demanded crossly, pulling at the door-handle. She blew on her hands, emphasizing how cold she was.

'Have you said goodbye to the old folk?' Petroc asked, climbing into the driving seat. It wasn't easy – his long legs had to fit each side of the steering-wheel. He was nearly eighteen and prayed he wouldn't get any taller. The seat was already pushed back so far no-one could sit behind him.

Lily climbed in beside him, 'No-one about. They don't care whether we get educated or not.'

Petroc grinned at her as he started the eager engine. '*You* aren't getting educated. I know you spend half your time up the lane in Josh and Rita's kitchen when you should be at school.'

'You can learn a lot in Rita's kitchen.'

'Not stuff you pass exams in.'

'You sound like Dad, you know that? She tells me real-life things.'

'Like how to roll a joint and grow your own? Sex a newborn goat and cook mung beans?'

Lily groaned. 'God you're boring. How did our parents manage to produce two people who were so different?'

Petroc laughed. 'It's a mystery. Ask Rita, she's bound to have a witchy theory.' Petroc slowed down as they passed Rita's farmhouse in case of straying livestock. Its roof had a shiny new patch of corrugated iron. He imagined Rita up a ladder with her hand-woven wicker basket full of nails and a mallet that was too heavy for her. All that wild black hair would blow across her face and her boots would slip on the dangerous tiles and she wouldn't care at all or even notice that she was teasing death. Rita's last year's daffodil-season find, Josh, a free and pretty spirit who dabbled lazily in restoring antiques and shivered miserably in inclement weather, wouldn't know where to begin with roofing pegs and a ladder. Rita wouldn't ask him anyway, in case he took fright at being asked to be useful. Lily was peering out of the window, eyes bright, hoping to catch sight of her mentor.

'School,' Petroc reminded her. 'Just do the exams and then you've got choices. You can go any-where.'

'Yeah I know. It's just . . . I don't want to go

anywhere, you know? Everyone expects you to want to run away from here, fast as you can to the nearest city. I don't.'

Petroc slowed the car round the last mud-caked bend. 'Here you are. One bus stop, complete with your doting admirer Fergus.'

'Oh thanks. Make my day. There's also one Spar shop, so money for Bounty bar?' She turned and smiled at him, her thin little face lit up as she extended her hand for cash.

He handed her fifty pee. 'That's part of my lunch money. Don't waste it.'

'That's the sort of thing the Queen was supposed to have said to Princess Diana about food. I'm *neither anorexic nor bulimic* Petroc, will you just get that?' The door of the car slammed and Lily's skinny legs stalked to the bus stop. Her clumpy shoes looked huge, as if she'd borrowed them from Olive Oyl. Fergus, a boy waiting ever more hopelessly for a growth spurt to kick in, grinned up at her. 'Poor sod,' Petroc said to himself, switching the radio to Pirate FM.

Kitty had allocated the best of the guest-rooms to George Moorfield simply because this early in the year he would be the only person occupying the converted barn. Refusing to be impressed by his fame, she'd told Glyn that he was to expect no special favours, especially after his fax had arrived. This notorious gentleman of literature had simply commanded 'I require *en-suite* facilities,' as if deep in Cornwall such a request might be a problem and that the words 'please' and 'thank you' might be unheard-of on the far side of the Tamar. 'He probably imagines a midden next to a pig pen and one cold tap behind a silage clamp,' Kitty had said.

The Barn had rooms for ten guests attracted by

34

adverts in *The Author* and *Writers' News* magazines. A large communal cooking-and-living area gave them a chance to get together and share work problems and ideas. They were usually struggling would-be authors in search of inspiring solitude, either escaping the demands of family life or making the most of holiday time from something in an office and dreaming that *this* book would be the one that brought them fame, fortune, prizes and film rights.

Being a painter herself, Kitty had at first thought they might accommodate artists, but decided ruthlessly that they were intrinsically messy and would spend too much time wandering the premises looking for the ever-better view. Writers, Kitty had pointed out to Glyn, had no choice but to be conveniently self-contained, though the previous scorching summer she had noticed several lying on the beach, closed notepads ready for inspiration by their side as they dozed in the sun. George Moorfield was by far the most famous client who'd ever booked in, and Glyn was keen that he should form a happy first impression and tell all his friends who he imagined would be equally celebrated.

'Play our cards right and this place could be right up there on the literary map. A sort of Cornish Bloomsbury,' he'd enthused to Kitty as they put final touches to the room. Kitty had doubts. One renowned author didn't make a salon. 'Do you think he'll be warm enough?' Glyn was fiddling with the radiator thermostat. 'I wonder if it needs bleeding . . .' he murmured.

'He'll be fine. It's like an oven. And he can always set up his computer or whatever he works on down in the kitchen by the Rayburn if he's in need of being cosier. There's only him so he won't be in anyone's way.' Kitty smoothed the heavy cream crocheted spread over the bed. The duvet beneath it was goose down, no-one could complain of being cold under that. The walls of the room were painted a warm butter yellow and the blue carpet, which was new and shedding the odd tuft, still smelled faintly of Homeworld's flooring showroom. The building was fearfully quiet and Kitty made a mental note to bring over a radio from the house. George Moorfield might have a fondness for listening to the Archers while he prepared his solitary supper down in the big snug kitchen, or even enjoy an unlikely background of faintly twittering Radio One while he worked.

'I wonder what Madeleine's bedroom is like,' she said as she took towels through to the small blue bathroom.

'What?' Glyn appeared at the doorway looking puzzled.

'Madeleine. That baby I had.' She didn't look at him. Her fingers fumbled with the loo-roll holder and she dropped the roll of paper on the floor. Glyn picked it up and handed it back. 'You haven't mentioned her for ages.'

Kitty sat on the edge of the bath. 'No. Well. It was just that Antonia's funeral got me thinking about her again. I think I've always assumed I could just check up on her for real, if I truly wanted to, any old time, though I know it's more complicated than that. But who knows how much time any of us have got?'

'Well they do that to you, funerals. They're a bit fundamental, all that here one minute, gone the next. And where? Gone where?' He was scratching the back of his neck, Kitty noticed. He always did that when he was nervous about difficult things being said. It wasn't that he liked emotions tidied away out of sight, as her parents had done, it was more that since he'd retired from dealing with school problems, he seemed to expect there to be nothing tricky to deal with for the rest of his life at home either.

36

Kitty persisted, determined to make him listen because, suddenly, it mattered.

'I don't even know if she's alive or dead. All those years ago all you were told was that it was the right thing to do, completely the best thing for the baby, giving it a proper family life. No-one said anything about all the wondering you do for the rest of your *own* life. Everyone made you feel that to do anything else would have been selfish.'

'Well they were right, weren't they? What could a teenager fresh out of school do with a small child?' Glyn interrupted. He was stroking her hair. Kitty flinched. She didn't want to be patted better and shook him off. '*This* life isn't so bad, surely? Rita up the lane had had her three boys by the time she was twenty-one. If I hadn't been so gutless . . . Anyway I started thinking maybe I should find out, you know, make sure the baby – girl – woman, is all right. If I don't do something about it I'll never ever know and then it will be too late. It might be already.'

Glyn sighed. 'Well you could, but suppose she's *not* all right? Not much you can do about it now, is there? There could be years of blame all built up in her.' Kitty glared at him. 'Or,' he went on, 'she might not know you exist, or she might know and not care because she's perfectly happy.'

'Well at least *I'd* know, either way.'

'Yes but that's the point isn't it, *you'd* know, and then what, back to what kind of normal? And also I'm sure she'd have to be the one who wants to do the finding, because I'm pretty sure you as the birth mother wouldn't be allowed to. And anyway, what's in it for her?'

Kitty stood up and pushed past him. 'I'll get some daffodils from Rita for this room. It needs a bit more cheering up.'

Glyn followed her out of the room and down the

stairs, too closely she thought, cross and criticizing. He was so headmasterly, so reasonable, so much too good at seeing both sides and cutting out the emotional content.

'There's ways of finding out. Julia Taggart would know. She seems to know bloody everything else. I might ask her. Or maybe Rita,' Kitty told him.

'Up to you. But don't say I didn't warn you, you don't know what you might be stirring up. Suppose she just sort of turns up here?'

Kitty shrugged. 'I don't think it quite works like that. But even if she did, wouldn't that be all right? I mean it's not as if the children don't know she exists. They've always known they've got a half-sister out there somewhere.' She smiled, recalling her mother's instruction that she would be wise not to tell anyone, not ever.

'And what if you make all the right connections and she *doesn't* turn up. What then?'

Kitty started walking across the yard to her own kitchen. 'Well then nothing will have changed, will it?' Behind her she heard him say, as if he hadn't decided whether she should hear, 'Oh but something *would* have changed, no question about that.'

Chapter Three

'Well of course Glyn's not going to be interested in some old baby from way back. Why should he be? It wasn't his.' Rita bustled about her cluttered kitchen, searching among the jumble of blue and purple glass jars on the shelf behind the sink for the one that contained the plain old ordinary tea bags that Kitty seemed so boringly to prefer. Rita could offer twenty different herbal selections and it irritated that her nearest tea-sharing neighbour was a PG Tips type. The pampered Josh's current favourite was ginger and ginseng (which he didn't suspect was to perk up both digestion and libido), with a dash of lemon to ward off his tendency to colds. Rita kept this in his special copper box that he claimed he'd found on a Peruvian mountain. She reached into the fridge and pulled out a jug of milk.

'Freshly squeezed goat?' she offered to Kitty, who, feeling she was being challenged to dare to ask for semi-skimmed cow, accepted.

Rita went on, 'You shouldn't expect him to be even slightly curious. Men let things go better than we do and then it's on to what's next. He probably wouldn't be that interested even if it *was* his.' There was in Rita's scathing tone more than a hint that she found men, apart from the adored Josh, unreliable, unfeeling and untrustworthy.

'Well *I'd* be curious if it was *his*, wouldn't you?' Kitty picked up a pair of small grey sleeping cats from the rocking-chair and sat down on a torn patchwork cushion with them on her lap. Lazily they stretched their baby limbs, extending hair-fine claws, and snuggled back down immediately, purring gently as if she'd never disturbed them.

'Yes but we're women. Of course we'd be interested, we have tender, enquiring natures. It's why your paintings are so full of detail.'

'We have overdeveloped nosiness, you mean.' Kitty realized as she said it that she sounded like her mother who, when it came to matters less delicate than bodily functions and pregnancy, liked to call a spade a bloody shovel.

'If you like,' Rita conceded grudgingly. 'Generalizing horribly, I think some men just shut inconvenient things out rather than poke at them like old scabs till there's blood and disaster everywhere like we do. And not only that, we then martyr ourselves clearing up the mess and absolutely demanding all the blame.' She grinned, her mouth slightly twisted as it always was, showing a glimpse of a gold premolar. There was a gypsyish look to Rita, something to do with flamboyance with colour and a Carmen-style swagger when she moved, as if she might, given the right amount of moonlight, moonshine and a camp-fire audience, break into a spontaneous flamenco. When she walked, her hips whistled up the air around her. Glyn had once admitted to Kitty, after a party, that Rita was pretty sexy, but only in a draughty sort of way. 'She could swish a bloke into bed,' he'd said, looking nervous.

Kitty frowned. 'You're right. And whatever I unearth now, there is no baby any more. Somewhere out there is a grown young woman, all cooked and finished.' She laughed. 'Glyn still looks at his own children sometimes as if he can't quite believe he's produced them, especially since they've been teenagers. Imagine how he'd feel if a fully formed adult turned up at the house looking for a mum who wouldn't have a chance of recognizing her.'

'And do *you* imagine that, how you'd feel, if it happened?' Rita's tobacco-coloured eyes were looking intensely at Kitty as if she had to hold her gaze to haul out the truth. Kitty didn't even have to hesitate.

'Well of course I imagine it. More now than I used to even. I'm sure everyone who's ever had a child adopted does the same thing. Over the years I've pictured her at different ages arriving on the doorstep: a sad little girl run away from being sent too early to boarding-school, or a stroppy thirteen-year-old having her first flukey go at finding me, easy as something out of Enid Blyton. And then a year or two back I kept expecting a cool nineteen-year-old to turn up, doing a casual detour after the backpack trip to India, checking out her real mother . . .'

'The one who brought her up *is* her real mother,' Rita reminded her softly.

'Yes, I know, I know.' Kitty gathered up the cats and put them back on the chair again. Her thighs were warm where their little bodies had lain and the outside chill damp air wasn't tempting. 'I'd better get going. Don't want to miss our illustrious guest arriving. Glyn's so excited you'd think we were getting royalty.'

Rita's eyes glinted and the twisted grin returned. 'I'm pretty excited too. I've read all his books and they're so full of complicated sex I'm wondering if he'll be short of company.' She put her hands on her hips and thrust her breasts forward in mock provocation. She was wearing an ancient rainbow-knitted sweater but Kitty imagined the fine cleavage beneath, cupped and lifted by the purple satin or lime green bra she'd seen flying brazenly on the orchard washing-line.

'Hey, he's only paying for the room. Don't go throwing in any freebies.'

'Are you suggesting I should charge for it?' Rita giggled, 'though I suppose a girl has to make a living . . .' *Girl* was pushing it; Rita wouldn't see forty-five again, surely explaining why she so treasured the idle (but young and vigorous) Josh who was probably upstairs now, still sleeping off Rita's attentions till she brought him tea and tenderness.

'I'll invite you over for supper, just as soon as he's settled in,' Kitty promised. 'But who knows, he might prefer Petroc . . .' She made her escape before Rita could throw a cold tea bag at her and picked her way through the mud in the yard towards the field where the last daffodils waited to be saved from running to seed. Rita's five small fields with their tumbled-down banks of mixed scrap iron, crumbling wall and bramble-woven hawthorn had a scrappy pre-war appearance, as if they'd been salvaged from a group of ancient cottage gardens. The daffodil picking was finished and these leftover flowers that had bloomed just too late had a desperate look to them, like debs at an old-style coming-out dance where there weren't quite enough men. Wordsworth's host they were not, these mud-splashed and pathetic, shivering and rather puny specimens. Lily looked just like that in winter, all pinched and trembling, Kitty thought, as her ancient Timberlands sucked and squelched their way through the puddle of coppery mud that had collected by the gate. Lily had limbs like strings and a new-found appetite for large amounts of fruit that she'd pick up from the dresser halfway through a meal and walk out of the kitchen with, saying she'd eat it in her room, she didn't feel like a big meal just now.

Kitty's fingers were sticky with dripping sap after picking an armful of the damp flowers, and she wondered if she'd bother going to all this trouble for some less legendary scribbler taking a fortnight off from the nine-to-five grind to indulge a fantasy. That would be the sort of client who would most appreciate a huge bunch of hand-picked daffodils, she thought. George Moorfield had the comfort of bestseller status and a bank account boosted by prizewinnings. As she stepped carefully through the least of the mud back to the road a large turquoise car, a strange mixture of what looked like a Bentley at the front and a pick-up truck at the back, sped towards her along the lane, heedless of any possible traffic round the bend ahead. Its wheels whooshed up an arc of muddy water which soaked Kitty's jeans.

'Shit! Stupid bastard!' she yelled after the car, setting out speedily along the road in the same direction. It could only be going to Treneath, there was nowhere else after that, unless the driver fancied whizzing on up towards the coast path and then up and over the cliff edge. She marched along fast and furious, keeping to the middle of the road. If the driver realized he'd taken a wrong turning and came back, she'd make bloody sure he had to stop so she could tell him what she thought.

Glyn counted out a hundred shallots and laid them out on the clean, empty staging in the greenhouse. He breathed in the soft damp smell of young lettuces, picked a crisp young leaf from the earthenware pot next to him and chewed it speculatively, trying to feel certain that it tasted so very much better than something imported from Guatemala that he could get in a supermarket. It was costing a lot, on the whole, all this going organic and growing their own. Much more than if they just bought vegetables at

43

Safeway. The fact that Kitty never pointed this out made him wonder, sometimes, if she was just indulging him, letting him play, like a child in mud. He had to make sure he thought of it as something separate from simply replacing shop veg, make it not just functional. There were plenty of restaurants that could be interested – the word 'organic' on a menu was a handy price-booster, especially with the sort of holiday visitors who liked to go home able to say, 'So *marvellous*, entirely local veg'. That was the sort of comment that went into the restaurant guides.

He loved the process of sowing and raising the little seedlings, the first magic sight of them sprouting, then potting them on at the two-leaf stage, holding them carefully by the leaves so as not to hurt the stems. He'd done a lot of damage that way at first, even though he'd thought he'd done it right and then he'd had to watch so many of them struggle, fall down and shrivel just because he'd been heavy-handed. Ignoring advice from five instruction books, on the grounds that he was an intelligent man and knew many things better than most, he'd also meticulously thinned out his first batch of carrots, thinking they surely needed more room than that, only to leave them as no-mercy prey for carrot fly. The various crops needed more attention than small children, and certainly far more than Lily and Petroc, with their teenage secret lives, were needing these days.

He glanced out of the greenhouse at the nine raised rectangles of earth in the walled vegetable garden. Together they looked like a block of good chocolate. The soil was rich and well-manured and the old stone walls kept the warmth in and the wind out, which prolonged the growing time. He was still picking broccoli from the year before, the garlic was already a foot tall and the cauliflowers had been bigger than the ones in Rita's medium field that she rented to the farm on the hill. He looked at the shallots waiting on the worktop. 'All in now, or stagger them?' he muttered aloud, pondering the problems of storing a harvest of several hundred when they all ripened at once. He should have started some off back in December, getting them in on the shortest day like the garlic.

'First sign of craziness, if you'll forgive the cliché.' The voice (male) was alarmingly close, right beside him, shoulder to shoulder and too chummy. Glyn felt instant fury that anyone should have crept up so close without him noticing, almost into the middle of his reverie. He'd assumed years running a school had given him a sort of second sight where being sneaked up on and surprised was concerned. It was something basic you just didn't let happen, like turning your back in a physics lab full of frisky fourteen-year-olds.

'I'm George Moorfield.' The man leaned back against the worktop, picked up a shallot and began casually unfurling the papery top of it as if it was a wrapped sweet. 'Amazing these things, aren't they? Did you grow them?'

'Not these, they're sets for this year's crop,' Glyn told him grudgingly. He'd looked forward to meeting this man, read his books which probed the problems of the Doubt-Racked Male and thought he might, just possibly, be something of a soulmate. Now he just wanted to snatch the baby onion out of George Moorfield's careless hand and put it back in line. The feeling reminded him uncomfortably of confiscating penknives from first-years. Recalling good manners he forced a smile and offered an earthy hand. 'I'm Glyn Harding, I suppose you didn't find anyone up at the house?'

'No, neither sight nor breath but the doors were open and I wandered round a bit and then came out here. The phone rang and I answered it – message on your kitchen table. I'm a bit early. Well, a lot early. Sorry.'

'Well yes.' Glyn wiped his hands on a ripped tea towel and led George out of the greenhouse, closing the door behind him firmly and not just to keep the warmth in. People should know that greenhouses, like sheds and attics and little huts down at the ends of paths, were private retreats, never to be invaded. He didn't mind about the wandering through the house, that was more public space, or the answering the phone – who could ever leave one to ring? It wasn't even eleven o'clock yet. He was pretty sure tenants weren't supposed to arrive till after three, though this one might have thought he'd be above mere instructions. Kitty usually dealt with the clients, and this one, well this was one he'd actually *read*, which made him feel he was talking to someone who wasn't quite real.

George Moorfield was wearing clothes that looked as if they'd been selected specially to be deliberately contrary to what was appropriate for some of the deepest countryside Britain had to offer. His suede boots were as pale as lion fur and his black leather jacket was so glaringly new it was still as stiff as cardboard. Its front barely met over the substantial portly belly that was squashed into denim shirt and jeans. It must have been a very uncomfortable drive, Glyn concluded, unless the man had worn an old tracksuit for the actual journey, changing into image-wear the moment he crossed the Tamar, like Joan Collins travelling on Concorde. The famous author looked several years older than the photo that appeared in his books, his long grey hair well received as if it had slipped backwards, exposing vulnerable pink scalp at the front.

'Kit will be back in a minute,' Glyn said, now

wondering what on earth he should do with him, 'And she'll show you to your room and all that. Come into the house and have some coffee.' The man had an extraordinary car, he noted, passing the strange blue-green Bentley parked just where it most inconveniently blocked the gateway. Glyn didn't comment, feeling that to mention the thing might seem depressingly parochial. They got their fair share of strange motors in Cornwall too. If you could stick a truck back-end on a Beetle, like the Neanderthal Josh bloke who 'worked' on Rita's land, it was surely no big deal to tag one onto a Bentley.

Lily's G-Shock watch said 10.30. She was hungry now and her stomach was going to rumble till break, all the way through Maths. She would eat half of the Bounty bar as soon as break started and see if the uncomfortable full feeling lasted all the way to lunch. She didn't like feeling hungry because it was something she couldn't decide to feel or not to feel, it was just automatic, so the feeling had to be kept just a little away from her, usually just a dry biscuit's-worth here and there, with only occasional giving into sweet temptation like today. She wrote her best poems when her head was full of the clanging panic of hunger. 'Thin as a nun' had come to her the night before when she'd been looking at her pale narrow body in the bathroom mirror. It made her think of sacrifice and purity and a no-sex state. She hated having periods too, for the same lack of controllability. They just came, all by themselves, bringing cramps and a terror of some disastrous bloody accidental embarrassment every month, whatever she did.

She didn't want to starve, but she knew from things she'd read and from the girl who'd had to leave school when she got so skeletal she couldn't stand, that there was a clever balance if you worked at it hard enough and were careful. She wouldn't end up like that girl, with peach-fur skin and a head like just a skull and tights that hung drooping off her legs, not a chance. But if she got it right and didn't eat just *quite* enough, the periods would go away and she'd be all right, *not anorexic*, definitely not that, but in control. Perhaps she'd have just a little tiny corner of the Bounty bar. Charlotte could have the rest. It would be greedy to eat the whole thing in front of her anyway.

She chewed the ends of her fine fair hair and thought about the summer. She'd be able to surf every day, and always feel exactly the same. She wouldn't have moods, cramps, blood, pads or any of that hassle. She'd be OK, she always had breakfast and she'd make sure her energy level ticked over. Well she'd have to, or she wouldn't even be able to lift her board, would she?

Smiling, she raised her hand to reply to a question that had been asked and answered about ten minutes previously, earning a rebuke for lack of concentration and a concerned narrowing of the eyes from the teacher. 'Sorry.' Lily smiled more broadly, her expression turning cheeky. The concern vanished, to be replaced with one of relief. Lily noted the alteration and understood it: teachers much preferred their pupils, especially sensitive teenage girls, to be merely naughty rather than suspiciously loopy. Their lives were difficult enough.

'Glyn! Glyn, whose is that car in the yard?' Kitty staggered into the kitchen shedding daffodils, shouting and kicking off her boots at the same time. She'd left muddy prints and sticky trails of sap all over the beechwood floor in her hurry to be cross with the stranger who'd splattered her with mud.

'Hi. George Moorfield. You were expecting me?'

Kitty adjusted a woolly sock and stood up properly to look at this house guest who'd arrived so unforgivably early.

'Mr Moorfield! Goodness we weren't expecting you till later.' She immediately wished she hadn't said that. It reminded her of her mother who, out of good old Christian charity, had liked to be sure people were aware of their shortcomings. She dropped the boots to shake hands, 'Excuse the mud – there's lakes of it out in the lane.'

'Oh dear, was it you I zoomed past so rudely? I'm so sorry – I was so afraid of getting lost in these teeny roads, the high banks and the narrowness made me feel just a bit trippy.' He had a rather drawly don't-care voice, she thought, like someone who is well used to being able to charm his way out of trouble. She recalled tabloid tales of two wives, each of whom in their turn had walked out claiming mental turmoil that they could no longer stand, presumably after that charm wore thin and tattered.

She pulled a vase from the dresser shelf and quickly shoved the daffodils in, arranging them rather uselessly.

'These are for your room which is ready if you want to come and see it,' Kitty told him. He stood up and gave Glyn a glance of amused conspiracy. 'Should they have water, do you think?' he suggested kindly.

'God I feel so *twittish*,' Kitty told Glyn the moment she got back from the barn. 'He must think I'm a complete lunatic – covered in mud, flapping about with waterless daffs and dropping boots everywhere.'

'Well it was his fault about the mud. He's got one of those knacks some blokes perfect over the years,' Glyn told her wearily, handing her a fresh mug of coffee across the table. 'He makes women go all

49

dippy and then they're grateful when he's all under-standing and sweetness to them.' Kitty looked at him, frowning. 'I hope you don't really think I'm that sus-ceptible. Anyway, I thought he was someone you admired,' she said. 'What happened?'

'He invaded my greenhouse.' Glyn laughed. 'No, I admire his books. No-one else does Thinking Man as Victim these days and gets away with it quite like he does. But it's a bit like meeting actors, they're always shorter than you expect. With writers, they're shorter in the sensitivity department and his hands have got drinker's twitch.'

'Actually he told me he didn't want to see so much as an empty wine bottle while he's here, in case he's tempted to take a sniff at it. He's come here to be very seriously off the booze.'

'Telling you his troubles, was he?'

'While we sat cosily on the bed, you mean?' Kitty grinned at him. 'No, just warning me not to invite him in for a g. and t. at sixish.'

'In his dreams. But there's the pub in the village, he must have passed it. If he's tempted, it isn't far. And the Spar has a decent chardonnay, not to mention six brands of vodka.'

'We could let his tyres down.'

'Only after he moves that monstrous thing away from the gate.' Glyn hauled himself out of the chair. He was carrying his shoulders very stiffly, Kitty noticed, as if George Moorfield made him feel old and decrepit. There couldn't really be anything in it, age-wise: Glyn was early fifties, and George was clearly even more than that in spite of the leather and Levis.

'He said there was a phone call and he'd taken a message?' Kitty searched among the junk mail and lists and loose bits of paper by the phone on the dresser.

'Oh, sorry, forgot – it's on the shelf, next to the blue mug.' Glyn pointed from the doorway, 'I'm going back to the shallots. Decisions must be made. See you later.'

Kitty smoothed out the scrap of paper on which George had scrawled Julia Taggart's number and started dialling. The usual irritating electronic voice told her that the number she was calling knew she was waiting and she hung up. There wasn't much left for her and Julia to talk about anyway; they'd discussed who'd worn/said what at Antonia's funeral on the drive to the station, and Kitty could only surmise Julia had some earthy piece of gossip about Rosemary-Jane that she'd forgotten to pass on, something that just couldn't wait till they next met in London. Minutes later, as Kitty was setting out to ask George to repark his car so she could get out to the supermarket, the phone rang.

'I did 1471,' Julia announced without saying hello. 'I am glad you rang back. You'll never guess what.'

Kitty laughed. Julia still sounded so like the eager schoolgirl she'd been when she'd discovered a secret romance between the gorgeous young Latin mistress and the visiting violin teacher.

'OK, what won't I guess?' she indulged her.

'Rosemary-Jane hasn't come back from the funeral yet. I've had her husband, Ben-that-you-used-to-know, on the phone wondering if she'd stayed with me.' Julia paused for breath then asked, more subdued, 'Is she with you?'

'Me? No of course not. Yesterday was the first time I'd seen her since she went off to shine and sparkle at Oxford. I didn't even know she'd married Ben-that-I-used-to-know, as you call him. I couldn't honestly claim to know either of them now, not in the being-adults-together sense.'

'Worse than I thought then.' Julia's drama hysteria

was rising. 'She surely couldn't have stayed with *him*. Not even Rose would be so callous.'

'With Antonia's husband, do you mean?' Kitty wondered, not for the first time, if Julia, divorced and with her solitary son away at Edinburgh, now had too little of substance to think about.

'Widower. And she's not the type to hang about waiting for the decent interval. He's a lone man; she'd be sure to pounce before someone else does.'

'Look Julia, I really wouldn't know.'

'Yes you would. You remember what she was like.'

'Julia, it was more than *twenty* years ago. We were into David Bowie and dyeing our hair purple!' What *would* Ben look like these days, Kitty wondered again.

'She married your bloke. *Kitty*, he surely wasn't the one who . . .' Julia suddenly said. She sounded as if this was the first time it had crossed her mind. Kitty could feel her pulse getting up speed.

'Oh, he and I had a brief thing, that was all, just a teenage number before he went off to do VSO.' With forced breeziness she headed off Julia's train of thought.

There was a pause, in which Kitty could have sworn she could hear the mechanics of Julia's brain ticking over.

'But wasn't that about when you, you know that bit of trouble . . .'

'That baby, do you mean?'

'Yes, that baby.'

'Oh I had the baby loads later. You know I only told you, or rather my mother told yours, Rose never knew and I hope she won't, even now.'

'Well *I've* never mentioned it. I promised, didn't I?' Julia needed distracting from speculation. Kitty thought quickly and got in before Julia could take things any further, 'Actually Julia, I was going to call you to do with all that. It was just a thought, really, I don't know whether you'd have any ideas.'

'Ooh what? Tell me now.' Luckily Julia was as easy to lead as a child's pony.

'If, just *if* I wanted to find out where the baby was now, is there some kind of organization where you can let them know you're willing to be traced? Because I think that it's the child who has to do the finding, not the mother. I'm not saying I'd want to, I just feel I need to know how to go about making it possible, opening doors. I think it's to do with feeling mortal after poor Antonia.'

'Hmm. I know what you mean. You just think people are always there, of your own generation anyway.' More ticking of Julia's brain cells was going on. 'Listen, leave it with me and I'll find out and ring you back. I'm pretty sure there was a woman up here in Richmond who met a long-lost son. It isn't necessarily all joy and bananas, you know. You might end up with disappointment.'

'You sound like Glyn! It's not as if I haven't thought it through. Ask anyone in the same boat, if you can find them, and they'll tell you they've gone over it a million times. And I might not do anything about it — it's a just-in-case sort of thing. So will you ask this woman?'

'I'll ask her. I'll let you know.'

'Thanks Julia. And Julia?'

'Hmm?' Julia sounded eager to go now, on to the next thing, a nice bit of sleuthing.

'I'm sure Rosemary-Jane will turn up soon. She always did.'

'Yes I remember. Like an alleycat slinking home. With her knickers in her handbag and her tights on back to front . . .'

Chapter Four

Petroc had always understood that having a car was a great and essential woman-puller. It was something he couldn't remember *not* knowing, same as the way he knew stinging-nettles hurt and that Coke tasted nicer than milk. He'd seen the power that local boys on the summer beaches had when they'd got their own wheels. Holidaying girls from distant dusty towns, flicking their Sun-In hair and tweaking the ridden-up bottoms of their bikinis into place, didn't want some bozo with a bicycle to take them clubbing. They didn't want to be *walked* back to their B and B where their giggly mates peeping from behind net curtains could see they'd only pulled a sad under-age yokel with legs for transport, however muscly and gorgeous those legs might have looked down on the daytime sand. Sunshine kit required a wetsuit that was truly sleek in all the right places, a Kamikaze board that was for serious creaming on the waves, not just for posing, and, top of the range, a Cal-look rainbow-paint-job Beetle horsed up with some ludicrous 1800cc fuck-off engine and wheels the size of the ones on Rita's tractor. He'd seen girls roll over and pant for the guy last year who'd turned up on Fistral beach with exactly that. Not much was special about the bloke himself, but, starting up, that car had sounded like big cats mating and its exhaust had smelled of rude hormones.

Petroc was the first in his year to pass his test and he was daily grateful that his grandmother was given to indulging him with generous presents. As he sat in the college library reading up on the importance of the Industrial Revolution in *Tess of the D'Urbervilles*, he could see his adored Mini down below in the car park waiting, like Lily's cat on the gatepost, for their end of the day reunion. There might be many places in the nation where this car wouldn't rate high on desirability, but in a county where most villages were lucky to see two buses a day and none at all after dark, the Mini was a true prize.

'Not going into Penzance are you?' Jamie Kent's perpetually beery breath wafted in front of Petroc and he recoiled, waving the air.

'Jesus, Jamie, are you using pints of Tinners for mouthwash?'

Jamie grinned, his big over-pink face like an eager Labrador's. Glyn had once said that Jamie already looked prime for his first heart attack. 'No-one in their right mind will ever sell him life insurance,' he'd added, as if Jamie, at seventeen, was likely to care.

'Got to have lunch somewhere haven't I?' he said to Petroc. 'I leave the non-drinking to you drivers. Anyway, *are* you going to Penzance? Caniver lift?'

'Well I wasn't, but I suppose I need a couple of things. OK.'

'Good – and Hayley and Amanda too?'

'Amanda Goodbody?' Petroc's hands grew hot and he prayed not to be blushing. Never was a girl so perfectly named.

'By name and by nature.' Jamie smacked his chubby lips. Petroc knew it was beyond hope that Jamie would organize himself to crush into the back with big, bouncy Hayley when he could haul Amanda in to squash up next to him and jiggle his

55

great rugby-player thigh against the most delectable girl in the college. Petroc sighed, feeling used, being Jamie's transport by proxy for the purpose of his trying to pull Amanda. There wasn't much hope that Jamie would succeed, of course, which had to pass for compensation, but then from what he'd heard, there wasn't much chance of anyone short of a Rock God pulling *her*. She had a waist-long flag of soft pale hair, the bleached-out white-gold of a sand dune, and one of those pearly mouths that looked as if it had just said the poutiest bit of 'oh'. Even girls looked at her. He wondered where she and Hayley were going in the town. He couldn't imagine them wanting Jamie to give them a yes/no opinion on some dress they'd found in Beauty and the Beast. Still, a quiet word offering a return trip just to Amanda might secure him the possibility of hanging around the town till she took a whim to go home, then at least her spectacular legs would be alongside his as he drove, and with his being so long, their limbs might just crash into each other a bit.

'Do you think George is OK over there in the barn all by himself? Not lonely or anything?' Kitty put down the *Times* crossword and looked across the room at Glyn. 'I know what he said about drink but I wonder if we should invite him up, just for some coffee or something.'

'Hmm, maybe, whatever.' Glyn was noncommittal and clearly not listening. Kitty grinned. She should know better, she realized, than to try to talk to Glyn when Manchester United were one nil down to Southampton on TV.

'Though this might be the time of night he does most work. Unless he's a morning sort. It's only that we never seem to have just one all by themselves. He must be rattling around.' No reaction from Glyn. 'Or

56

he might have hung himself from that rafter in front of the Rayburn.'

'I'll go over and see him, shall I? See if he wants anything?' Lily asked, wandering into the room carrying an apple from which Kitty could see only a tiny bite had been taken. For supper Lily had eaten just one small lamb chop but a reasonable quantity of broccoli, no potatoes. Kitty realized she was now noting all that she ate. In the pools of lamplight in the sitting-room Lily's face looked all hollows and shadows, like a bruised skull. She'd always been thin, it was hard to work out if she was imagining that the girl looked somehow *less* of herself than she used to. She wondered if she should have tried to get her to eat more, or would that be putting pressure on and make her fight against it even more? At this stage it might be better to ignore what she ate, just carry on as usual, expecting her to turn up for meals and at least eat *something*, like normal people did. There'd been no rush to the loo to do any secret throwing-up, anyway. The thought almost made Kitty smile. Lily had always so hated being sick that she would, if she felt it was even remotely likely, wander the beach groaning loudly and breathing so deeply she almost passed out, just to try to get rid of the awful nausea. It was impossible to imagine her being able to do it on purpose. What was possible, though, was to imagine Lily starving herself to a state of near-hallucination in an attempt to stimulate her brain to celestial heights of poetry.

'He won't want a serious type of drink, obviously,' Kitty carried on musing to whoever might be half-listening. 'But he might like to feel it's OK to mingle a bit if he wants to.' The first half of the match had finished and a heavy-metal ad for a Real Man's car came on. Glyn pressed the remote and turned the sound down.

'The writers don't usually come in here and mingle with us,' Glyn reminded her, looking faintly hostile. He made a bit of a ritual of getting through several cans of Budweiser when he watched football, and resorting to coffee or fizzy water just to keep an alcoholically challenged guest feeling comfortable would render the match unwatchable. 'They usually make their own entertainment. Once you start letting them in . . .' He sounded as if he was talking about stray cats.

'Well, making your own entertainment's fine when there's more than one of them. We've never had a lone author out there before.'

'If he'd wanted to be with people, he could have gone to a hotel. Or just stayed home and let the pursuing wives catch up with him.'

Kitty sighed and gave up, returning to a tricky anagram.

'So *shall* I go?' Lily persisted. 'Is no-one going to answer me?'

Kitty put the paper down again and looked at her. 'No don't go, Lily; it's OK. I expect Glyn's right. We should leave the man in peace.' Lily went to the window and peered out, bored, into the darkness. There was more than enough peace out there for anyone if you imagined nothing but trees and grass and the sea, frozen for the night like a dismal painting. But you only had to do a bit of listening to work out that there wasn't anything that was really peaceful at all: there were owls and foxes and mice, and sea birds roosting on sea that wouldn't rest, and the waves that always had something to say and small, pinching winds that wouldn't let the trees sleep. It was only ordinary people who thought that darkness meant everything stopped; creatures, plants, poets, they knew better. She crunched her apple extra loudly so her parents knew she was still breathing.

Kitty recalled what she'd read about about George Moorfield's most recent novel. She hadn't actually read the book yet, but it would have been hard to miss the enormous number of reviews and interviews it had generated. Something about the kind of extended family, she recalled reading, where *not* to have sex with every single member would have been, as the *Sunday Times* had put it, 'significant as a sin of omission'. Lily would want to show him her writings. It was easy to catch herself speculating what he might want to show her.

'There's someone in the yard. And the car's not Petroc's,' Lily announced as an arc of headlights reflected on the mirror over the fireplace.

'Perhaps our illustrious guest is already stir crazy and has imported some "own entertainment" of an interesting sort,' Glyn chuckled. 'I'll go out and point them in the right direction.'

Kitty flipped channels while Glyn was out of the room and was therefore caught watching a brash and trashy game show as Rosemary-Jane hurtled into the room some way ahead of Glyn, who padded in behind her looking cross.

'They made me leave!' Rose announced. 'His bloody family just didn't understand!'

'Whose and what?' Kitty asked. Glyn reclaimed his chair, turned back to the football and turned up the volume, making it rudely clear he couldn't be bothered with proper introductions. Kitty got up to manoeuvre their guest out of the way of the football. Rose followed her, shedding a wondrously expensive-looking sleek camel coat and chucking it carelessly at the newel post at the bottom of the stairs as they went through to the kitchen. It dropped in an elegant heap, like something cast off by a 1930s movie star, and Kitty ignored it. She felt much the same as Glyn did about unexpected visitors, especially rather late in the evening. How difficult was a phone call?

'Tom's family, you know, Antonia's husband. Widower, I should say, though the word's too dire, poor man. I thought I'd stay on, you see, after the *thing*, just for a few days to help settle the children, just doing my bit as a family friend and then these *aunts*, his side of the family, naturally, turned up and insisted I should go, and go at once. They lined themselves up like guard dogs. And it's the *middle* of the *night*!' She parked her slim bottom on a chair by the table, placed her pointy chin in her hands and sighed loudly, a deep hard-done-by gasp of despair. Her eyes swivelled, taking in her surroundings, all pale maple and sunshine paint. 'Super kitchen,' she commented in a tone of mild surprise, as if good design was not to be expected west of Weybridge. Kitty took a bottle of white wine from the fridge and a couple of glasses from the shelf and settled herself at the table next to Rose, prepared for a long bout of listening. 'Middle of the night' was an exaggeration, especially as Rose must have been driving for well over an hour already, and the wrong way for London. A faint TV roar and a delighted yell from Lily told her she'd just missed Manchester United equalizing.

'So how come you're still down here and not back home?' Kitty asked, trying to feel calm yet politely interested. Back home with Ben. She tried to imagine again what he might look like now. The 'remarkably average' comment her mother had so disparagingly made furnished her mind only with a medium-sized, mildly paunchy executive in a greyish dull suit, some round-the-edge hair loss and no face at all, just blank pink cloth like a rag doll with unravelled features. He'd had, at eighteen, peculiarly soft downy skin as if he'd already been lying about his age and had actually barely started shaving. His mid-brown hair had had a stubborn curl at the ends, making him furious that he looked a bit like a housewife with a bad perm when he'd tried to grow it long.

Rose placed her hands flat down on the table and studied her nails which were painted a subdued pale pink, perhaps in deference to Antonia's demise. It was easy to imagine them painted a vibrant pearly cyclamen. 'Well if I went home *right now*, I wouldn't get there till about three in the morning. I mean it's more than three hundred miles to Highgate.' (More exaggeration, Kitty noted with a grin.) 'So I rang Julia on the mobile from the car for suggestions about hotels, seeing as she's a walking encyclopedia, and she suggested you.' Rose took hold of Kitty's wrist, making the glass in her hand tremble dangerously. 'You don't mind, do you darling? I mean it's just for a night, though I know it's all a bit out of the blue after all these years.'

'No, of course I don't mind. It's hardly as if we're short of accommodation.' It would have to be the sofa bed in her attic studio though, she thought, unless she trudged out in the dark and made up one of the beds in the barn. 'Do you mean these aunts just turned up and chucked you out right there and then? What on earth were you doing?'

'Nothing! Just my absolute very best as a family friend, same as anyone would,' Rose squealed, her eyes innocent and wide. 'Poor Tom's distraught, doesn't know what day it is, the children were wandering that great place like lost cats and after the funeral when everyone had gone, well, I just felt they couldn't be left like that. It was so big and so empty. Someone had to make sure those children hadn't run out of Coco Pops and that the dogs were let out.'

'But why you? Were there no staff?'

'There's a dopey au pair who's trying to book a flight home, three dailies who come in – you saw them, the ones handing out drinks – and a couple of garden chaps, oh and the farm staff of course, but no *family*. I couldn't believe they all just went off home. Quite honestly, I was glad to see the aunts.' Kitty couldn't help grinning and Rose's eyes widened again. 'No, truly,' she insisted. 'I am just a friend, you know. Ever since we made that programme. BBC2, you might have caught it, Antonia and I got on terribly well. I was due to go back to research another show, but now I don't suppose . . . Anyway, the aunts had been to the funeral and gone home, and then just turned up back again as if they'd had a powwow and decided I was the sort who'd nick the silver. Someone must have phoned them.' She frowned, trying to pin a name on the traitor. 'Ben knew where I was, you know. Well, I mean I hadn't told him I'd be anywhere else.'

'I don't think he did know, actually. Julia rang.'

Rose laughed. 'Well he will by now then, now that I've spoken to her. Can you imagine her having any piece of information that she doesn't broadcast?'

'Oh it happens. occasionally.'

'Talking of which . . .' Rose reached into her handbag and hauled out a pale grey leather Filofax. 'In here somewhere . . . oh yes, here it is. Julia asked me to pass this on to you. Some number about adoption. She said you should ring it and they'll be able to help.' She handed the slip of paper over to Kitty who read on it the address and phone number of the Post-Adoption Centre, a north London address that couldn't be far from Rose and Ben's own home.

'Very mysterious. What's it for?' Rosemary-Jane looked intently at Kitty. 'Are you adopting a baby? Are we allowed at our age? Or are you looking for your real mum? I never did think you looked much like yours.'

Kitty folded the paper and took it to the dresser

where she placed it carefully in a box covered in shells that Lily had made at school.

'It's no to both of those. Just something for a friend,' she replied to Rose. 'Have another drink and I'll whip up a mushroom omelette for you. Then I think if the football's finished, you should meet the rest of my family.'

'What time do you have to be back?' It was a passion-shattering question to nuzzle into Amanda's ear but Petroc had to ask, just so he could make an effort to pace himself and stay awake for the long drive back to her home. Getting her back here had been strangely easy and he kept expecting things to turn difficult. He'd spent the evening not believing his luck, since Hayley had got the train back to Redruth and Amanda had said yes to his offer of chips in the Penzance harbourside car park, sharing them with the greedy gulls, all through the couple of hours in the pub spending every last bit of his month's lunch money on her rum and Cokes.

It was pitch starless black in the yard at the back of the barn, and Amanda was keyed up and giggling from the last few hundred yards where he'd switched off the headlights and relied on instinct and the protection of the saint of showing-off to get him down the last part of the lane and through the gateway so he could park out of sight of the house. His mum was a great one for inviting people in: ambushing visitors the moment they walked in through the door, encouraging his and Lily's mates to come and join them downstairs and chat, when all they wanted to do was dash through the hallway, rush up the stairs and hurl themselves into the privacy of their own rooms where they could just hang out and where conversation was not something to fill spaces with. If they went in, his dad would sit Amanda down and ask her about university choices and think he should still give her advice, and his mum would offer her coffee and then look at the length of her skirt as if she was calculating how very few inches long it was.

'No particular time,' Amanda whispered. 'They don't much care what I do. I expect it's because I'm adopted,' she giggled softly, joking about it as only a securely loved child could. Petroc knew he had a half-sister somewhere out there in the world who perhaps also made lightweight, careless comments like that. Occasionally he wondered if she looked like Lily, all skinny and water-coloured, or if she was darker and more solid like him. Amanda's perfect pouty mouth was breathing warm and damp on Petroc's neck and he weighed up whether to slide a hand through to her skin now while they were snugly close in the car, or wait till they could get even more comfortable inside the barn. She might cool down on the way in and decide to become all sensible and prim. Or she might not. 'Though I've got to be up early for the milking. My turn, Wednesdays.' She pulled away a little and smiled, biting her bottom lip. Her face and hair looked ghostly against the black night and the looming building.

He groped in the side pocket for his trusty Maglite, reached across and pushed her door open. 'Come on, I'll just show you round. There's a brilliant room for parties. I've got great plans for this barn next time the parents go away.' He tried to make it sound as if his mum and dad spent half their lives flitting off on Concorde, leaving him and Lily to organize a social life worthy of London's best clubs. All he really cared about just now was that the barn, out of season, provided an enviable choice of many empty bedrooms. Amanda was the third girl he'd sneaked in there like this. The other two had been gratifyingly impressed.

'Are we really allowed in here?' Amanda clung to

Petroc's hand as they crept in through the barn's back door and she stumbled on the step in the darkness.

'Course we are,' he said, 'it's only another part of home. I'm only not putting the lights on because I don't want the parents to start thinking there's burglars and come out looking.'

'Would they mind, if they did and they found us?' Amanda had a soft Cornish accent, less strident than the local girls who picked Rita's daffodils, more like something that you heard on television when people were trying to sound West Country combined with posh.

'So who have we here?' A light snapped on, leaving Amanda and Petroc blinking helplessly. Amanda squeaked and clung to Petroc, hiding her face in his shoulder as if it made her invisible.

'Shit. I'd forgotten,' Petroc said, looking the amused man in the eyes and attempting a smile. 'Are you George Moorfield?'

George treated him to a sardonic grin. 'And are you burglar or squatter or,' and his head inclined towards Amanda who was now gazing at him with blatant interest, her mouth unprettily gaping, 'just looking for somewhere private for a shag?'

Amanda giggled and Petroc felt foolish and caught out. 'I'm Petroc, Kitty and Glyn's son. And I forgot you were here and I'm really sorry to have barged in. We'll go now.' He tugged on Amanda's hand but she didn't move.

'Are you really George Moorfield? I've read all your books. I think they're wonderful, especially *Framing Cain*,' she gushed. Petroc sighed, sensing imminent defeat. George ran his fingers through his long sparse hair and gave her the kind of smile Petroc assumed he kept for charming intellectually uppity arts-programme interviewers.

'Why don't you two come in and join me for a

drink?' he oozed at Amanda. 'Tea or coffee though, as I'm off the other stuff for now.'

'I should get you back home. It's getting late,' Petroc tried lamely to claim her back. 'And you've got to get up for the milking tomorrow, you said.' She looked from him to George who put up his hands in mock surrender. 'Up to you entirely. Or maybe you two would prefer to dash up the stairs and take advantage of room eight?' Petroc glared but he continued, 'After all that's what you came here for, isn't it? I do remember lust you know, even at my age. Especially at my age, come to think of it.'

Amanda looked flustered and took hold of Petroc's hand again. 'I do have to get up early,' she said, 'so maybe we should just go.'

The air was damp and chilly in the yard. Amanda climbed into the Mini, drew her legs up onto the seat and wrapped her arms round them. 'George Moorfield!' she sighed, 'I've always really deeply admired him. When he writes about sex, it's not like, you know, just prose. He does something with the words so it's like sacred or something, even higher than poetic.' It was the longest and most enthusiastic speech she'd come out with all day and Petroc felt depressed. The girl was clearly thrilled, but not by *him*. Well, not any more.

Petroc tried starting the car, the engine whining over and over. Furious with the whole world, he shoved his foot hard down on the accelerator. The engine still wouldn't turn over. 'I haven't read him,' he said flatly. Didn't intend to either, he thought, smarmy git. He tried the ignition again. 'Shit, I think I've flooded it. Now we'll have to wait.'

'Boring.' Amanda was grumpy now. 'Oh look he's coming out again.' She wound down her window and let in a blast of misty air.

'Having trouble? I could hear you not getting

started.' George Moorfield's lion mane of grey hair was horribly close to Amanda's face. Petroc scowled at him, sensing that 'not getting started' referred not just to the car. 'Just a bit flooded, I'll try again.' He did and the engine whined miserably. 'You're flattening it,' George pointed out helpfully. 'But I've got to get home!' Amanda fretted.

Petroc groaned, knowing what was coming next, and it did, 'No problem, I'll run you there, if you just give me directions,' the Great Author told her, opening the passenger door at the same time. Amanda scrambled out and grinned back at Petroc, looking, he thought, like a little rock chick abandoning the roadie for the lead guitarist. It was pointless to offer to go with them. 'My car's just through here behind the trees . . .' Petroc heard him say, watching miserably as a large hand appeared like a scuttling crab splayed against the pale beacon of Amanda's hair, guiding her out of Petroc's life.

Petroc slammed his hands against the steering-wheel, feeling like bashing his head against it too. He made one last feeble attempt to start the Mini, watching, as his engine struggled to turn over, the vast turquoise Bentley sweep past him out of the yard, with Amanda smiling like royalty next to the prizewinning writer. Petroc's only compensation was that George Moorfield, used to the well-lit, wide and direct routes of London, now had a twenty-two-mile round trip on some of the narrowest and most rutted lanes in Cornwall. He wouldn't dare take his hands off the steering-wheel, at least not till they arrived.

They were on the second bottle and Kitty had some questions that were not about Antonia's husband.

'Tell me how you came to end up married to Ben. I thought you'd have met some potential Nobel prizewinner at Oxford and never deigned to visit the dismal provinces again.'

Rose laughed. 'Oh, I met Ben in Paris when I was getting over the first husband. I'd married *him* straight from Oxford but he wanted immediate heirs and offspring and all that, which simply wasn't going to happen. We divorced and the next thing I knew his was the name destined to marry some pearl-necked dozy deb smirking from that front page they used to do in *Country Life*.' She stopped and sloshed more wine inaccurately into the glass. 'I expect they've got a whole litter of pink-faced little mouse-haired buggers by now. Probably *born* wearing velvet padded headbands. Anyway, I came across Ben at some wine-tasting in Paris, learning the wine trade from his old man, who soon conveniently snuffed it leaving Ben the deliciously thriving business. Coincidence about Paris, wasn't it? He remembered me from that pub we all used to go to near school.' She frowned. 'I didn't honestly remember much about him from then. He said he'd been out with you a bit.' She laughed, a harsh abrupt noise. 'I should sleep with your Glyn, then we'd be quits on the husband stakes.'

'You love him though, Ben I mean . . .' Kitty realized she was quite drunk − it seemed such a ridiculously sentimental question, as if the next thing they should do was to sob on each other's shoulders about the miracle of romance.

'Oh, love! How to define it . . .' Rose gulped her wine. 'Yes, actually I suppose I must do. We're the best of friends. You have to be when you don't have children, though we do have a dog. We prefer skiing and hot expensive holidays − and the boat. Oh and work. I couldn't be without my work.' She grinned and looked sly. 'It does mean I can get out and about such a lot. And I have to have that, absolutely have to.'

Chapter Five

'I'm glad she didn't stay long.' Glyn had said it more than once, as if chanting a spell to ward off any possible future visit from the demon Rose. Kitty was getting annoyed. On the easel in front of her was a half completed painting of Coverack harbour and before Glyn had clattered up the attic stairs she had been absorbed in picking out colours for the fishing-boats. Her paintings were bright and vibrant and often described in patronizing gallery blurbs as 'charmingly naïve'. She felt they should be under-taken in as light and happy a mood as possible if they were to gladden people's hearts and wallets, but here was Glyn like a mobile grey cloud, pacing the floor of her workroom and stirring up cooling air. He kept glancing out of the window as if half expecting Rose's silver BMW to flash into the yard again.

She was probably way past Exeter by now, Kitty calculated, driving too fast, carelessly flicking through radio stations or making phone calls. She wouldn't waste time concocting a credible story for the long-suffering Ben. And Kitty had no doubt he must *be* long-suffering – she'd now concluded that he was a man of routine and solidity who tolerated his unreliable wife for the pathetic excitement of her returning to him in need of a shot of stability and comfort. She would be more than tolerated, Kitty thought as she watched Glyn grumpily pacing, she would be positively treasured. Rose would easily have managed to keep an air of maddening elusiveness that had Ben still, after what must be twenty years, absolutely panting after her, body and soul.

There'd always been an interesting unreliability about her, bordering on sly deviousness. Boys had always fancied that aspect of her, back in their schooldays. So hard to pin down was Rose that the will-she/won't-she question about sex would be the last to come up with anyone who asked her out; they all had to start the guessing game with wondering if she'd even turn up. Kitty felt quite envious of this imagined Ben-and-Rose-excitement scenario: she objected to being lined up as the opposite by Glyn, lumped in with the safe and plodding and domestic and predictable. She pointed her paintbrush at Glyn, accusing, 'You're sounding like some boring old fart who doesn't want any new experiences in life any more. Just because you've officially retired, it doesn't mean you have to get dull and territorial.'

Glyn looked quite hurt. The skin on his forehead furrowed like the field Rita had let Josh plough so very badly the year before. He stopped pacing and went to the sink to scrape bits of Petroc's engine oil out of his fingernails with a palette-knife. 'Sorry. I just thought she was sort of flighty. Not a bit like you. I didn't know you had friends like that.'

Kitty was even more annoyed: he'd now damningly confirmed her private thoughts. 'Actually I *don't* have friends like that. You can't call someone a friend just because they were at school with you when you haven't seen them for a million years. Though why I'm not to be allowed "flighty" friends I can't imagine. I don't intend to feel in the slightest bit old and boring.'

'Now you're being contrary,' he pointed out.

'Better than giving into being bloody geriatric, especially at your age. Next, you'll be complaining when someone sits in "your" chair and grumbling if we don't have halibut every single Friday,' she countered. She squeezed a dollop of Winsor blue on to the palette and felt calmer. 'Did you manage to get Petroc's car sorted?'

'We jump-started it. He's not in the best of moods either. Must be something in the air.' Glyn looked down out of the window again. 'There's that George, wandering up the lane. I wonder if he'll discover Rita.'

Kitty looked out, down at the lane and along towards Rita's farmhouse. A corner of it was visible through the beech trees that were just coming into leaf. Kitty thought of them as half dressed, shivering in leaves too small and delicate. Only weeks from now she wouldn't be able to see the house at all. She could hardly wait, winter in the country was so desolate. When they'd lived in London, warmed by traffic pollution and heating blasting out from shops, she could almost ignore it. Here there seemed to be weeks of endless damp windy grey with just the occasional reward of a scintillating blue day of brave vivid sunshine. Even the sea, when it wasn't rowdy with storm, seemed to sulk. She pictured Rita sitting in her kitchen, sipping coffee by the wood burner and waiting for her young lover to finish sleeping. 'I think she's hoping he will. Josh might be starting to pall by now.'

'If you'd put your friend Rose up in one of the barn rooms last night, rather than cramming her in here with us, there might have been some fun goings-on with George.' Glyn, she was glad to see, seemed to have regained some of the usual cheery glint in his eye.

'I thought you were glad she'd gone. Just think, if

71

there'd been any of that kind of fun she might have stayed for weeks.'

'I don't suppose she would. The delights of metropolitan life call, I expect,' he decided. Kitty wasn't so certain. Julia had been more than hinting that any 'call', like an on-heat cat, would be from poor Antonia's husband, whatever Rose insisted about being just friends.

Glyn wandered off down to the garden to tend to his cauliflower seedlings and Kitty started on her painting. The phone number Julia had given her had been brought up from the kitchen and was now on a shelf beside her in the attic, tucked into a jar of sable paintbrushes. She painted the hull of the first boat and then went and picked up the slip of paper and looked at it again. She copied the number down, painted in the same blue gouache, onto a piece of water-colour paper, then pinned it to the big cork notice-board on which she kept pieces of inspiration: bits of coloured cloth, pictures from magazines, shells and slivers of wood from the beach and photos that might lead to a painting. It seemed a significant act. Nothing went on that board that wasn't meant to be made use of. For Kitty, pinning things up where she could see them was a sort of editing process: it might narrow down the selection of shades of yellow for painting the kitchen, or it might be to do with choosing oblong sunglasses or oval ones. She stood by the easel, sucking the end of the brush and looking at the painted numbers. It couldn't hurt just to find out what she should do, if, only if, she decided to try to discover what had happened to Madeleine.

She looked out of the window. Glyn was down in the greenhouse in the vegetable garden far below, she could just make out the shape of him, pricking out or potting on or whatever these mysterious gardeners did. She thought of his big gentle hands tenderly settling the earth round the fragile stems. Whatever she found out now about the baby, there wasn't any point discussing it with him at this stage. He'd only try to dissuade her, worried, she realized, that it might imply an unsettling. However he denied it, she'd been right that he liked life to be reasonably simple and predictable. It was for that he'd given up the trials and troubles of running a large school. She rinsed the brush, put it upside down in the purple jar that Petroc had made as a GCSE art project, and went to the phone.

'Surely it doesn't matter about exams just as long as I can read and write and count,' Lily was saying to Josh across Rita's kitchen table.

'You'll need more than that, otherwise you'll end up like me,' he grinned at her. He had very even teeth and she guessed that he'd had the kind of good and careful parents who'd taken him for regular ortho-dontic treatment, vaccinations and neat haircuts and then had to watch him turn into a drifter. She thought he looked very proud of himself, as if he was actually a cake that had turned out perfectly cooked without anyone looking at a recipe.

Lily knew she was supposed to care about getting good GCSE grades, had to care even more than the others, because of her father being a teacher. It was what teachers were for, for telling you you had to make *them* a success by working your own brains to a mush just to get their schools up the ratings so other parents would want their kids to go there. She'd told her mum she didn't feel like putting her-self out for the sake of unknown parents of children who weren't yet eleven. But then her mum had said there was no point failing all her GCSEs just for the sake of *not* impressing some unknown parents who wouldn't care about her either, and she supposed

73

deep down she was right, which made her feel weak and as if she couldn't stick with her own opinions.

Josh seemed to have got away with having none of the usual grown-up ambitions at all. He talked about the travelling he'd done, the bars he'd picked up work in, the finding out just enough about antiques and working with wood as if he'd learned it by chance. He wore Rita's old rainbow-striped jumpers and chewed holes in the sleeves just like Lily did. He hadn't grown out of things like that, the way adults were supposed to have, and he smelled of unmade bed like the boys at school, not proper men. Her dad smelled of sporty deodorant, fabric softener and earth and his hair wasn't allowed to stray into being too long. Josh's thick gingery-fair hair was on its way to turning into dreads and he wore odd-coloured old baseball boots with no laces and no socks. It was really cold outside, so Lily could only assume he meant to stay in all day, hanging out in the house's warmest place, like her cat when the air turned windy and chilled. Either that or he hadn't thought far enough ahead about having cold feet, which was another thing that meant he was being childlike. She would have thought of it, so she assumed she was already more sensibly adult than he was, which was depressing.

'You'll end up as one of life's rovers, doing odd jobs for silly women, or more likely men in your case, and living off your charm if you're intending to go the way he did,' Rita said, coming into the room carrying a tiny black goat.

Lily grinned, trying to work out whether Rita minded about Josh and his charm or not. It was hard to tell. Rita seemed to spend so much of her time teasing Josh and telling him off, like a fond aunt, as if she was cross with herself for falling for him. He didn't seem to take any notice. But as she passed the back of his chair, Rita's hand came out and she drew her nails across the back of his neck. Josh did an exaggerated shiver and caught hold of the hand. He pulled it towards him and bit into the soft pad at the base of her thumb. Lily winced, expecting a shriek of pain and toothmarks, but Rita was laughing, her mouth wide open and her face going pink, and pressing her body against the broad back of Josh. Her breasts spread out each side of his neck and made Lily think of those curved pillows she'd seen advertised for old people to read books in bed. She sensed sex in the air in a way you just didn't get at home.

All her friends' parents were like her own when it came to sex: just when you got to the age where you could cope with the possibility that they still *did it*, for fun, not for making babies, they gave absolutely no clue at all that this might actually be true. It was probably a 'not in front of the children' thing that Rita, whose children had grown up and gone up-country, had forgotten to worry about. It was the same with swearing, which Rita did loudly, all the time, and in front of absolutely anyone.

'I'd better go,' Lily said, yawning and faking bored weariness. 'It's nearly lunch-time and there'll be a bus soon.' She felt embarrassed and didn't want them to know. They'd laugh at her because, although everyone said Josh was quite young, to her they were like old hippies from way back and might accuse her of being prudish. Last summer Josh had swum naked in the sea every morning and taken his time walking back up the beach right in front of their house. It wasn't beyond possibility that he might just strip off any old time, even now in the early-spring cold. Rita wrapped her spare arm round Josh's neck and nuzzled his ear. The tiny goat, squashed between them, bleated a protest. Lily stood up and rummaged awkwardly on the floor for her school bag, eager to

75

leave before things could get any worse. Josh might
snake his hand up Rita's skirt, or take a bite at the
breast that was still leaning over his shoulder and
practically already in his mouth. She might as well
be not there.

'I'll give you a lift to the Spar bus stop,' Josh volunteered, disentangling himself from Rita. 'It's time I
went out and got on with the day.'

'No, no really, thanks it's OK. Bye,' Lily shouted
over her shoulder as she bolted out of the door. She
sprinted to the gate and out onto the road, not daring
to slow down and look back in case she heard them
laughing at her and her pathetic running away.
Though perhaps they weren't laughing at her at
all, she thought as she reached the lane and could
catch her breath. Perhaps now she'd gone they
were all wound round each other on Rita's big pink
sofa that was always covered with wolfhound
hair and old bits of embroidered cloth and frayed
crocheted blanket with loops of wool dangling for
the cats to play with. She stood still for a moment
and shook her head hard, trying to dislodge the
thoughts about passion and lust that seemed stuck
there.

'Hello. Are you Petroc's little sister?' Lily, startled,
opened her eyes and let the world which was still
shaking settle back to normal. George Moorfield
stood before her, looking as out of place in his surroundings as a haddock in a koi pond. Lily could see
he'd made not even the slightest concession to the
fact that he was so very far from Sloane Street. He
was shorter than she'd thought he'd be (it was
enough for his writing to have stature, she decided,
charitably), but more lined and grey, which she liked,
thinking it gave more of an air of having suffered for
art. She'd have hated him to look all smooth and
pampered, as if he got all his inspiration from just

lying in the sun watching cricket. Lily gave him a huge wide smile; this was the man who might recognize her genius. 'You'll ruin your shoes,' she said, hating herself for not thinking of something more scintillating for her first words to him. She looked down at the soft suede boots that now had waves of the lane's wetness, that had crept up and marked them like a high tide on clean sand.

'Who cares. I'll get some more,' he shrugged.

'Not round here you won't. Not like those.' She started walking again and he strode along beside her, hands in his leather pockets, taking one stride for every two of hers.

'I'll get some different ones then,' he went on. 'What do you recommend for the terrain?' Lily scowled slightly, but stared at the ground in case he wasn't really sending her up. She didn't know him, he might talk like that to everyone. He was a writer, they were strange. At least she hoped they were, because what use were they otherwise?

'You need a pair of Timberlands or Celts. Celts are boots, all soft and sheepskin but tough as well. Snowboarders and surfers and stuff, they . . . *we* . . . wear them. They feel like old slippers but they're OK in mud.'

She could almost feel him shudder, perhaps it was because she'd thought he might like the idea of slippers, as if he was really old. 'Celts it is, or they are, then,' he said. 'Thanks . . . what's your name?'

'Lily. And yes I am Petroc's little sister.' And I write poems and I want you to look at them and read them and then come and tell me I have insight and maturity way beyond my years and that you wished I was your daughter, she wanted to add. She looked up at him to risk seeing what kind of expression he had. Please, she begged whatever god was listening, please don't let it be 'amused condescension'.

Disappointingly, he didn't look as if he was thinking about anything. 'Amused admiration' would have been acceptable. She noticed his feet made no attempt to avoid the puddles, which pleased her because she'd have hated someone who she imagined should have higher things on his mind to pick his way along a muddy lane like a fastidious cat. At least he didn't have to worry about the price of shoes.

'Where are you actually going?' she asked.

'Wherever the lane leads,' he said.

'Well, seeing as we don't have a proper village even, no duckpond, no green, just a pub and shop, it just goes to the main road, nowhere special. But after that there's the road to anywhere in the world.' Embarrassing overstatement, she thought, feeling her face getting hot. 'Well, to Truro one way or Penzance the other anyway. So what's happened to your car?'

'My car?' he looked at her, puzzled. 'Oh, I see. Nothing's happened. Sorry, I thought you meant you'd noticed something wrong with it this morning, flat tyre or a wing fallen off.' He grinned at her. 'Writers' tendency, always to see the worst dramatic possibility. I just felt like a walk, see where I've set myself.'

Lily forced a smile back, thinking he sounded almost as pleased with himself as Josh had. But then he had a track record for more than just dossing about, anyone would be pleased to be George. He was always in the papers: 'Moorfield Against Monogamy' was one whole-page in-depth article she'd read, along with another called 'George's Dragons' where he'd been awful about his wives, and then there were the wacky lifestyle ones, 'A Writer's Room', 'Lone Living'.

'So, are these normal school hours?' he then enquired, eyeing her scruffy uniform with curiosity. 'Or shouldn't I ask?'

Lily weighed up the benefits of lies versus truth. 'I could tell you I had a free morning,' she ventured.

'And I could tell you the pig in that field there is just lining up for take-off. I won't tell your parents.' He gave a sudden deep chuckle and added, 'I seem to be making a habit of this, and here such a short time too.'

'Habit of what?'

'Accompanying beautiful blonde young girls and promising to keep schtum about what they're up to. Is Cornwall full of girls like you? Last night's had me driving about two thousand cross-country miles while she told me the plot of the novel she thinks she might write one day. Amanda someone. Not a bad plot either. If she doesn't use it soon, she might find that I will.' Lily felt heart-clanging envy. She could actually feel her hands getting clammy. Amanda Goodbody, two years older than her, had left their school for the sixth-form college with every boy fancying her, every prize for English and her first short story having won a national magazine competition. They'd all had to clap in assembly. Now she'd got in first with George. She looked along the main road and was, for the first time she could recall, genuinely pleased to see the bus. It would probably never, now, be the right moment to mention her poetry.

There was still a lot of detail to add but Kitty was already thoroughly pleased with the painting of Coverack. She always liked catching sight of her work almost unexpectedly, just glancing at it as she entered the room, rather than inspecting it close up and then getting too involved with it to be able to see it with fresh eyes. As she came back into the studio late in the afternoon, just to take a glimpse of it in the same way that an anxious mother does when checking a sleeping baby, she was struck by the blocks of vivid colour of the boats, the satisfyingly deep unnatural blue of the harbour water and the rich scarlet of the roof of the old lifeboat shelter. Close up, it still needed more work on the boats, varying tones added to brickwork, and some lobster pots and fish boxes piled on the quayside.

'You always make a pattern out of everything,' her foundation-course tutor had sneered at her. 'Set yourself free!' He just hadn't understood the all-absorbing calm of painting every brick on a wall, individual leaves on a tree. It might not be art, in the grandest meaning of the word, Kitty conceded, but it made her a reasonable amount of cash and, better yet, made her happy. It would be most satisfying if this tutor knew that postcards of her work were in every gift shop and gallery between here and Dorset.

Right now, though, there wasn't much point starting anything that would take more than ten minutes. Petroc's car, stranded with him at the college, was in dire need of a new battery. 'It's not just that it won't start, Mum,' he'd moaned down the phone, 'It's totally flat and even with push-starting it's going to keep on doing it.' Kitty, fearing for Glyn's back and blood pressure if he had to help get the car going every morning, agreed to pick up a new battery, drive over to the college and help Petroc install it.

Even after nearly seventeen years, since she and Glyn had left their small house in Dulwich and taken over his family's collapsing homestead after the death of his father, Kitty still found the distances that had to be covered for the simplest country errand daunting. Visiting the Truro Sainsbury's seemed to take more than half a day. You didn't just pop down to the Spar for an extra pint of milk without checking the fridge and the bread bin in case you later found you had to make another trek out. Her three-year-old

Fiesta had covered nearly sixty thousand miles, and at every garage economy-minded local drivers queued patiently in line at the single diesel pump. Right now, having driven five miles to collect Petroc's new battery and making her way another ten miles in the opposite direction, Kitty found herself wondering what it would be like to live again in a place where all one needed for life's efficiency and comfort was to be found in a five-mile radius. Urban politicians who whinged about housewives cluttering up the streets with the school run and gad-about weekend families polluting popular beauty spots clearly had no idea how real people in the country had to function without flag-down public transport.

Kitty drove up the hill towards Redruth station where an Intercity train heading for London was waiting to get going again. It looked far too big for the small station, making impatient revving noises as if it could hardly wait to get out of the county and up to serious speed. Among the schoolchildren who casually used the service just between Penzance and Bodmin every day, there would be many who had never travelled any further, never crossed the Tamar or seen a terminus bigger or busier than the harbour-side shed at Penzance. When Kitty had phoned the Post-Adoption Centre she'd been offered counselling, either locally or in London. She didn't want it to be local; the baby had been something from a distant time and a distant county. She could park right now, if she wanted to, forget about Petroc and his battery and simply get on that train.

A bus loading a rush-hour queue of passengers forced her to wait, and she recognized a tall slender blonde girl sitting on the bench across at the station outside the ticket office. Amanda Goodbody. Petroc had mentioned her name at his final school speech day when Kitty had been tactless enough to wonder aloud how a girl could so completely *not* resemble her parents. She of all people should have known better and when he'd said, 'Oh, she's adopted,' it had been inevitable. 'Even her mum calls her a cuckoo,' he'd laughed. Kitty had felt ashamed of her careless comment. The parents, she recalled as she waited for the slow procession of heavily laden bus passengers to pay their fares to the driver, had been classic Cornish farming people, stocky and with plum-skinned weather-battered complexions whatever the season. Amanda's hair was baby-fine and light, whereas her family's earth-brown hair resembled impenetrable nests of sprung wire.

'Hey! Mrs Harding!' Just as Kitty was about to move off behind the fully loaded bus, a streak of pale yellow flashed across the front of her car. 'Are you going anywhere near the college?' Amanda's eager blue eyes were peering through the window at her, so close Kitty could have counted her eyelashes. 'I've forgotten *Macbeth*!'

'Haven't we all!' Kitty laughed, opening the passenger door. A fresh scent of teenage skin and Body Shop soap wafted in with Amanda. 'I hope you don't mind. I was hanging round the station desperately hoping to see someone I knew, even if it's only really slightly. I've got an essay. Something about Lady Macbeth and motherhood.'

'*Was* she a mother? I haven't read it since school and I can't actually remember.' There was a gap in the traffic and Kitty pulled out and overtook the bus.

'Oh yes, she was. She says some stuff about breast-feeding anyway, though who knows what happened to the kids. Perhaps the babies died.' Amanda didn't seem remotely perturbed by the idea.

'Perhaps,' Kitty agreed. 'That might have made her jealous of that other one who had lots of children, the

82

ones that Macbeth killed. I hated that bit. What was it he said, "All my pretty chicks and their dam . . ." I always thought that was terribly sad. I remember sitting in class feeling quite tearful. It's about all I remember of the play.'

'Yeah, that was old Macduff,' Amanda told her. She fished around in her bag and took out some sticks of chewing-gum, offering one to Kitty who declined. Amanda peeled off the silver paper and folded it into a boat shape. 'I suppose my mum could have killed me,' she said suddenly, crumpling up the tiny silver ship between her fingers. Kitty, negotiating a right turn, was startled. They'd looked like a pretty close family when she'd seen them at the speech day, proud and happy parents, a daughter loving enough to allow them to hug her in public when her name came up for the English prize. 'Why? What have you done?' Kitty asked.

'Before she had me. Not this mum, not the one that adopted me, the one I was born with,' Amanda said. 'She could have had an abortion but she gave me away instead. I think I'm glad she actually went ahead and had me, but then you never know if you'd have got a chance to be someone else instead if you'd died, do you? I mean if your soul, or inner self or *me-ness*, whatever you like to call it, was going to exist anyway, you don't know if you'd have got a better deal if you'd been given another shot at it. Like karma, you *might* have been awarded a completely wonderful life just because it was owed to you.'

Kitty felt exhausted. The girl's train of thought was faster than Great Western.

'Come on, Amanda – look at yourself, beautiful, talented, clever, what more could you ask for?' They were pulling into the college drive, so Kitty assumed she could count on a short and uncomplicated answer. Amanda sighed. 'Paris?' she said after a small pause for thought. 'I wouldn't have minded being French. I do so admire Colette.' She sighed again as they stopped and she stretched her long legs out of the car door. 'You're right though, I am lucky. But I do wish I'd done A-level philosophy,' she said. 'I'm sure it would have helped.'

'It might have made things worse,' Kitty told her. 'Anyway, good luck with the essay. And with anything else you think you need it for.'

'Cheers!' the girl was out of the car and sprinting for the building. 'Hi Petroc!' she yelled as she ran.

'Huh,' mumbled Kitty's son, barely looking up. Amanda didn't even look back.

Chapter Six

The trouble with staying with Julia Taggart was that she liked to know exactly what you were there for. It was the price of the visit and, as Kitty preferred the comforts of staying at Julia's house to the dodgy anonymity of a cheap hotel, she was going to have to donate some information along with the flowers and contributory bottles of wine.

Julia, so long divorced and with only her own inclinations to indulge, hadn't yet moved on from the squashy over-stuffed décor of the 1980s and although the surfeit of curtain fabric and the number of cushions to be removed from the bed before it could be got into were slightly oppressive, at least Kitty knew this was one house for which she didn't need to pack the transparent hot-water bottle with the floating scarlet hearts in it that Glyn had given her last Valentine's Day. The spare-room walls in Julia's Victorian house in Richmond were painted the faded terracotta of old flowerpots, and the pile of the pale blue carpet was deep enough to lose even the flashiest earrings in. Kitty sometimes suspected that the rush to streamline her own home with stark beech floor and unlined calico, abandoning the cosy fitted carpet and padded curtains, had been an impulse not properly thought out. She'd been inspired by too many interior-décor features on the

American seaside look, all clapboard, linen and hot picnic summers. It was a look that required a serious input of sunshine, and sometimes in the mild but dank Cornish winter she felt her sitting-room resembled a skinny girl who'd worn a sleeveless silk frock to a chilly marquee wedding in early May.

'So, what time's your appointment?' Julia demanded over breakfast in her sunny kitchen which was the exact soft blue of love-in-a-mist. Behind the request, Kitty sensed a reminder to Tell All the moment she returned. Julia had never quite understood the word 'confidential', but there'd be plenty of time on the tube back from north London to work out suitable edited highlights.

'I can't think what you need to see a counsellor for, actually,' Julia, not waiting for an answer, commented as she poured coffee into artistically uneven rustic mugs. 'They can't tell you anything that you can't tell yourself. If you've decided you want to find your daughter what difference does it make what anyone else thinks?'

'I think the idea is that with this person I work out for myself the things I don't already know, if you see what I mean,' Kitty told her. 'Like why do I want to do this *now*, what's different from earlier. Why find her at all and what do I think either she or I could possibly have to gain from it, that sort of thing.'

Julia sniffed. 'There might not be anything to gain at all, not on your side. She might turn out to be one of those squawking girls who present kids' telly. Or she might be in prison for murdering her adoptive mother. You should be careful, digging things up. Or wait another ten years till she's more sort of fully formed. More like us, settled.'

'Digging things up' made Kitty think of an old Labrador rooting in the earth for a long-buried bone, scattering earth and trampling peonies. This thought was swiftly followed by the poignant image of a child's exhumed coffin, a dusty version of what she'd pictured during Antonia's funeral. Quashing her demons, she grinned at Julia. 'You sound just like Glyn. I think I'd rather risk it than not and if I want to see "settled" I can look in the mirror at my ever-increasing wrinkles and feel depressed. Don't forget I can't actually do any finding myself. I'm just opening the doors for her to do it, if she wants to. Of course she might not.' Kitty found she always added some kind of rider like that, even when she was only thinking, not speaking. It felt like touching wood or crossing fingers, except this time she hadn't quite decided which particular outcome she was touching wood for. Julia could easily be right, Madeleine could have turned out to be a complete disaster. Or not. Fingers crossed again.

She reached across the table for more butter. The croissants were fat and flaky and sinfully delicious, enough to make you sure that diets were only for those sad souls who were losing the will to live. Julia had gone out early to collect them from the French patisserie round the corner. In a moment of frank envy for the joys of urban life, Kitty thought of the huge old earthenware bread bin on the pitted wooden worktop at Treneath, which tended to contain nothing more exotic than basic wholemeal and Lily's favourite spongy white sliced. Sometimes she bought croissants in supermarket bags of eight and then put them in the freezer where they languished forgotten until they resembled fossilized pallid Plasticine and were long past any possible eat-by date. She could imagine the various versions of the Madeleine she'd conjured up for herself, peering into that bread bin: one version sneered at the lack of smart ciabatta and olive focaccia; another, less sophisticated Madeleine hauled out a half-defrosted

pain au chocolat and scoffed it down cold with coo-
ings of delight.

'So anyway, what time do you have to be there?'
Julia persisted.

'Eleven thirty.' Kitty sensed possible trouble.
Julia's sense of curiosity might make her suggest
going along as well. She'd say it was for 'support',
which was so very much a blackmail word in that the
offerer knew exactly how almost impossible it was
for the offeree to find a tactful way, *any* way, of turning it down.

'Oh good. That fits in.' Julia looked pleased and
started bustling about clearing plates and mugs while
Kitty was still finishing her last piece of croissant,
licking butter from her fingers. 'It gives you plenty of
time to get back after and get ready.'

Julia was being careful, as she rinsed plates and
shoved knives into their dishwasher slots, not to look
at her, but Kitty could just see the edges of a little
smile.

'OK, you've got that I-know-something look, Julia.
What are you planning?'

Julia looked up, wide-eyed. With her bobbed chest-
nut hair hanging like a spaniel's ears beside her face
and her pink-cheeked suggestion of guilt, she
reminded Kitty of the day they'd stashed one of the
biology lab's dissection catfish behind the gym radiator. 'Nothing!' she insisted, dragging it out to several
syllables. (Shades of 'It wasn't me' from way back
then.) 'Just a little surprise supper. Especially in your
honour.' Kitty recognized another blackmail phrase.
'I've just invited a couple of people, that's all, so we
won't have just each other to put up with all
evening.' Julia bent back to the dishwasher and
swopped a couple of plates round, pointlessly as far
as Kitty could make out. 'Just Rosemary-Jane and
Ben. Unless you feel you've seen too much of her

88

lately, just that she mentioned they might be out this way today . . . Oh and a chap called Martin from up the road who I wheel out when I need to make up the numbers. No-one special. Or do you think you might be too tired? I just thought you might find it fun to see your old ex again. That's all.'

Kitty grinned at her, defeated by Julia's cunning. 'No, I won't be too tired. I think I can manage north London and back without needing an early night. Though I don't for a moment imagine Ben will remember which of his girlfriends I was. It was hardly a great romance. Typical teenage thing.'

It was important to underplay it. Julia had shown staggeringly untypical reticence in not chiselling away to find out who Madeleine's father was, but it didn't mean one or two possibles hadn't crossed her mind. She wouldn't ask directly, that would be too simple and would involve no satisfying detective work. If Kitty simply said, right now, 'Julia, I think I ought to tell you, Ben was Madeleine's father,' Julia would be as disappointed as a child who demands and actually gets their Christmas presents early. Perhaps she hoped that plenty of tongue-loosening alcohol over dinner would lead to indiscreet reminiscing.

'Oh, he'll remember. Men only pretend they don't in case we've got something to hold against them. It's just like when they get drunk and claim everything's a blank and they weren't responsible. I had a husband like that.' Julia sighed and her face took on a rather remote, distant-memory kind of look. Briskly, she grabbed a J-cloth and wiped Jif round the sink as if scrubbing away the last memories of this sub-standard man.

'Now I've got today off work,' Julia said. 'So I'll just go down to the market for veg and over to Kingston for fish. Simple. I'll see you later.'

'So you're on your own then. I saw Kitty going off in her car yesterday with a bag and a look of travel.' George sat next to Glyn on the rock. Glyn shifted along slightly, regretting it instantly as he felt the seeping of a patch of damp through his Levis. It wasn't worth getting soggy just to make a point, but the beach was plenty big enough. George could have parked his bum anywhere. Why didn't it occur to him that a man sitting by himself on a rock might be there because he wanted to do some thinking in peace and quiet? Glyn had assumed a writer would be sensitive to moods. Presumably George was only sensitive to his own. That must be the problem with living so much in the inside of your head, you ended up thinking no-one else had anything going on in theirs. Lily, off school for an inset day, was further along the shore, perched in another patch of sunlight on a rock of her own, huddled up with her sweatshirt pulled over her knees and a notebook open. Glyn guessed she was writing something creative, sea-gazing for inspiration. Perhaps if he'd brought his garden journal and a pencil with him George might have kept a respectful distance while he planned his bean bed.

'She's left the car at the station in Redruth and gone to London for a couple of days. To see a friend,' Glyn told him grudgingly. Now perhaps George would go away and scribble something, which was what he was renting his room for, paying all that money. He was always wandering about, looking as if sitting down and actually writing something was the last thing he was there for. Weren't writers supposed never to be off duty? Shouldn't they carry handy notebooks around with them? Glyn was willing to concede that any kind of hand-sized computer might seize up from sand damage out here on the beach, but even Lily wouldn't be parted from a biro and a notepad in case a perfectly turned phrase struck. George, he could see, had given into the elements and was sporting a new pair of those sheepskin boots that Lily liked in a moss green shade. His chunky cream oiled-wool sweater was one of those sold as 'Cornish traditional' in Penzance. It looked so stiffly new it must have felt like wearing a doormat. Glyn would never wear anything like that; he preferred anything wool to be from the softest lamb, and ideally from Paul Smith.

'One of the most sod-awful things about London,' George stared out at the stripes of mauvey-grey sky on the horizon, 'is there's all those people and no-one to talk to just when you need to pass the time of day and make sure your powers of speech are still intact. You go down to the Kensington 7-Eleven for a *Guardian* and all they do is grunt and look as if they're about to call the police if you so much as comment on the weather. Here though, now here whenever I see someone they're up for a chat. Rarity value I suppose.'

Don't be too sure, was on the tip of Glyn's tongue. 'Curiosity more like,' he said instead. 'They just want to know what the hell you're doing here. Once you've been in the Spar a couple of times, everyone knows who you are and what you're up to. You'll end up desperate for a bit of Kensington anonymity.'

George laughed. 'No, it's OK, I like it. I suppose gossip is a sort of rustic hobby.'

Glyn felt uncomfortably as if he, a former habitué of Dulwich, was being called on quite unsuitably to defend rural habits. He wasn't really in the right mood: it was only mildly irritating, certainly not worth the effort of arguing about, that George assumed any old odd-bod from east of Plymouth must be just the most fascinatingly exotic creature to the culturally deprived peasants. He shrugged. 'Not really. Scratch the surface round here and you'll find most of the inhabitants are refugees from towns up-country. Rita in the farmhouse up the lane lived in Chiswick till ten years ago. That Josh she's got living there apparently has an old mum in Macclesfield.'

'Yeah, well we're all refugees. Everyone's got something to get away from, and I'm not just talking places.' George stared out over the sea and Glyn recognized a cue for him to ask a suitable question inviting confidences. He kept quiet. He didn't want to know about the carping ex-wives or writer's block or the difficulties of avoiding vodka. Whatever or whoever it was George was on the run from, he wasn't remotely interested, not right now. It was just the wrong moment. What he wanted to do was sit and think about Kitty and this long-lost baby that was nothing to do with him. He wanted to work out how he was supposed to feel about the possibility of being confronted by Petroc and Lily's half-sister.

It was all right for Kitty, whizzing off to meet the Post-Adoption people for counselling, to be dosed up with information and advice – at least she got to put her fears and ideas to someone. If *he* had turbulent feelings of his own about all this, no-one was going to help him calm them down. 'It's only just in case there's any chance of taking it further. I might not,' she'd said breezily as she left, as if there really still could be a moment where she'd decide to call it a day and give tracing the girl no more thought. It was about as likely as the FA saying they weren't that bothered about the next World Cup.

Over the weekend there'd been one of those momentous family suppers that he'd always associated with heavy television dramas. Whoever thought it a good idea to combine the consumption of food with the discussion of the most serious, life-changing events? That was something that, when he was safely

92

in an armchair doing the viewing, he'd always wondered about. He'd scorned it as a dramatist's lazy
device for gathering half a dozen diverse characters
together. Now he knew he'd always associate the
taste and texture of monkfish and coriander with
the feeling of being absolutely excluded, completely
left out from right inside his own family. It was like a
grown-up version of being last to be picked for the
rounders team, with the same heartburning anxiety,
the same stubborn waiting to be asked rather than
making what he wanted known.

When Kitty had said 'What do you think?' she'd
been addressing Petroc and Lily but not him. He'd
kept his eyes on her, waiting for her to turn his way.
Instead she handed him the dish of spiced rice (what
for? consolation?) and waited for the children's
responses. Petroc had been wary, fidgety, reminding
Glyn of pupils who'd been put on the spot with a test
they'd forgotten they should revise for. It might have
been because he was the elder one thinking he was
about to concede his leader's place. He'd gone on eating, clearly thinking hard and barely tasting what he
ate. Bits dropped off his fork and he picked at them
idly as if he'd already had a meal and was being too
polite to say so and offend the cook.

'Yeah, go for it. I'd like to meet her. We should,'
Petroc had eventually decreed and had then put
down his fork and left the rest of his food untouched,
all effort exhausted. In the gap where no-one spoke,
Cilla Black and *Blind Date* could be heard being
raucous and risqué from the TV in the sitting-room.
Lily had been straightforwardly thrilled and eager to
try to find this sister, childishly heedless of any possible problems. She wanted to see her *now*, she
wanted time off to go with Kitty to London as if
this 'Madeleine' might be brought home in a giant
carry-cot in a sort of reverse of her original adoption.

She was just too naïve to think there might be any dreadful consequences of all this. He, Glyn, with his appetite deadened, had sat and waited for his opinion to be sought and it wasn't. He was the one whose misgivings didn't count, the only one in the family who wasn't related to this child, or this young woman as she'd now be. If she was alive. If she wanted to meet her birth mother. If, for heaven's sake, she'd had such a miserable life she decided she wanted to move in with them and have another go at Happy Families. There were so many ifs to consider that no-one seemed to feel the need to discuss with him. He wasn't relevant.

One of the biggest ifs now scurrying backwards and forwards across his mind was the one that went: what if nothing comes of all this? It was too late for there to be nothing at all. Dire disappointment and a sense of abject failure might be the least of what was waiting for Kitty.

George Moorfield didn't even look at her. Lily sat like the Little Mermaid on her rock and fluffed her hair out the way Amanda Goodbody used to when she was at the school. Whenever you went near her, there'd been this waft of fresh shampoo in the air like some smelly spell she kept hanging about her to get all the boys to lust. Lily was willing to bet Amanda was still doing the same trick at the college, conquering a whole new set of besotted males. You shouldn't be that clever *and* that beautiful, that was like going back for second helpings of a delicious pudding while there was still a great long queue of people waiting for their first lot. God should have been more careful, kept things more even. Madeleine might be beautiful and clever like Amanda. Lily wondered if she would be able to bring herself to like her if she was. She'd try. Madeleine might have a beautiful, faultless nature too. That might be harder to like.

Lily wrote down a few unrelated words in a circle on her notepad. She wrote yellow, sentient, sap, coruscate, fleeting and triumph, at random, without stopping to think. She tried to detach her thoughts from the inside of her head so it was like automatic writing, coming from somewhere celestial, material from which somehow a poem would evolve. When it worked it was like being halfway into a trance. It wasn't working now. It didn't seem to be the right kind of day and it was too early in the year to feel properly warm outside, even in the sun. Probably, she admitted, it was something to do with the fact that she was simply sitting there on the rock posing as a poet but not, at that moment, feeling remotely like one. There was a stack of homework she'd been putting off till this day and she had difficulties with maths on her mind.

The maths made her think about Josh. It was all very well not minding ending up a drifter like him if there was some kind of choice about it, but suppose there wasn't, suppose she was just too dense ever to pass her exams and then hadn't got any choices at all? Decisions would have to be made right now, whether to get down to some serious school-work and spend less time on the sea or to go with her soul and aim to get the British women's surf championship out of the hands of Robyn Davies as soon as she possibly could. Right now the sea wasn't on her side. It sat out there on the turn of the tide, barely moving, lazy and flat. Today it would have to be the schoolwork, which was a pain because she'd have to eat a reasonable amount if she didn't want to be distracted all day by hunger pangs.

Glancing sideways to where her father was heading back towards the garden, she watched from behind her mirrored Oakley sunglasses as George

Moorfield hauled himself awkwardly to his feet and staggered slightly on the rocks that jutted through the beach's sandy surface. He still looked all wrong on the sand, in spite of the soft new boots and the bulky sweater that made him resemble a Tellytubby. Lily approved of him looking out of place. He was Town Man, an urban author who knew about agents and smart lunches and parties where everyone discussed their reviews and their agents and their spot on *The South Bank Show*. His flat had been in the *Telegraph* magazine one Saturday, all bookish chaos and erotic art. It was right that he should look bizarre out of his proper environment. When her first poetry collection was published, (before, during or after surfing stardom) Lily intended to be equally peculiar and be fêted around London in a pair of tatty Reef beach shoes, a Headworkx top and the floppy cream and black check drawstring baggies she'd seen through the windows of Big Wednesdays in Falmouth. She'd smell just slightly of the ocean (but definitely not of fish or bladderwrack) and be photographed for the cover of the *Sunday Times* magazine lying on the wet sand with the turquoise waves of Porthmeor beach lapping over her.

'Are you doing homework?' Now he was there, blocking out her sun. Lily had been dreaming away and was caught out yet again with no smart answers.

'Er, no, actually I'm waiting for inspiration. I write poetry,' she confessed, knowing instantly that she sounded silly and babyish. Amanda Goodbody would have simply smiled and said nothing and been thought enticingly mysterious. If she, Lily, had smiled goofily and said nothing he'd probably have repeated the question, louder, the way people do with small children who aren't concentrating. She waited, watching his face and daring him to laugh at her. George Moorfield nodded his head solemnly. 'I'll leave you to it then,' he said and then grinned, looking like Petroc used to when he'd broken something and couldn't help laughing. 'I'm not much of a one for poetry, myself. Frankly, I can't stand the stuff. Sorry.'

On the train Kitty tried not to think ahead to how she expected this meeting to go. She told herself, as she flicked unseeingly through her newspaper, that it could only go well. Only positive things could come out of it. It would be reassuring, like going to see a doctor when both of you know there isn't anything really wrong. She would be asked polite pertinent questions about her motives and why she thought finding Madeleine (or at least making it possible for Madeleine to find her) was a good idea. She had answers ready for all that, well thought-out answers that could only bring approving nods and satisfactory little ticks in relevant boxes on forms. There would be gentle comfort and warnings about not expecting too much, even to expect only disappointment. She was ready for that.

Changing trains at Waterloo for the Northern line, she made for a block of seats that were vacant apart from one slumped and dozing passenger where none of the silent standing passengers seemed to want to sit. Wary that there might be something disgusting waiting to be sat on, Kitty hesitated and met the eye of an old lady, straphanging and clutching the hand of a small big-eyed girl. 'I wouldn't,' the woman muttered to Kitty. Kitty glanced at the man. He was curled forward, awkward and twisted, his head hanging down. A thin stream of saliva was dribbling over the knee of his threadbare cord trousers and there was a more sinister patch of wetness collected around his shoes. He's only asleep, asleep and drunk, she thought. No-one spoke. No-one looked at him or each other. Kitty looked again. His back was bent over across his knees and if he was breathing it should have been easy enough to tell. A stench of neglect wafted from him across the carriage as the doors opened and closed. Once again a passenger went to sit down and quickly, more practised than Kitty was perhaps, thought better of it and swerved away to the other end of the carriage. Kitty thought of London's young lost people sleeping and sometimes dying in doorways. Maybe one of them was Madeleine. Of all the guises she pictured her in, this one had never crossed her mind. The next stop was hers. Only at the top of the escalator did she find a station official.

'There was a man on that train, I have an awful feeling he might be dead,' she told him. 'Is there someone you can tell?'

The man shrugged. 'We get them now and then. Not as bad as the Circle line. They can go round and round all day till someone complains about the whiff. I'll mention it, they might get him off by Finchley Central.'

'Thanks.' Kitty walked away, feeling she'd failed at something, though she wasn't sure what. A poor dirty man that nobody wanted to touch, alive or dead. He must have had some sort of family once, and then somehow perhaps lost them.

The little office was trying hard to be homey and relaxing, with its jolly pink tulips, comfortable, slightly shabby armchairs and a coffee-table on which Kitty noticed a newly opened box of paper tissues.

'Coffee? Or would you prefer tea?' The counsellor, Helen, was smiling, plump and mumsy in a gathered floral skirt and maroon chenille jumper. She bustled between the room and an annex where Kitty could hear the sounds of water and a kettle. Double glazing

98

muffled the sound of traffic from the main road and she felt quite safely enclosed in the warm room with this woman who had immediately told her that she too had once given away her baby.

'So. Tell me about your baby's birth.' Helen settled herself in the chair opposite and sipped her tea. 'Oh, biscuit?' She jumped up again and ran back through the doorway.

'No thanks,' Kitty called after her. 'It was very quick and hurt like hell,' she added.

'Stiches?' Helen sat down again and bit into a chocolate digestive.

'No, actually.' Kitty grinned. 'My mother didn't approve of that; she thought I was "getting away with it" as she put it. I suppose it confirmed her opinion that I really was a loose woman, quite literally!'

Helen laughed. 'You weren't though, were you. You were just unlucky, like me, like so very many others. Tell me what she weighed and was she bald like mine? He looked just like an egg.'

'Well she was seven pounds exactly, quite thin and long, and she had sort of pale gingery hair. I remember thinking that it might have some curl to it later.' As she said it, Kitty could almost smell the creamy hot scent of baby scalp. She wondered about the curls – had they happened or had Madeleine's hair turned dark and straight and flat?

'I've never talked about this,' Kitty realized, feeling slightly light-headed. 'I did after the other two were born. Everyone does, don't they? It's usual, it's what you do with your friends, I hadn't thought about it before. We weren't supposed to talk about it after because we weren't supposed to dwell on it. No-one back home knew, and your parents, well . . .'

'Adoptive births tended to be somewhat furtive and were supposed to be wiped from the memory,' Helen agreed. 'You missed out on all the natural

99

celebration you got with the later, "legitimate" births, all that essential new-mother bonding too. We women give each other that listening time to rant on about the uselessness of gas and air, or the wait for epidural top-ups. I always think it's as much part of the birthing event as the grannies knitting all those bootees.'

'There wasn't any of that either. I was in that ward, ten beds, for three days and my mother's face never betrayed anything more than hostile duty when she came to see me.'

'She did come, though. She must have felt something.'

'She wouldn't look at Madeleine.' Kitty's eyes were filling and she reached forward to the tissue box. Madeleine had spent most of her time in the nursery. 'In case you get too attached' had been the reason given by a shifty-eyed nurse who hadn't really known how Kitty should be treated. 'Too attached' might have meant letting down the childless couple who were counting on being able to give this baby a home. They'd been promised, so they were owed. There were single rooms for those thankfully rare mothers who'd lost their babies, but girls like Kitty were harder to categorize.

'Everyone else passed their babies around their visitors like gorgeous new dollies.' Kitty sniffed. 'Sometimes I just hated them all and I pulled the curtains around the bed, but I couldn't shut out the sound of all that gift-wrap. So much oohing and aahing over the teddy bears and Babygros. And everyone kept saying I was doing the right thing. For the baby.'

'Yes. For the baby.' Helen smiled. Kitty felt again the desolation of those days. The married mothers, triumphantly bloated with breast milk, had lain like vast queen insects on their beds, surrounded by cards

100

and flowers and a steady stream of joyful noisy visitors. Kitty had sat alone on her bed pretending not to watch, carefully embroidering the last silver stars onto the dress she'd made for this baby that she wasn't allowed to cuddle, missing the gossipy companionship of the girls from the home. As she thought about that time, she recalled the man she'd seen on the train that morning, the ultimate, desolate, result of having neither love nor care. If what she had done *hadn't* been the right thing for the baby, however was she to live with that?

Chapter Seven

Glyn stood back on the path to check that he'd put the bean poles in straight. The designer-crafted gardens he'd seen in smart magazines were currently favouring decorative wigwam-style arrangements, usually placed in symmetrically balanced corners of the garden or arranged centrally on beds as a focal point ('edging, filling and height' were the *potager* buzz-words). Stubbornly he preferred to stick with the traditional approach: a long structure like a denuded scout tent, using plain, fuss-tree bamboo cane held together with plain green string. 'The beans don't give a toss about fancy scaffolding,' he murmured to himself as he tied the last pole firmly into place. With luck, and with a good pitched battle against slugs and snails, it wouldn't be long before the whole thing disappeared from view beneath a mat of glossy bean leaves anyway.

The fresh air and the effort had given Glyn an aching back but new energy. When he'd finished in the garden, instead of going into the house to clean off the mud, he took a wander down the lane towards the field where Rita's goats were bleating softly just the other side of the wall. As he approached their noise grew louder and he heard the little ones scampering eagerly towards the gate, excited by the sound of his footsteps and the anticipation of attention and food. 'Hello babies,' he murmured to them, crouching down to stroke the pair of black and white heads that nuzzled eagerly into his hand. Behind them, their mother watched him warily, her eyes mistrusting.

'Cute, aren't they?' Rita, in a swirling purple patched velvet skirt, appeared next to him and joined him petting the goats. 'Both billies, sadly, but that's the way it is sometimes. I can't keep them, but I'm enjoying them for now. Perhaps we'll get a pair of girls next time.'

'Why can't you keep the boys?' Glyn asked without thinking. Rita's great open-mouthed roar of a laugh sent the little creatures scuttling back to their mother. 'Well, you can take the man out of the town, but you can't take the town out of the man!' she teased. '*Milk,* my dear, that's why. You'd soon find out the difference if you started milking this pair's father!'

Glyn straightened up, conscious of a twinge in his back from the work on the bean poles. 'Aching?' Rita was behind him instantly, one hand resting on his stomach (vanity immediately made him pull in his muscles), the heel of her other kneading into his spine just where it met his pelvis.

'Mmm. How did you know just the right spot?'

'It's obvious. You're a gardener, I'm a witch. No really,' she laughed, 'just common sense. It's where everyone aches when they overdo the bending.' She stopped rubbing and turned him to face her. 'I could do you a wondrous rub with some delicious oils.'

Glyn looked at her warily, wishing he didn't feel such outdated suspicion. Why did the idea of massage always seem somehow smutty to him? He was born in the wrong age. Kitty had had a course of aromatherapy massages just after Christmas and deemed it the most relaxing, calming experience ever. He just thought of tatty-edged postcards advertising

Busty Swedish Models and a fast-fisted toss-off euphemistically described as Relief.

'Yes? No?' Rita persisted, hands on her broad velvet hips.

'Yes,' he agreed simply, wondering what on earth he was letting himself in for.

'Right.' Rita became businesslike. 'You go home and shower the garden off you, wrap a towel round and present yourself on that big soft rug on your sitting-room floor in exactly twenty minutes. I'll go and get the stuff. Trust me,' she said, seeing his face registering alarm, 'you'll be making a weekly booking.'

When the train pulled into Richmond Kitty felt almost too exhausted to stand up and get off. She felt depressed and lethargic, wishing she was back home and walking on the beach where the air was sharp and energizing. Other passengers, with more sense of immediate purpose, pushed past her up the stairs, running to be first for the taxis and the bus queue. Outside the late afternoon was full of mild spring warmth and Kitty stopped by the flower stall and bought a big bunch of exuberantly over-frilled pink parrot tulips for Julia. She sniffed at them and their sappy scent reminded her that she missed Glyn and the earthy smell of things that grow that he seemed to carry with him all the time these days. All those things she'd said that day to the counsellor, she wondered how Glyn would have reacted if she'd sat him down and talked to *him* for an hour in the same way. How interested could he have been in a conversation about baby hair and a twenty-four-year sense of loss?

As she walked along the streets where so many gardens were enjoying the short spectacular blooming of plump magnolias, she wondered how long he'd have been able to sit still and silent and listen. Not for long, probably. Men looked squeamish when you started on birth stories. Rita had once said that they got that screwy-eyed look, as if you were about to produce (and possibly eat) a preserved piece of livery old placenta. Glyn might have looked at his watch, the way he used to do with the difficult ones on parents' nights who wanted a good half-hour more on the geography curriculum. But she should have tried, she realized, at least once.

Petroc and Lily had phoned to check with Surfline for the possibility of waves and taken their boards over to the north coast on the offchance that the optimistic recorded message wasn't out of date. Glyn was glad they weren't there to see him wandering the house wrapped only in a towel, pretending it was the sort of thing he did all the time, like some slick executive at a city gym. He felt rather foolish and part of him hoped Rita wouldn't bother to come. That would be the best thing, and then neither of them need mention the word massage ever again. Barefoot, chilled and with his aching back stiffening by the minute, Glyn went into the kitchen and started emptying the dishwasher, simply for something to do. He wondered if he should at least have put on some underwear. Perhaps she assumed he'd know you were supposed to, but then if he wasn't properly naked he'd feel silly if she then teased him for being pathetically over-modest, so uptight and English. She seemed to be taking an awfully long time.

'Hi! Sorry I was so long. Josh needed help moving a heap of wood across the barn.' Rita strode in, bringing with her a scent of lavender and damply rotting oak. Glyn inhaled deeply, savouring country smells, earth smells.

'I knew that rug would be just right,' Rita told him,

taking his hand and leading him like a child across his own sitting-room. 'Be careful how you lie down, go onto your side and roll carefully onto your front using your hand for support.'

'You've done this before,' he said, following her instructions.

'Well of course I have. You wouldn't want some hopeless beginner pummelling your flesh would you?'

Firmly but gently Rita arranged Glyn's arms beneath him and placed his head sideways on his hands. 'You're very tense,' she commented, rubbing the back of his neck and feeling for his vertebrae. 'Completely knotted. Obviously under strain.'

Glyn breathed out and tried to relax. 'Kitty's gone to London.'

'About the adopted baby?'

'You knew?' His head shot up and he found his face disconcertingly close to her knee. She was squatting beside him, the velvet skirt ridden up and showing winter-pale bare legs. She'd taken off her shoes and her large scruffy toes looked bony and vulnerable. The nails were horny and yellowed as if they'd endured a lifetime of nicotine stains.

'Of course I knew. We had a chat about whether she should go ahead or not. Did you think she wouldn't tell me? Or shouldn't have?'

Rita was burrowing in a deep bag, pulling out jars and bottles and doing a lot of pouring and mixing. The smell of almonds filled the air. Glyn, for a ridiculous moment, had the impression that she was going to use paint on his body, paint that would be indelible and show just where her hands had been. Not that it would matter, because this was all above board in a hippy kind of way that he'd missed out on all these years.

'Lie down properly and relax. I'm just going to go over you with a bit of this.' Glyn tried not to tense as

Rita took hold of his left foot. She kneaded quite hard at the base of his toes and he twitched. 'Ssh. It's OK,' she soothed. He looked up at the shelf over the fireplace. Things looked strange from floor level — it must be years since he'd lain down on the rug like this. He could see a chip out of the china on the underside of the big green vase of white daffodils in front of the mirror over the shelf, and the school photo of Lily that she'd been unusually proud of looked strangely distorted from that angle.

'Aren't you curious about her, then?' Rita asked, moving her hand up his right calf. Wherever her hands went his skin became warm and glowing, as if she was slowly cooking him with contact.

'About this old baby? I haven't been asked that before. I suppose I am.'

'What do you mean you haven't been asked? Surely you and Kitty have talked about it, what it'll mean if the girl ever turns up?'

Glyn felt Rita's hands shoving hard against his back. He relaxed against them, feeling that he was letting out more than aches and tension. 'No. We haven't,' he said, closing his eyes. Strangely they felt as if they might contain tears. His body was warm and tingling all over now and he felt cared for, cherished.

'It might affect you more than any of them, Kitty, Lily and Petroc.' Rita's soft voice was close to his ear. 'They're the ones who know where they stand.' She understood. He'd hardly had to say anything. 'Turn over now,' she commanded.

Glyn rolled over smoothly and easily, grinning to himself that the ease of movement made him feel like an oiled machine, albeit a machine that now smelled of lavender. Rita started work on his face, stroking away gently and lovingly. Glyn breathed smoothly and contentedly. If he was a cat, he thought as she moved down his body, he'd be purring. Without him noticing her move she seemed suddenly to be down at his feet, her hands working their way up his calves and on up his thighs. The only stiffness he now felt was in his cock, huge and hard, he was sure, as the Lizard lighthouse. He sighed contentedly as she slid the towel away and moved softly up astride him. Rita's oiled hands stroked the length of his straining penis with the same soothing skill that she'd used on his aching body and then she lowered herself and her naked velvet thighs on top of him. Her pubic hair tickled his balls deliciously as she took him into her body as if it was the most simple, natural continuation of the massage, her hands working his chest while her hips moved harder against his as their breath and bodies accelerated the pace together.

'How's your back now?' Rita asked later as Glyn tried to stop grinning.

'Fine. Thank you.' He opened his eyes and looked up at her. She was off him now, putting the towel back in place like a nurse sensitive to dignity. 'Do you . . .' he started.

'No, of course not. Not always, only when it's therapeutically called for.' Her grin was teasing.

'No consequences,' she then said to him as she packed away her potions. 'No telling, no guilt and no regrets, OK?'

'OK,' Glyn agreed drowsily. He'd been entirely (and literally) in her hands and hadn't even considered guilt and regret. Later he was sure he would – whichever way you looked at it, however generously peace-love-and-sharing Rita was about all this, he'd cheated on Kitty and he'd never done that before. But for now he was just shamefully delighted to have all his best prejudices confirmed. Massage really could be just the most devastatingly sexy event.

* * *

'You remember Kitty, of course, don't you Ben? Seeing as you went out with her once or twice, so Julia tells me.' Rose, her long folding body seeming to angle itself against both walls of Julia's narrow hallway, was looking coolly at her husband as if noting his reaction for later use. Rose was wearing high green satin shoes that Kitty had seen in a *Vogue* feature on Manolo Blahnik and which made Ben, beside her, look rather shorter and more square than she remembered him.

'Of course I do,' Ben said, putting out a polite hand to shake hers. Kitty took it and it felt damp like a fish. This was the man with whom she'd had her first orgasm, remote and courteous now like someone about to discuss the drawing-up of a will.

'I can *almost* see the mists of non-recognition clearing from your face,' Kitty laughed. She'd been wrong about his hair, which seemed as thick and as present as it had when he was nineteen, though it was lacking colour strength, like a cheap dark teeshirt that's been washed too much. He was still 'average' in girth, but in the substantial way more suited to a man of fortyish than one of twenty. His face had kept its slightly soft pudgy look, like a very old baby and with eyes that were wide open enough to make him look as if he was permanently alarmed. That was probably the result of all those years with Rosemary-Jane. She caught sight of her own reflection in the hall mirror and wondered how much of the teenager was left in *her*.

They went through to the sitting-room and Julia started bustling with the drinks. Rose paced about the room, inspecting Julia's décor, feeling the curtain fabric and idly picking a couple of petals from the large blue hydrangea on the desk in the window. 'That's a lovely shade of pink you've had the walls

109

painted,' she commented. 'You can get away with pink if you don't live with a man.'

Ben sat on the edge of the cream sofa opposite Kitty, looking nervous. 'I'm supposed to say you haven't changed a bit, I think,' he said, not quite quietly enough for Rose to miss.

'Well go on then,' Rose urged, prodding Ben in the ribs with a long purple fingernail till he flinched. 'Say it.'

'He can't, don't be silly,' Kitty said. 'Nor can I. I mean last time we met I had waist-length hair and Ben was, well . . .'

'Thinner?' Rose suggested, her eyebrows raised.

'Well, yes, but then we all were then. Real no-muscle thin. Even most *young* people aren't that skinny these days. No, what I was going to say was that back then he was into glam-rock eye-shadow and skinny leather trousers.' Ben groaned into his gin and tonic. 'Oh don't . . .' She grinned at him. 'Sorry if you'd rather not be reminded.' The phone rang and Julia darted into the kitchen. Kitty sipped her drink, wondering if the whole evening was to be spent in surface chat and half-accurate reminiscing. Only Julia could honestly believe that people who hadn't seen each other for such a long time would be sure to fall into deep and fascinating conversation the second they met up again, as if they'd been waiting all this time for just that moment. A devil in her wanted to blurt out that she'd spent two hours discussing the birth of Ben's daughter in north London that morning, but Julia had gone to a lot of trouble with a complicated sea bass recipe and could do without flashy distraction.

'Men. They're so unreliable aren't they?' Julia hurtled back into the room looking flustered. 'He can't come, Martin from up the road! He waits till now to tell me! He says he's got an urgent presentation to prepare for work tomorrow and he's very sorry.' She poured herself a large glass of wine and gulped at it. 'Very sorry. Huh. Well *I'm* sorry Ben, it's just you and we three women. I hope you don't mind too much.' She smiled at him prettily, daring him to say that yes, he did mind.

'Just you and Macbeth's three witches then darling,' Rose drawled from the depths of the most comfortable chair. Kitty could just see Ben's left eyelid twitching.

'*And* they're having a party next door, the people on the corner,' Julia went on.

'Oh, can't we go to that?' Rose asked tactlessly. Julia glared at her. 'Actually, it's rather insulting, they called round earlier to apologize in advance and said there'd be quite a lot of noise but they couldn't ask me to go to it because they knew it wouldn't be *my sort of thing.*' She finished her glass of wine very quickly, tipping her head back too fast so that ruby drops slid down her chin and were hastily smeared off with the back of her hand. Kitty feared for the safe cooking of the fish. 'I mean they hardly know me, so how can they tell I wouldn't enjoy it? They've put masking tape all over the kitchen windows too, so I can't see in. As if I'd look . . . They're no younger than us, they're professional types like me and I can hear their music and it's the same sort of rock classics and opera mixture that I like . . .'

'Don't take it personally Julia, they might be having karaoke night with their tennis-club cronies or a reunion of last year's Club Med in Sardinia. *No-one* would want to see that. You've probably had a very lucky escape,' Kitty soothed.

'Yes you're right,' Julia conceded. 'Who needs them? Now come through to the kitchen and let's eat.'

Kitty was sitting opposite Ben. As she was taking her first forkful of prosciutto, she caught his eye and he smiled at her, a shy, secret smile, too reminiscent of how he'd looked as a sixth-former. It looked most odd on a man over forty, too much as if he was trying to be coy in a way that his mummy might have been thrilled by when he was little. Her mind went way back to a conversation they'd had years ago, lying on the grass in the local park watching parents with young children. 'Don't you think everyone looks like an animal?' he'd said. 'That woman must have been a squirrel once, and that curly little kid looks just like a poodle.' Then he'd stroked her face, gazing at her just about as fondly as any eighteen-year-old girl could hope for in a boyfriend, and said, 'You look a bit like a Shetland pony.' Kitty munched her rocket salad and remembered that she hadn't felt particularly insulted. You took sentences like that and extracted the best possible way of interpreting. If he'd smiled nastily and told her she was snakelike she'd simply have chosen from that the smooth, slinky and lithe attributes. She'd had shaggy blond hair back then, which might just look a bit mane-ish, and she assumed Shetland ponies had large limpid eyes with massive lashes. She'd been careful not to blurt out that he reminded her of a rabbit. He wouldn't have liked that and she'd been careful with his feelings.

'I'm supposed to set fire to this . . .' Julia slurred over the sea bass as she poured a reckless amount of Pernod over it. 'Says it needs flambéeing. S'old-fashioned, like steak Diane, 'member that? Who *was* Diane d'you think?'

'You can't do that Jules, you're too pissed. Let Ben do it,' Rose said, shoving Ben hard in the side again. His poor bruised ribcage must look like someone had spilled ink on it, Kitty thought, grimacing in sympathy. Dutifully, he got up and went to Julia's aid. 'Sit down, I'll finish it off for you.'

'And I'll get the potatoes out of the oven,' Kitty said, joining in.

'I'll just stay here and be an admiring audience with Julia.' Rose poured herself and Julia another glass of wine. 'Do you remember that time we got Antonia drunk on the school trip to Blenheim?' she giggled.

'You're not to speak ill of the dead,' Julia warned.

'What's ill? Apart from Antonia. Ill *and* dead! And God, was she *ill*!' They fell against each other, convulsed with giggles. Kitty put the dish of *boulangère* potatoes on the table and sat looking at them. She remembered the incident well enough. 'And she drank all of it!' Julia was shrieking, 'it was her own fault.'

'Shouldn't have been so greedy. If she'd sipped it she'd have tasted the rum in the Coke.'

'She nearly got expelled,' Kitty reminded them. 'She probably only drank it at all because she thought we were being nice to her.'

'Should have known better by then,' Julia spluttered.

'Wasn't it a horrid mess, all that sick on the coach? It kept sliding about,' Rose giggled. Tears had spread her mascara down her cheeks and it had caught in the fine lines of her skin, just like, Kitty thought, seaweed stuck in the ripples on the sand.

'Anyone got a match?' Ben was still playing with the bass, pushing it here and there with a spatula the way Glyn always did with anything on a barbecue.

'Here.' Rose handed him her gold lighter, not looking at him, but smirking and biting her lip, just the way Kitty remembered her when she'd offered the rum-laced drink to poor Antonia. The flame that leapt out was spectacular, shooting way up to the ceiling and licking all round Ben's hand, which he pulled away too fast, spilling the bottle of Pernod all over the fish and into the flames.

'Shit!' he roared, backing towards the sink and turning on the cold tap.

'My curtains!' Julia shrieked, flapping at the burning cloth with a tea towel.

'A bit clumsy, Ben.' Rose commented.

Kitty grabbed the small fire extinguisher that Julia had hanging on the wall by the door and aimed it at the cooker. It fizzed for a few seconds, produced a pathetic stream of foam and gave out. Rose flung the contents of the kettle at the curtains and Julia squealed again.

'Fire brigade?' Rose's voice was excited.

'No, I'll deal with this. You three out. Now.' Ben was moving fast, scooping the three women out through the front door.

'It's freezing and people opposite are staring.' Rose stood on the pavement, hugging her body and stamping her feet. 'Let's go to next-door's party and keep warm.'

'Good idea,' Kitty agreed. She followed the sounds of music and a good time up the path next to Julia's and rang the bell.

'Mick's here!' someone on the other side yelled, opening the door wide and standing back.

'Ah. Not Mick,' said the voice, shutting the door quickly.

'That was Martin!' Julia shouted. 'And did you see . . . ?'

'All those studs,' Kitty marvelled.

'And the leather mask!'

'I saw a naked bottom and some boots,' Rose said solemnly.

'No wonder I wasn't invited.' Julia sounded quite regretful. Kitty took hold of her arm. There was a chic and inviting café bar just across the road. Ben would find them in there if he escaped alive from the kitchen inferno. There'd be food and she was starving. 'Suppose they had asked you,' she comforted, 'you wouldn't have had a thing to wear.'

Rosemary-Jane smirked. 'I would,' she said. Kitty grinned at her. She didn't doubt it.

'Drinks,' Julia said the moment the café door was open.

'You'd better have a Coke,' Rose told her, 'unless you want to get pissed enough to do an Antonia.'

Kitty bought spritzers for her and Rose and a diet Coke for Julia. The menu looked reasonably promising with mussels and lasagne and a selection of chicken dishes and salads. There were quite a lot of customers but Julia bustled her way through to a free table and sat down heavily.

'Shall we wait for Ben?' Kitty said, studying the menu.

'Heavens no. If I spent my life waiting for Ben I'd never get anything done. I love him dearly but he's one of life's plodders, everything at his own stolid pace.'

Her mother had been on the right lines then, Kitty thought. Staring at the menu she thought about all the sticky summer days they'd spent together, curled up in his single bed while his mother was out at work, typing for the local education authority. The sun had blazed away outside and they had lain there, sweaty and pale, touching and kissing and experimenting and being pleased to have each other like this at just the right time for learning the sexual ropes. They'd known it was to be temporary, which made it more exciting somehow (nothing of the 'stolid pace' about him then, she recalled). Ben had had his flight to Africa booked since well before he'd met her and neither of them was going to claim it was the kind of love that could shatter long-laid plans.

Just as they were about to order Ben arrived. He

115

brought with him the scent of fire and cold night air.

'All done. Though the kitchen's a bit messy,' he told Julia, putting her house keys into a puddle of spilt wine on the table. Rose tutted loudly, picked them up and wiped them down Ben's thigh. Presumably used to this sort of thing, he ignored her, 'I smothered the fire with towels but the smoke's made the whole house smell a bit. I left the windows open.'

'Burglars,' Julia grumbled. 'I'll be robbed.'

'No you won't,' Rose reassured her. 'Say thank you nicely, Julia.'

'Thank you Ben,' Julia smiled.

'So,' Ben said as Rose went to the bar to order. 'I suppose living in Cornwall you saw quite a lot of that poor Antonia woman you were all taking the piss out of?' he said to Kitty.

Kitty thought about Rose at the funeral, angling her long body towards Antonia's widower. The words 'indecent haste' came to mind. 'Actually, I hadn't seen her, *haven't* seen her since we left school. Julia only dragged me along because she was curious. As ever.' She looked hard at Julia but Julia's attention was elsewhere, her head turned so that the salient details of the row the couple behind her were having were going directly into her left ear.

Ben's eyebrows had shot up in surprise. 'Really? But Rose said you were practically neighbours. She's been working down there you know, a garden programme.'

'Everyone thinks you're only ten minutes from everyone else if you live in the same county. I did know about the programme.' Ben was asking for different information, she could see it in his anxious eyes. She didn't have it to give, only an awful sense of power that if she voiced her suspicions she could make this man very unhappy.

'Antonia had three children, Rose told me,' he

116

said. 'Poor things. Imagine losing your mother like that.' She felt touched, recognizing real sympathy for these children he'd never met.

'We haven't got children.' He was watching Rose exchanging easy chat at the bar with a blonde Australian barman. She was pulling at strands of her highlighted hair and then pointing at his, apparently deeply involved in discussing tints. 'I didn't used to think she minded that much though,' Ben added.

But what about you? Kitty thought. Really, she no longer knew him well enough to ask. She never had.

Chapter Eight

Kitty had been back from London ten days and Ben had phoned six times to talk about Rose. He was driving Kitty crazy and she'd taken to shouting 'I'm not in!' at the first ring. Of course no-one in the house took any notice. Petroc just looked depressed and growled, 'It won't be for me,' which she took to mean it wouldn't be Amanda and if it was anyone else he didn't care anyway. Lily and Glyn always seemed to be on their way out of a room, not so much as turning back with curiosity, when the phone rang.

'When I think, all those years ago he simply disappeared to do his VSO and never even sent me a postcard,' she complained to Glyn after the first four calls. 'He must have been looking through Rose's address book. I can't imagine him coming straight out with it and saying, "Hey Rose, what's Kitty's number these days, I think I'll call her a hundred times and talk about the affair I think you're having."'

'It's for you. Your admirer again,' Glyn smirked, handing the phone over to Kitty soon after breakfast. Tee-heeing at her and making mocking kissy noises, he drew a fat heart on the Post-it pad on the dresser, scrawled Ben's name on it and added an arrow through the middle, then stuck it on the cupboard door. He went out to the car to go off to do a stint filling in for a depressed colleague at the college,

118

whistling cheerily, and Kitty could hear him shouting hello across the yard to George.

'Well, you know what Rose is like . . .' Ben was sounding defeated as usual. Rose was away working, back in Cornwall filming something about mulch and manure at the Lost Gardens of Heligan and far too near to Tom for Ben's peace of mind. Kitty assumed she was getting lumbered with his confidence purely on the grounds that she was at the moment geographically closer to his wife than he was. There must have been other, closer friends of hers he could be sounding out, because really she *didn't* actually know what Rose was like, not these days. She only knew what she thought Rose might be like. For Ben, apparently, that was good enough.

'Perhaps I should have gone with her, but pressure of work, you know. And someone's got to keep the dog company at night.' Ben laughed weakly, as if even he knew how pathetic he sounded. She imagined him with a lonely takeaway, at one end of a long kitchen table, feeding chicken tikka scraps to an equally miserable-looking basset hound. Then she pictured the two of them curled up together on a sofa from which Rose had long ago banned the dog, watching a video about wronged husbands and revenge, stuffing themselves with sour-cream flavour Pringles.

Kitty shoved a cushion onto one of the kitchen chairs and settled herself into it, resigned to a long session of counselling. Ben was one of those people who liked to get well stuck in for a phone chat, going in for moaning in one long uninterruptible stream. He'd probably got himself all ready to call her with a mug of coffee and a scheduled space in his office diary. In her experience, men weren't usually keen on telephones. If Petroc and Glyn were typical, they simply made whatever arrangements the call demanded, or in Petroc's case grunted unintelligibly for fifteen seconds, then hung up. Rita had once said that a low phone bill was the best thing about having sons and not daughters.

Kitty wished she was up in the studio, where at least she could be adding a few seagulls to the Coverack painting while Ben talked. Just within reach on the window-ledge behind the sink was a bottle of Lily's nail varnish, so she entertained herself painting her left toenails purple. When Ben eventually took a breath she cut in quickly. 'Well Rose is working too, isn't she? It's not as if she's swanned off for no reason. Suppose it was the other way round and she had suspicions about you; how would you feel if she tagged along to all the wine auctions just to keep an eye on you? It would be like having your mum along at a scout camp.' She tried to keep it light, though there was only an outside chance she'd achieve a quick cheer-up breakthrough with him and be able to get back to work.

Not much painting had been done in the couple of weeks since she'd got back from London, having decided it might be a good idea to spend a bit of time with Glyn and convince him she wasn't about to run off back to the city and move into a flat with Julia and Rose in an effort to recapture some sort of lost school-buddy idyll. Nor, she made it clear, was she going to brood about Madeleine and race up the lane every morning to meet the postman's van in case all the form-filling and list-registering had worked and the girl decided to write a letter. What would it say if she did, she wondered as Ben prattled and she mopped purple globs of varnish off the table, 'Hello Mum'? 'I'm now on the Adoption Contact Register,' she'd told Glyn and the children. 'If anything comes of it, well fine. If not, well fine as well.' Glyn seemed convinced, though she wasn't quite so sure she was.

'And you'd think after so many years,' Ben was droning on. 'Perhaps if we'd had children. Perhaps if it had worked out with you and me . . .' Kitty started sketching Lily on the back of a bank statement. She could see her through the open doorway, sitting outside on the wall wearing her wetsuit and looking out at the sea, her fine pale hair drifting this way and that in the breeze. In a moment she would slide silently into the water and paddle out into the waves on her board, using reserves of strength that hardly seemed credible in someone who looked so fragile.

'And she's taken all her make-up: the going-out sort, not just the stuff she puts on quickly for work.' Kitty sighed impatiently and prodded at her big toe. The purple stuff was nearly dry but had turned a nasty insipid bluey-mauve, as if she'd been stepped on hard by a big pony. Ben was whining now, there was no other word for it. If it was Petroc she'd tell him to get over it, find someone else.

'You know, maybe you should just give up on her,' Kitty said callously, her mind on Petroc and his gloom over Amanda. 'Maybe all the worst possibilities you can think of are absolutely right and your marriage has simply run its course.'

'Oh. You don't really think so? Not deep down?' Ben prodded for signs of hope. Kitty felt as if she'd smacked a puppy.

'Look Ben, why don't you just ask her? It can't really be worse than just imagining, surely.' It could though, she knew that. No-one wants to be told that the worst they think is true. It was so much more comfortable to keep pretending that the best might be true instead.

Lily didn't care that it wasn't safe to be surfing alone. It was her beach, nothing the sea did here could surprise her. If someone was with her she'd only have to feel responsible for them, especially close to mid-tide when there was a vicious undertow over by the rocks on the west side. There was a medium offshore wind and the waves were coming in clean and just big enough, early-morning perfection. The sounds of the sea were muffled through her winter helmet and her webbed gloves helped her paddle through the water, out beyond the rock-line, with the grace and speed of a cormorant. Petroc had told her that in her full cold-weather kit she looked like a seal, all cased in neoprene like this. But seals were fat and they lumbered and wobbled on land. Lily felt she was more of an eel, slinky and slim. She got that from her mother who was just starting to admit to being middle-aged now but hadn't got the spread. Somewhere out there, she thought as she paddled along, she'd got a sister and she didn't even know what she looked like. She hoped she looked like her, so if they met they could see each other reflected, know how each felt in their own skin. Also she could see what she might look like in a few more years – decide if she liked what the future held and make arrangements, eating-wise and hair colour and such, if she didn't.

Pulling her concentration back and forgetting about this mystical Madeleine, she kept her head down on the board, feet together, streamlined and low, feeling no aches or strain as if only this one thing was what her body was built for. Knowing without looking that she had reached the right place, she turned the board sideways and lay on the waves. On its way from beyond the horizon, she could see, was the perfect set as if it had just been waiting for her. She smiled, steadied the board and braced as the first wave came, let that one go and then took off on the second. It was better than flying. Someone at school had said it was better than sex, though this particular someone was one who might not be relied on to know. It was like running across the surface of the sea, the ultimate walk on water. 'Eeeeagh!' she shrieked as she made a perfect cut-back before planing right up onto the sand. She picked up the board and shook her hair out of the helmet. That was enough for now. It couldn't be beaten, not on that day.

'Do you think that's what Jesus was doing?' George was on his rock in a patch of thin sun again, bravely barefoot this time. She was sure he must be pretty freezing – he looked all stiff as if he'd been there the whole night. He reminded her of the summer holiday-makers who even in the dankest sea mist still came to the beach, because that was what you did every day for a fortnight.

'Was *what* what Jesus was doing?' she called as she walked up the sand.

'Was Jesus the first surfer? You know, walking on the water?'

'Did he have a board?'

'Don't think the Bible mentions one.'

'Then he wasn't a much of a surfer, was he?' Lily stood in front of George, looking down at him and dripping cold sea water on his pale feet. City feet, she thought, guessing how much it must have hurt him to step across the gravelly yard and the layer of crushed shells, pebbles and weed at the top of the high-tide line. Serve him right, she thought, for not having the soul for poetry. She reached for the cord behind her back, pulled down the zip of her wetsuit and wriggled her shoulders and arms free from the neoprene. Her soaking rash-vest clung to her thin body and she shivered. George grinned up. 'Listen, I'm sorry about the poetry, about not being keen. If you want to show me some of your writing I promise to ignore my prejudices.' Lily could feel herself blushing scarlet. She hated him instantly. He was patronizing and he'd wrecked her mood.

123

'No fucking way,' she spat at him and stormed back to the house. Where the skin on her shoulders and back had been cold it now felt as if it was burning, as if she could feel George watching her walk. She felt aware of how she moved, seeing in her mind her skinny legs in their tight black casing. She wished the sand would part and she could walk down into a pit and cover herself. There was nothing worse, nothing at all worse than feeling like a total fool.

'Rita's here! Be quick Lily, you'll make her late,' Kitty was calling up the stairs. Rita was in the kitchen by the window, watching the blue tits squabbling over the nut feeder hanging from the cherry tree. 'It's coming up to blossom time. All swollen buds and sexual readiness,' Rita murmured. She was sitting inelegantly slumped with her legs apart and her purple crushed-velvet skirt draped across her thighs. Kitty thought the big expanse of fabric looked as if something was missing from her lap, a baby perhaps, or a basket of fruit, whatever they used to hold in those dark old paintings of unsmiling, put-upon women. Rita was wearing flat, round-toed sandals, half blue, half red, like children's holiday shoes, with enough room inside for her toes to splay comfortably. The shoes were scuffed and shabby, the stitching along the thick crêpe soles was coming undone, and her navy wool tights drooped over the straps. Sad shoes, Kitty thought, shoes for feet that no longer had the heart to dance. How different they were from Rose's frivolous Manolo Blahniks that she'd worn at Julia's. Those had been shoes to seduce by, shoes for tautening the leg muscles and making you think of sex. If she'd packed those for Cornwall, she was definitely up to no good. She wouldn't trouble Ben with that particular question.

'What's wrong Rita, you've lost some of your sparkle?'

Rita managed a half-hearted smile. 'Not much. Just that it'll soon be summer and Josh will be off.'

'Why? I thought he seemed pretty settled.' Kitty laughed. 'You've made him very comfortable.'

'He's just like the cats,' Rita said, watching Lily's ginger cat pacing stealthily along the beach wall, slinking low to creep up to where the blue tits were feeding. 'They only want to be in snuggling up to you when it's cold, making you feel loved and special. Come the summer he'll be off hunting just like they do and I'll be all on my own again.' She stood up and stretched, stiff. 'Where's Lily? She does want a lift to school doesn't she?' She sounded unusually impatient as if she wished she hadn't said anything.

'Talking about it doesn't make it happen you know,' Kitty told her.

'Doesn't make it not happen either, does it?' Rita sighed. 'Perhaps I shouldn't have had the children so young, then these middle years would still have some purpose. But everyone I knew was hauling a baby around with them when I had the boys. Toddlers were an essential part of the scene at all those summer festivals. All their little plump bodies running around naked. Mine had daisies in their hair. You never thought about them growing up and turning into accountants and teachers and stuff.' Her twisted grin lit up her face again. 'Malory, the eldest, he rang the other night and told me he's taking a party of year nines on a geography field trip to Swanage. And he's worried they'll misbehave. He's turned out so straight I can't believe he's mine sometimes.'

Amanda was being as friendly and normal as if nothing had happened and Petroc found it very hard to deal with. All the times he'd seen her since what he called in his head the Night of George, she'd just been casual, saying hello and then walking on by with Hayley or someone like she always did, and he'd had to be as if none of it mattered or had even happened. He had a feeling that if he said anything, reminded her how close they'd got to some serious sex, she'd go blank and look at him as if he was loopy. Perhaps it had all been some wanker's fantasy he'd had. A big sticky horny dream. He wanted to get her alone somewhere and do some talking about what, if anything, their relationship actually was, or could be, but she was like something slippery and couldn't be cornered. He'd think she was being evasive if she was anyone else, because anyone else would do silly-girl drama things like suddenly turn and stride off the other way if he met them in a corridor. He could deal with that all right, because he'd be the one in control of it all. But Amanda just chatted on, or not, as she always had, borrowing 20p for the phone if he was the nearest, or offering her own notes on Wordsworth's *Prelude* to anyone who wanted them, including him. He was simply not special.

Now though, during the morning break she brought an extra cup of coffee to the table where he was reading the *Daily Mirror* sports pages and asked if he minded her sitting with him. He grunted a casual ''s OK' at her but could feel himself getting as warm as if he was sitting on a radiator that had just been switched on. She was being *sisterly*: that seemed to be the only word for it, as if absolutely no-one in the whole building meant more to her than anyone else did. It blocked off all possibility of getting back to anything more intimate. Inside his head a voice of the Petroc who secretly absorbed every blokey word of *Loaded* in Smiths was doing some up-front laddish reasoning with her, saying, 'So. Shall we go on from where we left off, with my hands up your shirt groping for your tits?' But back in the college canteen the real-life pink-faced Petroc sat and pretended he couldn't give a flying fuck about anything but this all-absorbing report about British hopefuls for that summer's Wimbledon. What he *should* do, it suddenly occurred to him, was ask her about the adopted thing, about whether she'd ever wanted to go and find her first mother, just to see what she was like. He could tell her about his mother's given-away baby, who now might possibly turn up. He didn't think Kitty would mind – at home, since she'd got back from London, it seemed like something that was a now-topic, one with a bit of hope and expectation in it, not a rather sad past one like it had before. It would be something important he and Amanda could share, something special to link them. He took a breath but he'd spent too long thinking and she got in first.

'I've started my novel,' Amanda announced. She was drinking her coffee from a spoon, the way Lily used to with hot chocolate when she was six.

'Yeah? What, writing one you mean?' He tried to stop looking at her mouth, opening and closing round the spoon, licking and tasting. She laughed, *at* him for being stupid, rather than the sharing-a-joke type. 'Well *of course* writing it. I'd hardly tell anyone if I was just reading one, would I? That wouldn't be news.'

'Right.' Petroc sipped his coffee and racked his brains for a clever angle on novel-writing. It might be that he was the first, the only one she'd confided this to, so his interest had better be deep. It might be as good a piece of confiding as the adoption stuff. Nothing original came to mind. 'What's it about?' was all he could come up with.

'A sort of millennium Lolita. Rather sinister and dark.'

'Oh, paedo-porn.' He really thought that was more than clever enough, given the spontaneity of thought, but Amanda got up quickly and swished about with her hair and her bag and a jacket that she pulled so fast off the table that her coffee, most of the cupful, fell over and soaked his newspaper.

'You're such a *boy*, Petroc. I'm really surprised at you.'

'What have I done?' Petroc mopped at the mess with his sleeve. He would reek of stale coffee for the rest of the day and be reminded of this hopelessly failed encounter. Jamie was approaching with a leer and the kind of lolloping swagger he liked to amble up to girls with. Amanda pushed past him and he made a sympathetic face at Petroc. 'Upset the queen bee, have you? Let me guess, I bet you said something like, "Let me put my tongue in your ear." Subtle. Or perhaps it wasn't ear . . .'

'Piss off, Jamie.'

'Ooh! Petroc-loves-Amanda!' he sang.

'Which bits of those words "piss" and "off" are you not getting, Jamie?' he growled, squeezing greyish liquid out of his sweatshirt sleeve. 'Though you might be right. I might just as well have tried the unsubtle spell-it-out method of pulling her. Perhaps that's what it takes.'

Glyn had a long lunch break, for which he'd phoned Kitty and suggested she meet him at the Tate in St Ives. There was enough time; the classes he'd taken over from Maurice had now been cut to the minimum, doubling up the numbers where feasible and simply cancelling the ones with habitual low attendance, all to save money. Poor Maurice was out of action with serious depression brought on, Glyn soon realized, by the deathly futility of trying to drag the most unwilling and barely literate students through the final stages of GCSE English Language. The oral exams were coming up soon and each pupil made so much effort to avoid preparing for a practice run, choosing a subject for discussion and giving a four-minute talk on it, that during the first period he'd made six of them present an ad lib speech on avoidance of work. Now he was looking forward to lunch.

He drove his scruffy mud-encrusted old Volvo carefully through the narrow streets across the back of the town and down the steep lane towards Porthmeor beach. There were several spaces in the car park, tourists hadn't yet arrived in numbers large enough to make a difference, but Kitty's Fiesta wasn't anywhere in sight and Glyn felt mildly annoyed: he was the one with a class to get back to. George's bizarre turquoise Bentley, though, was parked up on the road above the beach. 'On the lookout for inspiration, I suppose,' Glyn muttered as he locked his car door and gazed, as he always did, across this strip of the finest pale sand and out to the sea that was the most perfect, most unEnglish shade of turquoise. If this beach was a fabric, he'd always thought, it would be up there with the best cashmere, whereas the scrubby strip of foreshore, loved though it was, in front of Treneath would probably rank with, say, denim or calico.

'Hey, Glyn, aren't you coming up?' Kitty was up on the road looking down at him.

'I thought you hadn't got here yet,' he said, climbing the steps towards her. He hadn't expected to see Kitty just then, and managed to catch sight of her for a second or two as if she was a stranger. The wind was blowing her thick fair hair wildly across her face. He liked her like that, unkempt and cosmetically careless. She had large, expressive brown eyes that looked all wrong framed and tamed with make-up.

As her hair blew around he could make out her joyous smile and the glint of delight in those eyes as if she was more pleased to see him than she had ever been about anyone else. He'd wondered such a lot lately what exactly, maybe something more than the funeral of Antonia, had prompted the decision to make it possible, after so many years, for her lost child to find her. It had crossed his mind that if she thought there was something lacking in her life, it might be to do with him. 'A retired man is a diminished one,' his own father had warned him when close to death from the cancer that had hurried so quickly to fill the awful gap of bored inactivity left after the giving up of his all-absorbing work in the Home Office.

'I got a lift in with George Moorfield.' Kitty laughed. 'He's meeting someone but wouldn't say who. Keeping up an image of a mysterious and complicated life, I suppose. I thought perhaps you might be able to drive me halfway home at least. I can get a bus the rest of the way, if there's one around.'

'Sure,' Glyn said, putting an arm round her and pulling her close. He could smell her Clarins body lotion and for a moment he closed his eyes and breathed in the reassuring scent. The first pangs of Rita-guilt hit, as if it was a flu bug he'd known he'd been incubating but had hoped would never come to anything.

'Hey look down there.' Kitty suddenly stiffened and pointed down the beach. 'I wonder if that's who I think it is . . .' she said, squinting hard and shading her eyes from the sun. 'It is. So George was meeting that Amanda girl that Petroc likes. Sleazy old sod, no wonder he wouldn't tell me. Poor old Petroc.'

Glyn gazed out to where she was staring. George was sprawled on the sand, at last managing to look as if it was something he did every day rather than perching gingerly as if there was a cunning freak wave out in the ocean, destined to swirl up the beach and wash him away to the next life. Beside him, clutching a folder, sat Amanda Goodbody, her arms wrapped round her knees.

'He looks like a lovesick swain at the feet of a goddess,' Kitty commented.

Glyn chuckled. 'Rather an old and porky sort of swain,' he said. He didn't refute the goddess bit, though, Kitty noticed, but then what man would?

The gallery was full of schoolchildren, swarming and circling and chatting as they filled in activity sheets. Their bits of paper fluttered and waved and were dropped on the floor. A furtive collection of small boys sniggered slyly in a corner in front of a painting of a fat pink naked woman, lying on a beach. Kitty thought she looked as if she'd been tragically drowned and washed up on the sand, but the children giggled and grimaced at and pointed at her breasts and the blue and purple seaweed that trailed through her pubic hair like party ribbons. It reminded her sharply, and with deep retrospective shame, of an appalling incident in the school gym changing-room, with a miserably naked Antonia (who'd foolishly braved the showers) held captive and spread-eagled on the cold tiled floor, while an attempt was made to race a pair of snails along her thighs. 'First one to her fanny's the winner,' stipulated Rosemary-Jane. Kitty, watching the small boys, shivered guiltily, remembering her cruel self remarking that the snails would never make it, there were too many dents and dimples. She turned away and made for the café entrance. Glyn, who had never known her as anything but grown-up, kind and reasonable, grinned sympathetically at the children's teachers who glared back at him with protective hostility.

'They probably think you've followed the kids in and you're waiting your chance to sneak one out to the beach,' Kitty said as they went into the comparative peace of the café.

'It's more likely they were expecting us to make some complaint about the noise level,' Glyn said, picking up the menu and wondering if he fancied vegetable lasagne or a smoked-salmon bagel. 'There's a common look of defensiveness that all staff on a school trip have. It comes from being thought to be forever in the wrong.'

'Is that how you feel?' Kitty asked as they sat down.

Glyn thought for a moment, wondering quite what the subject was. 'I haven't done a school visit for years, so I guess you're referring to an all-the-time feeling. Usually no, I don't, but just lately, I have to say that yes, I do feel as if I don't quite fit.'

A woman with frizzled greying curls was at the next table reading *Northanger Abbey*, the book propped open with a salt pot. She was taking large bites out of a big untidy sandwich, scattering shards of tomato and shreds of lettuce all over her plate along with messy drips of mayonnaise. Kitty sensed she wasn't really reading: she was peering just too intently at her book and had pushed her hair behind the ear that was closest to her and Glyn. She reminded her of Julia in the bar, forever vicariously alert to the goings-on of others. She wondered if Julia had any idea that Ben was phoning her almost daily. She was almost tempted to ring and tell her, ask her to give him a call and take over as chief sympathizer and counsellor. Glyn hadn't noticed the woman listening. She prodded his arm and tipped her head just a tiny bit in the direction of the scattered sandwich.

'Is it because of the baby?' Kitty said loudly. The

woman looked up and met her gaze, an incredulous expression firing from her wide blue eyes. Glyn glanced sideways and grinned wickedly. 'Yeah, well there's the baby, and that old lover of yours being back in your life.' He leaned towards Kitty and murmured, 'Do you think she's just nosy or researching for a novel?' Kitty giggled then said loudly, 'It's not my old lovers that's the problem, more their *wives*.'

'Or their children.' Glyn suddenly sounded more sombre. Kitty waited, a forkful of lasagne suspended between the plate and her mouth. Far more quietly he said, 'Years ago, way way back you told me who that baby's father was, which was all right then because I don't suppose it crossed your mind you'd ever see him again. I'm quite good at maths, especially the two plus two variety. I do have a memory you know, I do know that the fool who married your friend Rose and who keeps phoning is Madeleine's father. If she *does* turn up, are we going to get him as well?'

Kitty put the fork down. 'He didn't know at the time. There's no reason to lumber him with the truth now. Rose doesn't know either, of course.'

Glyn looked angry. 'What do you mean "of course"? Just how elective are you women about who you tell what to? When Julia rings she always sounds as if whatever she's about to say comes with a "Don't Tell Glyn" sticker all over it. But you didn't mind popping up the lane and discussing this Madeleine with Rita.' His hands were stretched flat on the table, white with tension. The woman at the next table quickly gathered up her book and her bag and swished past to the door. As it opened the sound of laughing children with no complicated histories drifted in.

'Your ex-baby might feel she's entitled to the truth. If she's looking for her birth mother, what right have

133

you got to keep the secret of her birth *father*?'

Kitty stared out of the window over the many-greyed slate roofs of St Ives. Everywhere you looked in the town, the sea was always just there, both a means of escape and a way of keeping you trapped on land, depending on your mood.

'You wish I'd never started looking for her, don't you?' she asked eventually.

Glyn didn't even hesitate. 'Since you ask, at last, yes,' he said.

Chapter Nine

Kitty was the only one home when the girl arrived.
She had spent the morning up in the studio sketching in the outline for a painting of St Michael's
Mount and was in the kitchen eating a tuna and
tomato sandwich for a late lunch. She'd brought the
finished painting of Coverack downstairs with her
and propped it up against the dresser shelves so she
could get an idea of what colour frame would suit it
best. Josh had suggested all her work should be
framed with bleached driftwood, with more than a
hint that he'd be the ideal person to do the making,
but Kitty thought that was just too folksy and twee for
work that was already primitive enough.

The *Archers* theme tune was dying away and the
kettle was just boiling when Kitty looked up from
the sequined swimwear on *The Times* fashion page
and caught her first sight of the girl, out there in the
yard. Kitty hadn't seen her arrive, hadn't seen
whether she'd come up from the beach or in through
the gate from the road. There was a stillness about
her as if she'd just sprung up from the earth she was
standing on, big and unfitting like a sunflower in
a wheat field. She was in the middle of the yard,
keeping quite still and looking around slowly, as if
very carefully taking in where she was and making
certain she missed nothing. For someone who was,

on the face of it, trespassing, she seemed very relaxed, not nervous at all that someone might call out and challenge her presence. Her hands were deep in the pockets of an unbuttoned long baggy cream jacket that was in dire need of dry-cleaning and she didn't seem to have a bag or anything with her, as if she'd just come up from a stroll along the sand and had simply felt irresistible curiosity.

For several minutes, during which Kitty poured water into the teapot and stirred it around idly, she watched and wondered as the girl stared at the house, turning to have a long look at the barn off to the side. Then she bent to stroke Lily's cat Russell, which rolled on the ground and across the girl's high-heeled espadrilles, rubbing his broad ginger back into the dusty gravel and waving his tail as she patted his tummy. The girl's hair was a deep rich red, darker than Antonia's had been, thick and wavy. As she leaned down to play with the cat, Kitty noticed the way the heavy hair fell forward into stranded clumps as if it, like the coat, was long overdue for a good wash. Russell's paw reached out suddenly and made a swift grab for the dangling tendrils and she squealed, jumping awkwardly backwards and staggering on the too-high shoes. Kitty stood by the window, watching and waiting and very very still. The tea-spoon was still in her hand, the warmth from the boiling liquid slowly making itself felt on her fingers.

'Fucking cat!' the girl shrieked, gathering up the fat hanks of hair and pushing them roughly behind her ears. The cat stalked off with its tail high, leapt gracefully up onto the beach wall and sat with its back to the house and the girl, starting a dignified wash to its paw.

'Hey, you bloody bastard animal!' Before Kitty could rush out and stop her, the girl had picked up a pebble and hurled it after Russell. It missed, but only just and the cat slid down the wall and out of sight onto the beach, probably under the impression that the girl had thrown something for him to chase, the way Lily did.

'What the hell did you do that for?' Kitty flew out of the back door, the warm spoon still in her hand. The girl turned round and looked at her, but stayed just where she was. Kitty stopped a few safe yards from her. This was a big-built young woman she was confronting, one not in the best of moods and who slung stones at small cats.

'Well? Why did you throw that at the cat?'

'It scratched me.' The voice was now hardly more than a whisper, but there was no mistaking a well-practised tone of aggrieved justification. 'It's its own stupid fault. Stupid cat, I wish I'd hit it.' Her mouth was turned down at the corners into a sulky pout that looked as if it was habitual. She was older than Kitty had first thought, certainly beyond her teens and well old enough to have grown out of this kind of childish whine. 'I hate cats,' she added, in case there should be any remaining doubts. Her eyes were surprisingly sparkly, Kitty was alarmed to see, as if she really was hurt but was doing her best to seem hard to cover up. Kitty went closer, half-expecting the girl to turn and flee.

'It was only doing what cats do. It didn't mean any harm to you on a personal level, I'm sure.'

The girl gave a loud sniff and looked down at her feet. One of her toes had come through the fabric of the shabby black espadrille, showing badly chipped silver nail polish. The shoes were tied on with long black ribbons that wound too tightly round her ankles, cutting into chubby flesh that was mottled bright pink and white with the wind. It wasn't warm enough yet for bare legs and Kitty ridiculously imagined the girl falling asleep, like something in a fairy tale, or a hibernating hedgehog, on the last warm day of the previous summer and waking up months later in the same clothes.

'Were you looking for someone?' she asked her eventually; this might, it occurred to her, be one of George's cast-off women, very much down on her luck and hell-bent on revenge. There was another loud sniff and the glittery eyes stared hard at her. They were very blue, very piercing and the angry challenge in them reminded her of Lily when she was lying about having finished all her homework.

'Yeah I am, actually. I'm looking for my mother.' It was boldly said, no trace of a whine this time.

'Oh, well I haven't seen anyone. What does she . . . where might she . . .' Kitty's mouth went dry and her heart thudded. 'You can't be, surely . . .' she muttered, wondering if she'd ever make sense again. She stood very very still, waiting either for the sky to fall in or for the girl to laugh and ask what the hell she was gabbling about. This wasn't how it was supposed to be. There should have been phone calls, letters, distant, polite, reasonable stuff, with everyone having time to consider, and the right things to say and a mutually agreed time and place. There should be a feeling of nervous excitement, a bit of dread and a lot of worried anticipation, all stirred up together before a meeting, preplanned and properly organized. When she'd asked if this, this type of turning up out of nowhere and pouncing might happen, she'd been told it was extremely unlikely. She'd sensed a weary but kind smile in the voice of the man on the Adoption Register phone who had said it, as if he wanted to add, 'Oh, all the mothers ask that and I know I shouldn't say it, but really people just read too many of the wrong sort of books . . .'

'Can't be what?' the girl demanded. 'I can. I can be whatever I want. Or *who*ever.' She shoved her hands

138

back into her pockets and pulled the coat round her bulky body for comfort. She was staring hard, and waiting; silent and antagonistic.

'You'd better come in.' Kitty turned abruptly, stiffly, and led the way into the kitchen. She pointed at a chair at the end of the table. 'You sit there and I'll make you some tea.' She knew she sounded brusque and hated herself for it. And *tea*, how clichéd and detached and English to come up with nothing better to offer than that after twenty-four years. There was probably a tone somewhere between tenderness, regret and jubilation that would be appropriate. Something that could express quite simply all the years of imagining just this one person turning up and claiming her. Right now though, she was only aware of underlying panic, a terror of doing things all wrong. All the might-happens, all those first-meeting scenes that had been going through her head in the past few weeks had been no real preparation. She'd had things all ready to say that she now couldn't even begin to recall, things to persuade a given-away child that she wasn't the most evil and selfish mother in the world.

'I hate tea. I want Coke.' The childish sullenness was back now, as if the earlier aggression had exhausted her. 'And I know who you are. I can tell by your hands shaking. You're Katherine Cochrane. You're my mother.' She didn't look up as she said it, but pulled Kitty's *Times* towards her and gazed down at the sequined swimsuit as if she was very seriously considering buying it.

Kitty reached into the freezer for ice. Her arms felt like metal bars, her hands were still shaking and her fingers stuck to the ice tray. She wrenched them free, needing the sensation of quick pain to make her feel this was real.

'Yes I am, or at least I was . . . then. It's Katherine

Harding now. Kitty.' Bizarre, she thought, to be introducing herself to her own daughter. 'Are you . . . what are you called?'

'Huh?' the girl looked up at her as if she was crazy, her mouth twisted into a sneer. 'What the fuck d'you *think* I'm called? Sodding Nigel or something? I'm Madeleine, aren't I. Like you called me. Christ, I only got two things from you in my whole bloody life, my name and this.' She reached deep into one of the coat pockets and pulled out some crumpled fabric, then shoved it across to Kitty. Kitty took hold of it carefully and smoothed out the material. It was the tiny dress, the silver embroidered stars looking to her now as if a child from another century had sewn them under the guidance of an exacting governess. Kitty put her hands over her face and big hot tears soaked their way through her fingers.

'Don't drip on it,' Madeleine grumbled, pulling the baby dress out of Kitty's reach. 'I thought you might not believe it was me if I didn't bring something. Lucky there *was* something. I've got my birth certificate as well, in case you're still wondering, not that you're probably interested, not that much. I've had the certificate for years but you weren't exactly making it easy to find you.'

Kitty reached for the box of tissues on the dresser and blew her nose. Madeleine was staring at her quite coldly, sitting perfectly still with her hands wrapped round the glass of Coke, dragging all the icy coolness into her palms.

'So why *didn't* you look for me before? Soon as I was eighteen? You could've. I've been waiting for you to, checking in every single week with E-Mail from wherever I was. Didn't you want to? Didn't you wonder what had happened to me?'

Kitty felt the words 'Didn't you care?' elbowing their way through the questions. She sat down opposite Madeleine, poured herself more tea, bracing her unsteady wrist against the table edge.

'I don't think there's been a day since I gave you up that I haven't thought about you,' she replied honestly.

'Then why did you do it? I couldn't do it.' Madeleine frowned. 'No real mother could. Not one who was any good.'

It was all going too fast, Kitty thought. There were things she wanted to know too, like had Madeleine been happy. What were her parents like, where did she live. One word wrong and this girl, so volatile and brittle, might stalk right out of her life again and never come back, never tell her anything at all.

'You don't know what it was like back then,' she told her. 'From my background, how things still were. We were still "unmarried mothers". "Single parents" was a term that came along just that little bit later. *Too* late. I never got the chance to feel like I *was* a real mother.' She thought for a moment while Madeleine waited. During the pause Kitty half expected her to cut in with all the easy accusations about feebleness, lack of feeling. She went on, 'All the girls in this home we'd been sent to, we were treated like something damaged, no good for anything. You can't believe how much a bunch of eager Christians can lay on the notion of "unfitness". You had to try to put things right by doing the best you could for the baby. Believe it or not, the message was that only the worst kind of selfish mother would want to keep her baby and bring it up all by herself. You had to give up the baby to someone who could give it a better life, that was being a *good* mother. I think that's a classic example of Catch-22.'

'Yeah but, shit, it wasn't *that* long ago. I thought all that flower power and stuff made it all right to have kids on your own.'

141

'Not in my dad's parish, it wasn't,' Kitty almost laughed. 'All that hippy stuff was just about past by the time I got pregnant and it had terrified them. My father, your grandfather, he used to say, "Peace and love are all very well *in theory*." And this from a vicar.' Kitty recalled the day he'd said this, barking at her over the Sunday roast lamb. She'd sniped back that she thought the whole point of Christianity was peace-and-love in *practice*, at which her mother had cut in with her usual 'Stop trying to be clever' and the argument had spiralled into something about if they'd given up wanting her to be clever, then why wouldn't they let her go to art school, to what they thought of as a den of drop-outs?

Madeleine was trying not to laugh. 'Sorry,' she spluttered as the giggles welled up. 'A *vicar*! Shit, my grandad was a vicar! I wonder what he'd think of me. I'm not exactly godly. Mum wasn't either.' The giggles stopped abruptly and she said, 'Did she get me from one of those church adoption things? I mean don't you have to promise to bring up the child to be churchgoing and good? We sometimes went to weddings but . . .'

Kitty wondered whose weddings they'd been, family ones, aunts, cousins or just her mother's down-the-pub friends. Had Madeleine been a bridesmaid? It was easy to imagine her sulking in satin and roses. These were more things she couldn't know about. She wished she could have written down the things to ask, the silly, superficially irrelevant things like had her mother brushed her hair with a special top-of-the-range bristle brush, the type that cost a fortune, or had she just had a series of plastic spiky ones that got lost down the backs of chairs. Kitty studied her face, trying to capture and savour each feature. She looked quite a lot like Petroc – her top front teeth crossed slightly like his and her chin had the same tiny cleft but she was on a bigger scale. Not taller, but broad and big-boned. Her cheeks were plump and over-pink and there seemed to be a lot of body packed under the bulky coat. *My first baby* Kitty thought, wondering what to say next that wouldn't drive the girl away again, make her disappear back to wherever she'd come from, satisfied to have been disappointed, relieved to return to the woman she called Mum.

'You were adopted through a Christian charity. I hadn't a clue what they expected from parents in terms of religious commitment. All they went on about was "a good home".'

'Like a stray cat. You've got other children. My brothers and sisters.' Madeleine's tone was accusing. Her eyes had gone hard when she'd looked at the wall calendar hanging on the end of the dresser. Kitty glanced at it, following her gaze. 'Petroc dentist' was down for next Friday, and 'Lily – overnight at Charlotte's' had been written the week before.

'So you managed to keep *them*,' Madeleine stated, staring at Kitty. Her eyes had gone glassy again, the way they'd been out in the yard.

'They came much later. Petroc's only seventeen. Lily's fifteen. Things were different.'

'You mean you were married. And not *that* much later. I'm only twenty-four.' Madeleine gave a sudden snorting laugh. 'What sort of a name is *Petroc*? I bet he hates it. I bet he gets the piss taken.'

'Petroc was a Cornish saint. There's quite a few with that name round here.'

'I still bet he hates it though.'

'Well, he did go through a phase of calling himself Pete,' Kitty admitted.

'Troc would've had more style. And *Lily*,' Madeleine sneered. 'Sounds like one of those old women drinking Guinness in the corner of some old brown pub. *Lil.* An old bag in a knitted hat.'

Kitty laughed, picturing again the rows of crocheted hats in her father's congregation. Several of them might well have been called Lil, Lilian. Their first names had never been mentioned. Her father had cooed in his oily fashion over each and every one of them, lingering too long on the after-service handshakes with '*Dear* Mrs Ellis, tea urn on the boil?' or 'Oh Miss Pemberton, such *flowers*'. Thus he perfected the art of making seduction out of the impersonal and ensuring the small essential comforts of church life were taken good care of.

'They'll be home soon,' Kitty said suddenly, 'Petroc and Lily. He'll be picking her up from school about now. No it's Friday though isn't it? She'll be here later, on the bus.' She was rambling, almost incoherent in her effort to explain a family life Madeleine hadn't been part of. Madeleine probably wouldn't want to know. Kitty seemed to have forgotten how to be sensitive.

'Oh he's got a car then. More than I had at seventeen.' Madeleine tore a narrow strip off the edge of the newspaper and rolled it up between her chubby fingers. She had beautiful fingernails, perfect clean ovals. Kitty had a sharp clear vision of a little girl standing on tiptoe to reach a tap, carefully washing her hands, patting them dry on a towel and making an experimental mess with too much hand cream.

'I suppose you want me to disappear before they turn up?' Madeleine made a move to get up, but Kitty quickly reached out and grabbed her wrist. Surprisingly, given the girl's bulky size, her fingers met round the slender bones. 'No! Please, don't leave. There's so much to say, to find out about . . .'

'About each other?' Madeleine snarled, finishing her sentence. 'I know what I need to know. You're alive and well and you've been perfectly happy

144

without me.' She grinned suddenly. 'Though maybe I'll hang on for a bit, have a look at my brother and sister and watch them getting the shock of their lives.'

'Yes, please stay.' Only reluctantly did Kitty let go of the wrist. It was skin that had been close-knit and new the last time she'd touched it. 'Actually, they not only know you exist, have known since they were little, but I also told them there was a chance you'd find us. They know I've been doing the research it takes for you to find me.'

'Oh.' Madeleine slumped back in her chair, disappointed.

'And where will you go to anyway?' Kitty asked. 'How did you get here? Did you drive or get a taxi from Redruth?' Even as she said it the words seemed ridiculous. The girl looked as if she could have barely afforded the bus fare from Penzance, let alone a cab.

'Train, bus, then I hitched a lift from the main road, with some old hippy woman who said she knew you. She said mad things, like she knew who I was and good luck, though I didn't tell her anything. She had one of those fake-mystery smiles, like I'm supposed to think she's telepathic or a witch.' Madeleine laughed, 'Actually when I got out of her car I got out really quick, 'cos I really thought she was going to kiss me or put a spell on something. She was well weird.'

Rita, Kitty deduced. Rita who was right now probably fidgeting and pacing with curiosity and asking Josh how long she should give it before she popped in to borrow a spanner and find out what was going on.

'Anyone in?' Kitty jumped. George's big shaggy head appeared round the kitchen door. Absurdly Kitty thought how much he resembled an Irish wolfhound. 'Sorry, didn't mean to interrupt.' He hovered in the doorway, staring at Madeleine and waiting to be introduced. He must be bored, Kitty realized, in need of even the smallest diversion. 'Hello George. This is . . . this is my daughter, Madeleine,' she said as clearly and steadily as she could manage. Madeleine was already out of her chair and giving George the smile she might have been keeping in reserve for a better mother than Kitty. 'You're George Moorfield! Amazing. I've read all your books!' She stood in front of him, looking like a starstruck admirer and George beamed at her, shrugging slightly and trying unsuccessfully to look faintly modest.

'And I think you're a horrible, pathetic, overrated pornographer,' she went on, keeping the smile going in a strange contrary way. George's expression whizzed from startled to amused, bordering on delighted. Kitty felt like warning him that to laugh might be a mistake. 'I suppose a shag's out of the question then?' he muttered, not quite far enough under his breath.

'No,' Madeleine said.

'No?' said George, puzzled.

'No, it's not out of the question. You're not un-fanciable,' she continued bluntly. George scratched his head and grinned stupidly, stumped for a reply. Kitty's sense of unreality was getting worse. In need of something to do to remind her where and who she was, she picked up the half empty can of tuna from the worktop and went to put it away in the fridge. It didn't say it was dolphin friendly, she noticed, pathetically trying to make some sense of what was going on and failing. She didn't particularly like dolphins; they all had the same false and indiscriminating smile which was a simple genetic accident of the jawline that made fools feel loved. Madeleine

146

was grinning at George as if she'd never met anyone she loved more in her life, and at the same time slating his life-work.

'Er, I just wondered if there'd been any post?' he eventually asked Kitty, keeping a wary eye on Madeleine.

'Sorry George, if there had been I'd have brought it over.' Please go away, she willed him, closing the fridge door loudly in the hope that it would sound like a hint. She heard something fall over inside it, something messy from the top shelf splashing and clattering to the bottom. An egg, probably, demanding maximum effort for clearing up which she felt was well-deserved, seeing as she didn't seem to be handling anything too well just now.

'Right. Just that I'm expecting the beginnings of a divorce. Er . . .' George continued staring at Madeleine for a moment or two, then backed out of the door. 'See you . . . around? Are you staying?' he said to her, looking worried in case she said yes.

'Yes. Well probably,' she told him. As the door closed Madeleine's smile vanished and she turned on Kitty. 'The man you married, the father of these two kids you've got, is he *my* father too?'

'No he's not.' Kitty felt exhausted. She wished she could put Madeleine in a cupboard for a few hours while she collected her thoughts.

'I shall want to know about him. And about why you've got George Moorfield's mail being delivered here,' Madeleine said. 'You can tell me later though, maybe tomorrow.' She leaned back against the dresser, hugging herself into the coat again. 'Can I stay?'

Petroc's car swished across the gravel into the yard, skidding slightly as he braked and turned at the same time. Glyn did that sometimes, showing off like a schoolboy when he was particularly happy about things. He hadn't done it lately. Kitty felt sick.

'Of course you can stay, we can all . . .'

'Yeah I know, get to know each other.' The sneer was back, but with less venom. The door opened and Petroc hauled his college bag through it, hurling it hard onto the table.

'Oh. Hi,' he said, looking at Madeleine with no particular interest. There were often strangers in the kitchen: writers, stray walkers, people off the beach who were desperate enough to ask to use the loo.

'Hello little brother,' Madeleine said.

On the bus Fergus had told Lily she was a scraggy cow which was particularly uncalled-for when she'd just given him the best part of a Crunchie bar. Lily stamped angrily up the lane from the bus stop, ignoring Russell who miaowed eagerly and trotted along fast beside her, desperate to be stroked.

'You should eat more,' Fergus had said as he gobbled it quickly, shedding flecks of gold honeycomb down the front of his Quiksilver fleece. Then he'd come out with the classic. Lily strode faster, more furiously, thinking about it. 'You'll never get a bloke to fancy you till you grow some tits.' As if, she thought, turning off into Rita's gateway, as if she cared, as if it was completely compulsory for every girl to provide a pair of globular toys for some fumbling adolescent jerk.

'Hi! You're in a hurry, you OK?' Rita was out by her front door, tidying up the dried-out leftovers of last summer's plants. Where she'd cleared out old leaves, new soft green growth was coming through the earth. It had made her envious, that nature could let plants renew themselves annually like that, but not people.

'I'm OK.' Lily turned off the road onto Rita's path and flopped down on her doorstep, looking at her splendidly skinny legs arranged in front of her. 'I'm thinking about men and balls.'

'Oh yeah?'

'Footballs, cricket balls, *their* balls, big round bouncy breasts – all the things they like to play with. Don't they ever want more grown-up toys?'

Rita sat back on her heels and laughed. Lily could see her fillings glinting bright gold, like the inside of Fergus's Crunchie. 'Well of course they do. Sometimes they like long sleek cars, it's hard to part them from the TV remote control and I'm told that up-country, where these things actually work, they can't go out without clutching a titchy dick-sized mobile phone. Why, what's brought this on?'

'Someone, someone stupid and pathetic, said I was too thin for boys to like. As if I care.' Lily folded her legs under her and wrapped her arms around her knees.

Rita stopped grinning. 'To be honest you are get-ting a bit Bambi-like,' she ventured warily. 'But I expect you're in a growing phase, stretching a bit.'

'I don't think so,' Lily told her, concentrating on twisting her shoelace round and round. 'I just don't want . . .'

'Don't want what?' Rita prompted gently.

'Anything much.' Lily looked up and shrugged, grinning at her. 'Can I stay for supper? Then you can see that sometimes I do actually eat. I'll do the dishes.'

Rita stood up and arched her back, stretching her body with her hands on her hips. The gesture reminded Lily of joky versions of pregnant women. The thought of pregnancy almost made her shudder, the ultimate in loss-of-control – a runaway body, two, your own on the outside and the wild greedy one inside, sapping all your nutrients and leaving you feeling sick and wasted and huge and dead.

'Actually, I think you ought to go home,' Rita said eventually, 'I gave a lift to someone who was going to your place. If she's still there you might want to see her.'

'Mysterious. Who is she?'

'Go and have a look. She might have gone by now, but you should still go, just in case.' Rita reached out a hand and hauled Lily up from the step. She gave her a quick hug and stroked her hair. 'Go on,' she urged, giving Lily a small push. 'Look, your cat's still waiting by the gate. And take care of yourself.'

Chapter Ten

Glyn stared at the display of spades and tried to feel like a wise old gardener with years of hard-acquired knowledge (perhaps even several weathered generations'-worth) behind him. The only immediate differences he could see between the various implements were the prices, and the fact that some of them were in appropriate shades of cabbage green while others were in shiny stainless steel or toy-like primary colours as if they were for hugely oversized children to build sandcastles on the beach. Around him, people mooched about pushing their equally toy-like green plastic trolleys containing a couple of strips of too-early bedding plants, packets of seed, cartons of lawn food or some bright new thornproof gloves. Amateurs, he sniffed to himself, then felt remorseful. Maybe not one of them would have to dither over the selection of a simple spade, more than possibly any of them might be able to look at him scornfully and say, 'That's the one you want, mate,' no hesitation.

He picked out one with a pale, shiny wooden shaft and a blade in a tint that brought to mind the British racing-green Austin he'd once owned, felt its weight and wondered what, exactly, he was supposed to be feeling *for*. Which was better, a lightweight tool that would probably bend to uselessness after a few hours

151

but make the effort of lifting the earth easier, or a vast heavy one that would still be going strong when Lily's grandchildren were digging their own allotments, but would give him a spine like a figure seven in minutes? Green would disappear into the foliage the moment he leaned it against the hedge, but scarlet looked frivolous, a plaything for the weekend fun-gardener who'd probably think bastard trenching was a Mafioso way of getting rid of troublesome enemies.

'Tricky, isn't it?' Glyn was startled out of his reverie by a woman's voice extremely close to his ear.

'Decisions, I mean. Goodness, you *are* Glyn Harding aren't you? I mean when you've only met someone once . . . though I'm pretty good at faces. Please don't think I accost strangers generally.'

The owner of this face was smiling confidently at him. She wasn't really going to allow him *not* to be Glyn Harding. She looked familiar. Predatory teeth and eyes that gave the impression of seeking out trouble. He remembered.

'Sorry. I was miles away. Rosemary-Jane, isn't it?'

'Rose,' she corrected briskly. 'Names like Rosemary-Jane are only OK for the under-nines; so very Milly-Molly-Mandy, I always think, don't you?'

'Er, I hadn't considered really.' Actually he had, many times, during the months when Petroc, at about twelve, had failed to persuade any of his schoolfriends to start calling him Pete. He'd been quite alarmingly troubled at the time, so much so that Glyn and Kitty had tried to please him by going along with the new name. But it had sounded false and self-conscious, calling 'Er, *Pete*, supper's ready!' up the stairs. Now, though, Petroc seemed to be quite proud of his name. Perhaps he'd grown into it, or found that girls liked it, or had simply met several people with worse ones and was relieved not to be called Horatio or Marmaduke.

'Nice jacket,' Rose murmured, a speculative finger reaching out for a second and giving the light wool fabric a brief stroke. 'Armani?'

'Kenzo, in a sale a couple of years back.' Glyn felt childishly pleased at having his taste in clothes approved by a woman so obviously urbane and knowing. Rose was wearing a sleek charcoal grey trouser suit that would have looked more at home behind an executive desk than it did in a mid-Cornwall garden centre. Beneath the jacket was a simple scoop-necked top. She wore no jewellery except for silver stud earrings, no fussy scarf, just a frosting of streaky gold hair hanging on her shoulders. Glyn wondered what on earth she was doing there and the ridiculous thought shot into his mind that she'd perhaps been tailing him. She might want to stroke more than his sleeve. The thought was troubling, just like the ones he now and then had about Rita, but not unexciting, though on balance he'd still prefer her to be several hundred miles away, sorting out things with her husband so Kitty could be let off counselling duty.

'So which of these pretty spades are you going to buy? Or are you just window-shopping?'

'I'm going to buy the middle weight at the middle price.' Suddenly decisive, he hauled out a blue one out from the rack. He presumed that would also count as a middle colour too. He wasn't really sure if it was exactly what he wanted, but what he *did* want was not to be quite so close to this woman's overpowering perfume. It was unmistakably mistress-scent. Her poor forever-phoning husband was probably right to have suspicions.

'I'm out here researching. Officially anyway,' she

153

said, walking with him towards the checkout. 'Actually I just felt the need to get out and about by myself for a few hours. Not long enough to venture as far down the county as your place, sadly, but I might drive to Fowey on the way back and take a look at that place where Daphne du Maurier lived.' She giggled, her hand to her mouth like a caught-out schoolgirl, 'I'm supposed to be checking out the price of compost bins for the programme and a location where we can film a short piece on them. Thrilling huh?' She giggled again and then went on, 'I could have just phoned around, or got my PA to do it, seeing as that's what she's paid for.' Glyn had his mind on the items *he* wouldn't be checking out if she hung about much longer. You didn't drive this far just for a spade. He'd got a long list of things like rabbit-proof netting, heavyweight secateurs, a selection of piping and comfrey liquid fertilizer that required solitary concentration and he wasn't going to get through it without getting rid of Rose.

'Programme?' he murmured vaguely, sorting through his wallet for the right credit card.

'It's called *Where There's Muck*. Garden secrets of the rich and/or famous?' She smacked his arm lightly. 'Don't tell me you've never seen it. That would be just too disloyal.' Rose was pouting. She was wearing very shiny lipstick, with a careful pencil outline that was just a bit too contrasting. Probably something she'd picked up from a makeup artist on a programme, he assumed, though he knew she produced rather than presented this show that he now felt guilty for not having seen.

'Sorry, I have to confess I haven't actually watched it. My TV tastes are simple, they run to football, cricket and *University Challenge*.'

'I bet you can answer all the questions.' She smiled at him, those big teeth making him nervous.

'I bet you can too,' he countered. 'Though don't you find . . .'

She interrupted quickly, laughing. 'I know what you're going to say: you can answer absolutely everything but *only when* there's no-one in the room to be impressed!'

'Exactly.' Glyn paid for his spade and they walked out together into the car park. He recognized Rose's silver BMW parked opposite his scruffy Volvo and wondered again if this was such a coincidence.

'Your husband phones sometimes,' Glyn ventured.

'Oh, Ben's a great one for offloading his worries.'

Glyn hadn't mentioned worries, and immediately wished he hadn't mentioned Ben, either. He hoped she wasn't going to do confiding, not of marital problems anyway. He'd had all that back in his head-teacher days, when depressed, defeated women would come in to explain that little Toby's or Tanya's sudden lack of progress might just be something to do with Daddy taking off with the skinny waitress from the Jolly Mariners. 'Trouble at home' was all he needed, by way of coded information, but was never handed so precise a statement. Once an abandoned wife, or occasionally a husband, got as far as the chair beside his desk, they somehow couldn't resist the urge to use him as something between a counsellor and a confessor. His secretary had kept supplies of tissues in the stationery cupboard, specially for the purpose.

Glyn reached his car and stood by the door, Rose still beside him, wondering how impolite he could bring himself to be, if he could just get in and wave and smile and drive away. Instead he waited, jangling his keys, but not very loudly. Rose had taken up a strangely angular position, her elbow leaning on his car roof as if she was pinning it down, stopping it moving. 'The trouble with Ben is he has a romantic view of the past. He thinks everything is running downhill too fast for him these days. He's one of those men who still has his degree certificate hanging on his study wall and a collection of rugby-team photos from the days when he was young and fit. I don't think he'd be able to lay his hands on our wedding photos though.' She had a look of sorrow, just for a few seconds, but it was enough. She'd got him.

'Have you got an extra hour or so?' Glyn heard himself asking. 'You could leave your car here and I'll drive us down to the pub at Mylor harbour for a swift half or even some perfectly respectable tea. It's not really grockle season yet, so it should be pretty quiet.' Kitty wouldn't mind how late back he was, she'd be pleased he was making an effort with one of her friends and after he'd dropped Rose back to her car again he could get on with his garden-shopping with a clear conscience. Rose was climbing into the Volvo before she'd finished saying yes, though she might well have instantly regretted it as she noticed its filthy state and was discreetly wiping the dust from her jacket that had attached itself to her when she'd carelessly leaned on the roof.

'Sorry about the mud. We don't much go in for car-washing round here.' Glyn started up the elderly but dependable engine and headed towards the main road.

She grinned, 'Sorry for being so crassly city-ish. By the way, did Kitty tell you, if Ben didn't, I've been seeing a bit of Tom Goodrich, Antonia's widower while I'm down here? It's the least I can do, poor man.'

Glyn gave an encouraging 'Mmm'.

'We weren't terribly nice to Antonia when we were at school, to be honest. I expect Kitty told you *that* anyway.'

'I think she did mention it, no details though.' Glyn had forgotten how far it actually was from the garden centre to Mylor. What on earth were they going to find to talk about after the next few minutes?

'Bit late to do anything about it now though, isn't it?' he said, negotiating a double roundabout.

'What, about Antonia? Yes of course, but one can hope to make up a bit, you know, somehow . . .'

'To soothe your conscience?' With the woman's *husband*?

'Whatever helps.' Glyn wondered, if she thought there was something to be made up, how she intended making up the spiritual deficit to Ben when the time came, or would she keep postponing the moment of pay-off indefinitely till the grim reaper came to collect his back rent? He could just see her, arguing the toss with St Peter at his gate, saying 'I was just trying to be *nice*' as if that made it all all right. Not for the first time he wondered about heaven's door policy – were the amoral allowed more leeway than the *im*moral?

'I've been here before,' Rose admitted as Glyn brought drinks out to their table beside the river. 'Ben and I took a boat a couple of years ago, sailed from Falmouth to the Scilly Isles . . .'

'Isles of Scilly,' Glyn corrected automatically.

'What? Oh, right, and then back up here, up the river. This place was swarming with families, masses of children. They all seemed to be called Jasper and Sebastian and from places like Putney and they all had absolutely thousands of pounds' worth of exactly the right sailing clothes, you know all state-of-the-art life-jackets and those dinky red jackets and Docksiders and stuff. Sweet.'

Rose, catching sight of a young couple entwined on a bench near the pub door, continued abruptly, 'You knew, of course, that my husband and your wife had a teeny walk-out together way back at the end of our schooldays?'

157

'I did know,' he said, smiling. 'But I didn't know if you knew, if you see what I mean.'

'Oh yes, well I expect everyone did. I wasn't actually around then. Went straight from school to work for Camp America, taking care of little brats with tooth-braces and spoilt New Jersey whines, and when I came back it was time for Oxford. Julia's the one who kept up with everyone. Ben spent a summer with your Kitty then went off to do good works in foreign parts, and apparently Kitty went off somewhere too. She might not even remember where she went, but I bet Julia Taggart does.' Her face, then, lost its smile but she said brightly enough, 'Ben and I don't have children. We have a poodle. The big sort, standard. I don't think of him as "my baby" though, like some women might. I mean he's our third and you don't replace your kids when they snuff it. They're dogs, pets, simple as that.'

Glyn studied her face as she sipped her spritzer. She wasn't looking particularly pensive, just casually interested in her surroundings, as if she was used to having this conversation early in new relationships, it was just a couple of sentences to be got through. It seemed quite awful, he thought suddenly, that he knew about a baby her husband had fathered, and yet neither Ben nor Rose had any idea. I hope this girl never turns up, he caught himself thinking.

No-one actually made the Little and Large joke, but it hovered unsaid in the pale cool sitting-room, lurking like an unmentionable smell, such was the contrast in appearance between Lily and Madeleine. Kitty had wondered how on earth she was supposed to introduce this new sister to her children but, with a staggering intuition that must get lost in the complex manners of grown-ups, both Petroc and Lily knew immediately who Madeleine was. Petroc was formal and polite, nodding and smiling and saying hello as if this strange large young woman was just another of the visiting authors, and likely to leave the room any minute with the instructions for using the Rayburn or whatever it was she'd popped over from the barn to collect. For a second or two, Kitty had even thought he was going to offer to shake hands.

Lily, running in half an hour after Petroc, already had the light of excitement making her eyes shine. She flew in through the back door shouting, 'Where is she? Does she look like me?' and grinning eagerly.

'You don't look *at all* like me,' Lily announced after about ten seconds of innocently rude staring. Petroc and Kitty exchanged glances. Lily was slowly circling the blue sofa on which Madeleine was perched, like a small sleek fox round a frightened pony. Lily glared across Madeleine to Kitty, fearful that she'd raced in and made a dreadful mistake, that Rita might have got things all wrong with all those hints and secrecy, and this might only be the person collecting the Christian Aid envelope and not the sister she'd never ever met.

'I expect we look like our dads,' Madeleine ventured, hugging herself into her jacket. Kitty thought she'd never seen Lily look more terrifyingly fragile. Her legs, even in her black school tights, were as thin as reeds. It would take more than the pair of hers to make up one of Madeleine's. Lily's fingers were so small they could be snapped by a clumsy toddler, whereas Madeleine's looked strong enough to strangle a cow.

'Are you staying?' Lily asked finally.

'I might. For a day or two, if no-one minds.' Madeleine shrugged.

'You can share my room if you like. There's a spare bed for my friends and it's still made up from when Jenna didn't stay last week,' Lily offered, suddenly finding the need to look for something in her school bag.

'Or there's the sofa bed in the studio. Wouldn't you rather . . .' Kitty cut in.

'No, that would be nice. I'll share with you.' Madeleine's voice was gentle and soft now and she was smiling at Lily as if she was something that had been a surprising pleasure to find. All the earlier hard bravado had gone.

'I'd better get my bag of stuff. I left it on the beach.' Madeleine stood up. She moved awkwardly and looked terribly tired. Her bulky body seemed too stiff to open out to its full height and her hair drooped across most of her face. Kitty felt dreadfully sorry for her. The courage it must have taken to make this visit, the sheer guts to have managed that early display of feistiness when inside she could only have been quaking. What would happen, Kitty wondered, if she went and simply hugged this big exhausted girl. Uselessly, her hands fluttered as she spoke, unable to decide whether to risk being pushed away, worried about what she might be taking on if she *wasn't* pushed away. This was, after all, someone else's daughter. A grown-up young woman, someone who was far too old to need 'taking on'.

'Petroc will go and get your bag, if you just tell him where you left it. Why don't you go upstairs with Lily and she'll show you where you're sleeping. You could have a bath if you like, and a rest if you want one. There's plenty of time before supper.'

Madeleine sighed wearily. 'I could sleep for weeks, actually.' She turned and grinned at Lily. 'Come on then, little sister, show me where my bed is.'

'I didn't know you had another sister.' Petroc, ambling along the sand looking for the rock behind which Madeleine had stashed her bag, was startled by George Moorfield skulking against the wall. Petroc stopped and looked at him. The man was starting to look more than a bit crazed: his hair was wild and getting matted as if he'd either lost the will to find a comb or was sneakily experimenting with the cultivation of dreadlocks while safely out of sight of his London companions. One day, just as Petroc had last summer, George would unthinkingly climb onto a train in Penzance wearing a sea-stiffened brine-reeking old sweater and a raggy pair of jeans with beach oil on them, and get off at Paddington into a puzzling swarm of smart crisp suits and rushing fools with mobile phones.

'I didn't know I had another sister. Well, I knew she existed, but never expected to meet her,' he told George, kicking at a crab claw. 'I probably shouldn't be telling you this,' he added. It was easy though, out in the half-dark. The wet slapping sound of the sea made him think of easy tears. If George, just then, asked the right questions, Petroc would probably confide his entire soul's-worth of problems.

'Oh I see. You mean it's "family stuff"?' George mocked. 'It's the curse of the English, the feeble insistence on secrecy. It makes for a humid, claustrophobic existence in my opinion. Collections of wondering folks in their nests stuck together by their moist little don't-tells. That way lies incest of, if you see my point, a metaphorical kind.'

Petroc stared out to sea. He didn't quite get the point, as it happened, but didn't want George to know that in case it somehow came up in conversation with Amanda. He muttered an all-purpose 'Yeah', intended to convey empathy.

'Of course without all the little intrigues and mysteries I'd have nothing to write about, would I?'

'Suppose not.' Petroc hadn't read anything of George's and felt much as he had at his GCSE French oral when it had become clear that he hadn't learned any French.

George picked up a pebble and hurled it at the sea. 'You're lucky,' he said. 'You're lucky, though you're probably too young to know it, having a good family and then getting an extra one too. It's like getting seconds of the world's best pudding.'

'Nothing to stop you having a family is there?' Petroc wanted to go back in the house, he was hungry. He didn't want to be sympathetic to a man who'd so easily nicked his woman.

'I've had two goes at wives,' George said, 'but not at children. Down here makes you realize something about being on your own. In London you think it's through choice. "Lonely" in London is self-indulgence, like bitter chocolate. Here it's wondering where it all went wrong.' With that, George strode off back towards the barn. Petroc, peering through the dusk gloom, wondered when he ever actually did find time to work. He's always out and about, he thought, recalling the sight of the monstrous car that afternoon pulling up outside the college and collecting Amanda Goodbody. He'd looked at the outline of her knickers against her tight trousers as she'd leant into the car and shoved her bag across to the back seat. Jamie had caught him looking, and had leered and muttered, 'M & S high-leg, seamless. I'd guess black, possibly cream or blue, and she never wears plain white except for tennis,' like a punter eyeing up the form of a racehorse.

Petroc found the bag behind a rock only just above the high-tide line. It was a battered, dark green rucksack and one of the straps was frayed almost to the point of breaking, giving an impression of plenty of use. Petroc knew nothing of Madeleine, it occurred to him, nothing at all. If he'd ever given her just that little bit of thought, he'd pictured her as a

162

gingery-gold little baby a few days old, the way his mother had described her. He hadn't thought about her out in the world having a parallel life to his own, though he presumed Kitty had.

The battered bag offered a selection of possibilities. Maybe she'd been something keen and committed like a sea cadet, hauling the bag on weeklong hikes over the Brecon Beacons, or maybe she'd Euro-railed in university vacations. If she'd been to university. Or lived rough, sleeping behind Waterloo station with her head on the rucksack and the straps twined through her hands in fear of thieves. He didn't look inside, although the bag was heavy and bulging with interesting shapes like a Christmas stocking. There wasn't any point looking, because with nothing of her life to refer to, the contents couldn't possibly give him any clues about her. The bag itself might even have been borrowed. He heaved it over his shoulder and made his way slowly back up the beach.

It was perversely attractive, the idea of starting over with a blood family who knew nothing about you. Madeleine, if she wanted to, could invent for them a whole growing-up of absolute fiction. They'd never know. Right now he wished he could do that with Amanda, just turn up all fresh and new and have her take him as he wanted to be found, rather than as the inept mess that she'd come to know. He could have drip-fed her all sorts of enticing lies if he hadn't known her since they were eleven. It would be interesting to see what Madeleine volunteered in terms of information, because presumably they'd only find out whatever there was she wanted them all to know.

'So you do eat meat? That's a relief, so many people, young ones especially, are veggie now. I mean it's only spag. bol. and I could do you something else if you'd prefer it . . .' Kitty was conscious she was gibbering. Madeleine was a strange presence in the kitchen, sitting at the table staring silently at Kitty as she chopped and stirred and made many trips to the fridge and back because her mind wasn't on the food and she kept forgetting things. Kitty had to keep reminding herself that this person was real, this large and scruffy young woman was The Baby. The Baby *then*, but now The Woman, everything in between was simply a void. How they related to each other could only start from here, from whether they even decided they wanted to or not. Strange there should be such an element of choice about someone you had actually created.

'I do eat meat, though not often — we didn't have red meat much at home. Mum liked chicken and fish better.' Kitty tried not to let her hand hesitate as she sliced tomatoes. 'Mum' Madeleine had said — evidence of a real past. *She*, Kitty, wasn't her mum. Of course she wasn't. She was just an official Birth Mother, something on paper who was supposed to have given up her feelings along with her baby. Madeleine looked uncomfortable, hot and sticky from her bath. The ends of her deep red hair were damp and corkscrewed and she kept tugging at them nervously. She'd put on a pair of black leggings and an all-enveloping long black shirt but the crumpled cream jacket was still there too, as if she needed to keep herself ready to leave instantly if she felt she had to, or maybe she was just over-conscious of her shape. Perhaps there would be something that Kitty had to say, some unknown phrase that Madeleine was waiting to hear that would make her feel satisfied she'd found out all she wanted to know, and then she'd be out of the door for good. The only thing Kitty was sure of was that it wouldn't be easy or appropriate attempting to have a deep conversation that could cover the essentials of twenty-four years while she whisked up the salad dressing.

'I'll do the table shall I?' Madeleine volunteered, looking around for a drawer that might contain cutlery.

'Oh, yes OK, that would be nice, thanks.' Kitty smiled at her, encouraging. Either Petroc or Lily usually did it. They seemed to be keeping out of the way, perhaps being tactful so that Kitty and Madeleine could do some sort of belated bonding. Or perhaps there was just something on TV. She must try not to analyse.

Madeleine wandered round the kitchen, opening and shutting cupboard doors in her search for plates. Kitty left her to get on with it while she washed the lettuce, though she followed Madeleine's progress round the kitchen, trying to see things as if through her eyes for the first time. She admired the corn-flower-blue plates as Madeleine took them from the dresser shelves, noted how much the beech handles of the knives had faded from over-fierce dishwasher detergent, and ran her eyes over the collection of hand-thrown mugs that hung from the dresser hooks. If Madeleine commented, she was ready to explain her taste, discuss pattern and form and the mood-lifting qualities of colour. Running through her head, too, was the thread of some kind of fantasy in which Madeleine played the part of a daughter who had always been around since birth, but had simply moved away as grown-up children do.

'Did you paint this?' Madeleine's voice cut into her thoughts. She was standing with a handful of glasses, studying the painting of Coverack which was still propped up on the dresser.

'Yes. It's what I do; local views, things tourists like. I sell prints and postcards through galleries, and

165

originals in shows a couple of times a year.'

'The Grandma Moses of Cornwall,' Madeleine commented. Kitty didn't detect any sarcasm and hated herself for anticipating it.

'We've got that in common, anyway. I did a degree in Art History,' Madeleine told her. 'And I paint too, but abstract stuff, nothing like this.' She smiled at Kitty. 'It's not bad.'

'Well thanks. What do your parents do?' Kitty asked. The word 'parents' came quite easily – a word she'd half expected to stumble over.

'Dad died. He did something electrical in a firm near Brighton. Mum works in the bank, always has.' Kitty felt absurdly cross that the baby she'd sacrificed hadn't had its adoptive mother's constant and undivided attention each and every day. 'And I've got two brothers,' Madeleine volunteered hesitantly. 'It was like, after they got me they could suddenly have their own, properly. And then they got divorced.' They should have given you back, Kitty immediately wanted to say. She felt outraged and cheated. She'd given up her baby because they'd promised her Madeleine would have a stable family home. With life's prize of someone else's child, the ordinary sordid messes of break-up and divorce simply shouldn't have been in question. Of course no-one, she should have seen, could have made that promise of perfect family existence in the certainty of being able to keep it.

'Perhaps they should have given me back,' Madeleine startled her by saying.

Kitty heard Glyn's car pulling into the yard. Her heart was beating very fast and her hands, chopping spring onions for the salad, felt clumsy as if she'd been given someone else's fingers to try. 'Dad's here.' Lily crashed into the kitchen, knocking against Madeleine who was putting glasses on the table. One flew out of her hand as Lily pushed the kitchen door too wide and too fast. 'Oh sorry!' she yelled, stooping to pick up the broken shards of glass from the floor.

'No don't, you might hurt yourself. Let me.' Madeleine bent at the same time as Lily and their heads collided. 'Sorry!' Lily said again. They stood up, giggling and rubbing their bruises.

'Oh Madeleine look, you've cut your hand on the glass.' Kitty reached out to see how much damage there was and Madeleine and Lily, still giggling, collected round her by the sink. Glyn opened the door awkwardly, carrying his new spade, a roll of wire and a six foot length of pipe. Blasts of cool sea air wafted into the room with him. No-one took any notice. His daughter and a stranger and his wife were laughing together at the sink, running water over a bleeding hand, though whose it was and why it took three of them he couldn't see. They looked very self-contained. Even when they finally turned round to look at him, they did it all together, lined up with their faces still full of a shared, exclusive joke. The strange girl leaned back against the sink, her jacket gaping and her shirt caught behind her and pulled tight against her body. He stared at her stomach which almost seemed to be pointing at him, round and stretched as a new balloon.

'Glyn.' Kitty, instantly serious, came forward and stood beside him, linking her arm through his and dislodging his spade so that it slipped and sliced painfully into his shin.

'Glyn, this is Madeleine.'

'Oh,' he said, still staring at the girl's tight front. Watching the direction of his gaze she'd put her hand over the bulge, stroking it protectively. 'And not just Madeleine,' was all he could find to say. Kitty looked from him to the girl and back. Big girls could hide their pregnancies so well, skillfully bulking their bodies and clothes around the swelling. A friend of Petroc's had kept her secret from her family till the day she went into labour. Madeleine glared at Glyn, her eyes narrow and hostile. It crossed his mind that if she'd been a cat he'd be ducking out of the way of spit and claws.

'So I'm a bit pregnant. What's it to you?'

'How much is a bit?' Kitty hovered between Glyn and Madeleine.

Madeleine shrugged. 'Six and a half, seven months. Bit more maybe.' She smiled suddenly. 'You'll be a grandmother,' she said to Kitty. 'Bet you weren't expecting that.'

Chapter Eleven

Glyn could see Rita from the bedroom window. He climbed out of bed, stood naked in front of the cool glass and failed entirely to be even slightly aroused at recalling Rita on the rug. He assumed it was because he'd decided that that didn't count as real sex. He tried to put it on a simple level of shared comfort, intellectually not unlike a six o'clock gin and tonic after a tricky day. Real sex would have involved all the moves for getting closer, possibly a dinner, lots of flirtation, intent and pursuit. There'd been none of that. There was, though, part of him that couldn't stop guilt from being sieved through the self-justifying, and his bare toes curled with anguish at the thought that Kitty would not see it any way but as an appalling betrayal. He was a man of his age, he thought with depression, nothing more than a silly cliché.

Through the branches of the beech tree that were rocking up and down in the sharpening sea breeze he could see Rita with the wolfhound shambling along beside her, walking quite fast along the lane towards the shop. She and the dog kept looking at each other as they walked, as if they were having a conversation. Glyn wished he was out there too, breathing something fresher and less constricting than the household air. Kitty was already up, down in the kitchen checking out various breakfast options that Madeleine might like, mindful of vitamins and nutrition for the baby.

'You'll drive the girl away again,' he'd groaned to her with supreme early-morning thoughtlessness the moment he'd sensed her beginning to fuss, heard her tossing and turning too early to get up and muttering about muesli and the need to get whole milk instead of semi-skimmed.

'If she hasn't already gone,' had been Kitty's pessimistic response and Glyn had felt bad.

'Sorry,' he'd said, but to an empty room.

Just now, Kitty spent most of each night waiting to hear the click of the closing latch as Madeleine, either disappointed with whom and what she'd found or simply satisfied and selfish, slid out of the front door and disappeared for ever from their lives. Even when they made love he could sense her attention just slightly askew, out of the room and along the corridor as if she was checking on a baby's living breath. It took the edge off eroticism, though considering what he had recently done, he felt he could hardly complain.

Showering quickly, Glyn realized he was accumulating quite a list of things to make amends for. Awash with guilt was the apt phrase that came to mind as he squeezed the last of the shower gel from the bottle. The pun failed to please him, a sure sign that his guilt was entirely justified. He was being horrible to Kitty whichever way you looked at it, unfaithful, unsupportive, moody and, with Madeleine, not particularly welcoming. The two of them edged round each other like lions waiting to battle it out over the carcass of a zebra.

'I'm going to the shop for a paper,' he told Kitty, joining her in the kitchen. 'Anything else we need?'

'More bread perhaps?' She peered into the bread

bin and hauled out a heel of something wholemeal and solid. 'Yes, more bread. I think Madeleine likes this sort . . .'

'Madeleine likes, Madeleine likes . . .' the words marched through Glyn's head in time with his own steps thudding fast along the lane.

Rita's wolfhound was tied to a rail outside the shop. Glyn hesitated, then went in. He didn't want to start avoiding Rita; he could imagine what sort of fool she'd make him feel if she suspected he might be. He could imagine her saying, 'Such a fuss over a bit of sex!' as if he was a silly adolescent. He skirted round the inside of the shop, picked out what he needed and met her at the door as both of them were leaving.

'Hello Rita, how's things?' he said, falling into step beside her as she and the dog started to make their way home. She looked preoccupied and vague, mildly unkempt too, he noticed. 'Fine,' she said brightly.

'We've got a visitor.' Glyn could hear himself not sounding thrilled. 'Though I expect you knew all about her coming before I did.'

'So it was her!' Rita smiled, pleased with herself for getting it right.

'It was Kitty's adopted baby, if that's what you mean by "her",' he agreed.

'Don't you like her then?'

He shrugged. 'What does it matter what I think? She's here, holed up in Lily's room. They giggle in the night. She and Kitty talk rather carefully in the kitchen – Kitty trying not to be too obviously asking heaps of questions, Madeleine grunting a few grudging yeses and noes. She stops and stares at me like a great moody teenager when I walk in. You wouldn't think she was twenty-four.'

Rita smiled. 'You're not exactly sounding all that

grown-up yourself, Glyn. In fact I'd say I'm hearing a jealous little boy.'

'Hah!' he barked. 'Well you would say that wouldn't you? Bloody conspiracy of women. All that "What would *you* know" etcetera as if you've all got the secret of the heavens and we don't deserve to share it.'

'Oh come on. That's not what I meant at all. Anyway, how's Kitty taking it all? That's the important thing. And what's the girl like?'

Glyn slowed down and looked up at the sky, considering a reply. Rita had simply confirmed his certainty that Madeleine's effect on *him* was just not 'important'.

'She's . . . well she's not like the other two. I suppose I shouldn't be surprised at that. She's also what she calls "just a little bit pregnant", just a teeny matter of about seven months. Apparently her mother doesn't know, she's been living in Scotland with a sod, she says, but he's long gone.'

'But Kitty knows.'

'Kitty does,' he agreed. 'And Kitty's delighted.'

'About the baby?'

'About knowing about it. She denies it, of course, but she's all gleeful, like it's their secret bond or something. I don't know why I'm telling you this.'

That wasn't true. It was because he just had to tell someone. The uncomfortable feeling that he didn't quite belong in his own home had grown steadily since that very first across-the-kitchen glare from Madeleine. He'd got it all wrong, blurting out the hopeless, unwelcoming thing instead of feigning some kind of second-hand delight on behalf of Kitty. It had only been because dropping the spade had hurt his shin. It had actually drawn blood, but no-one had rushed to mop *that*. Now he and Madeleine existed in the house in an atmosphere of wary truce, sidling round the kitchen giving each other far too much space or making for opposite sofas in the sitting-room and having nothing to say. Clumsily, he'd made one attempt at getting to know her, asking her, as teachers inevitably do, about her schooldays and exams.

'School was shit,' she'd snarled, barely looking up from the *Sunday Times* magazine, 'exams were fine. OK?' and that was it; she'd abandoned the magazine on the floor, stalked out to find Lily on the beach, leaving him feeling he was worse than a vicious interrogator with a desk and a harsh light and a wish to send her to her death.

Kitty was so elated she was blithely unaware of anything amiss. 'I can hardly believe we're all together,' she'd said, snuggling up to him in bed a couple of nights after Madeleine's arrival. Who exactly were 'we'? he'd wondered, keeping silent so as not to burst her happy-bubble.

'Kitty's lucky. The only person she's ever lost and she gets her back,' Rita said glumly as she reached her gate.

'Well she did lose her parents, a few years back.'

'Yeah but . . . you know what I mean. Josh has gone. I can sense it. He's been looking out over the sea like somebody shipwrecked for the past week. He was up before me this morning, out doing stuff with his car. He won't be there when I get back – he's not the sort to bother with goodbye.'

Rita was staring out across her garden towards the first field and the barn. No sounds of Josh being industrious came from it. Only the goats in the next field were bleating softly to each other. Hesitantly, Glyn put his arm across her sagging shoulders and she leaned her head against him. Her thick dark hair, blown by the wind, was woven through beneath the top layer with many strands of the purest white. It looked pathetically vulnerable, like a black kitten rolling on its back and exposing skinny pinkish-white underparts.

'He's probably on the beach,' Glyn suggested, 'or gone to see George.'

'No,' Rita said, 'it's a different kind of silence. He's gone.'

Petroc was in the library rethinking his reading of *Tess of the D'Urbervilles*. Tess's illegitimate baby had died, but suppose it hadn't? Who would have taken care of it? Perhaps it would have grown up in the sprawling muddle of the Durbeyfield family, thinking of Tess as some kind of much older sister and maybe she'd never have told Angel Clare the truth and then maybe they'd have lived on quite happily and of course there'd have been no story. He'd heard of families arranged like that even now. There'd been a boy at infants' school with a mother who'd always seemed more than a bit too old, with tight chipolata curls instead of the long careless hair that the other mothers had. 'Our little afterthought' he'd once heard her calling him to another school-gate mum. Petroc had been far too young to know what she was talking about and had imagined 'Afterthought' was just an embarrassing middle name. Years later when they were both at the comprehensive the boy had been having Thursday afternoons off for counselling because he'd just found out that this woman was his grandmother and his wild sister Sally, who'd hung round the Newlyn fish market since she was thirteen larking about with men, was really his mum.

'Are you working or can I sit here?' Amanda Goodbody had managed to come into the library, cross the room and actually pull up a chair without Petroc noticing. Usually he could sense her presence from out in the corridor long before she entered a room. Lily would say it was her Issey Miyake perfume but Petroc secretly preferred to think it was the targeting of pheromones or even something mystically cosmic.

'Sorry. You were concentrating and I've spoiled it.' She had already sat down. Her knee brushed against his under the desk before he'd had time to notice whether her legs were bare or if they were encased in denim.

'I was thinking about Tess.'

'Tess?' Did she look just a smidgen alarmed, he wondered; did it cross her mind for a second that he'd flipped for someone else? Or was that wide-eyed look just amazement that he was actually working?

'I was thinking about her baby, the one that died in the book.'

'Oh, that baby. Yeah I know.' Amanda had lost interest and was delving in her bag for her own work. Books spilled out and mingled with his. Sheets of music cascaded across the desk and he noticed how small her hands were as she collected them together.

'I had a sister, years ago . . .' he started. Amanda's hands went still and she looked at him, fearfully he thought. 'No it's OK, she didn't die.'

Amanda sighed and dumped her bag noisily on the seat beside her. 'Good. That's all right then because I'm late with the Eliot essay and I don't want to be rude but sympathy does take so much time.'

'She's turned up. She's staying with us,' Petroc babbled while she opened books and propped *The Waste Land* up against her bag. 'We've never seen her before and she's twenty-four and pregnant.'

'Oh that's the one! George was rambling on about someone. I can't say I listened properly.' Amanda beamed at him, eyes bright and crinkled. She'd get big crow-foot lines one day, he thought, and her hair would coarsen and go grey and she might run to fat. She wasn't perfect, there was no caring in her. Inside her head was a lot uglier than the outside.

Petroc felt feeble. Adoration for her was dripping away like blood, leaving him weak. He'd enjoyed his long obsession, could hardly recall a time before it. If only it had been more fruitful. 'I just wondered, seeing as you were adopted too, whether you might like to come and meet her. Perhaps you could talk to her, you know, having all that in common . . .' his voice trailed away.

'No,' Amanda said. She'd stopped smiling. Her face was set into its Madonna look, all flat and pale and flawless with no expression, no life, no interest.

'No?' Perhaps she thought, wrongly for once, that his motives were suspect.

'No. I don't want to meet her. We've got nothing in common. It would be like inviting your mum round to meet mine just on the grounds that they'd got blue eyes. You don't lump all gay people together, do you? Or French ones, or black ones? Her experience will be nothing like mine. We're just a pair of kids brought up in a pair of families. Nothing else. I've never even felt the slightest urge to find my birth mother.' Amanda shrugged and reached into her bag again, pulling out her pencil case. She took out a black fountain-pen and a ruler and wrote her essay title at the top of a blank sheet of file paper. Petroc watched as she underlined it three times. Over-emphatic, he judged. Self-important even. Before she'd teamed up with George Moorfield she'd probably only have ruled one line like the rest of them.

'Of course I might try and find her it I suspected she was someone fantastically famous, because that might be interesting and possibly even useful,' Amanda said, looking up. She'd put on her most stunning smile. Petroc looked at her, testing out his new indifference. It was still there. The smile didn't bewitch him any more. He didn't actually like her very much. He smiled back coolly and then took a quick glance round the library. Several other girls, previously of no more interest than the brown and cream striped window blinds, were dotted about at desks, some working, some chatting, all potentially more than a bit alluring. Just a brief radar sweep took in plump Hayley Mason, broad of thigh and with a blithely fashion-free dress sense but a stunning cloud of nut-brown curls, another girl whose long slim legs coiled with pretty gawkiness round her chair legs. No longer being slavishly besotted by Amanda Goodbody might be wonderfully liberating.

As Kitty drove into the multistorey car park in Truro she tried to detach herself mentally from the sheer ordinariness of what she was doing and capture the essence of the moment. Beside her sat Madeleine, quiet but apparently contented enough. She'd stopped thinking of the girl's frequent long silences as sulking hostility. If she hated the family that much she surely would have left by now, curiosity satisfied.

I'm here to buy baby clothes with my daughter Kitty thought as she steered the car up the slope to level five. She practised the words in her head as if she might need to say them. Perhaps someone from the village might be out in the town. They might stop to chat and look with curiosity at this big, pretty girl walking along with her. Kitty could introduce her, as she had on that first day to George. This time though, there'd be none of that awkward rush and confusion. Now she could smile and watch faces for reactions, savour this odd extra parenthood. *'My daughter, Madeleine.'*

'I haven't got much money, only about twenty

quid,' Madeleine warned as she got out of the car. She moved with difficulty, hauling herself out with both hands like someone who'd never been particularly lithe and was now, with the weight of pregnancy, finding even the smallest exertion tricky.

'Don't worry about the money. I don't think we'll be breaking the bank with a trip to Mothercare,' Kitty told her, adding, 'were you any good at games at school?'

Madeleine gave a short laugh, one that Kitty could tell didn't express amusement. 'Games? Jesus no. You had to be able to run fast for hockey and tennis and I couldn't. I was quite good at netball though, people got out of my way. Strange thing to ask.'

Kitty was thinking about Antonia lumbering around the field during hockey warm-up. 'Twice round the pitch and then twice back again!' had been the games mistress's way of killing the first fifteen minutes of those dreaded long-ago Wednesday afternoons. Poor slow Antonia had always still been sweating and gasping in one direction long after the others had turned to run the other way. Looking back, Kitty was sure the little warm-up routine had been specially designed with the humiliation of the congenitally slow in mind.

'I just wondered. Did you . . . did you get picked on?'

'God no. It wasn't cool to be sporty. Or not to be.' She shrugged. 'You could just be yourself, nobody cared.'

'Oh well, that's lucky.'

Madeleine was looking at her as if she was mad. 'Is it? I thought it was like that for everyone.'

'Not always. Listen, tell me what you've already got for this baby then we'll know what not to bother looking at.'

'Nothing.'

Kitty stopped walking. They were outside Marks and Spencer next to a busking trio of singing girls who were putting lots of effort into 'Three Little Maids from School'.

'You've got nothing at all? At eight months?'

Madeleine stuffed her hands in her jacket pockets and looked sulky. 'Maybe it's only seven months, or even less. Does it matter?'

'Where are you going to have it? The baby?' The girl was frighteningly vague. 'Edinburgh' had been the only information volunteered about where Madeleine had been since she'd discovered she was pregnant. She hadn't been home, she'd said, since it had started to show, so her mother didn't know. Her mother thought she was still working in a gallery and failing to phone home. Kitty didn't push it. She had no right to information at all, no right to ask for or expect any. Madeleine had said that the baby's father was American and he'd gone home to Denver. He didn't seem to be expected back.

Madeleine pushed open the door of Mothercare and looked back with a casual smile. 'I don't know where it'll be born. When the time comes I thought I'd just call an ambulance and trust them to know where to go.' Kitty felt appalled and her face must have shown it. 'Don't hassle.' This sounded more like a shaking-off than reassurance. 'I'm OK. It's not an illness.'

Kitty had absolutely no success in trying not to indulge in fantasy as she and Madeleine walked around the shop picking out packs of tiny clothes. In her mind she'd turned her studio into a nursery for Madeleine and the baby. She imagined a pale wooden cot where her easel now stood. She would paint a mobile of brightly coloured fish to hang from the sloping ceiling and the baby would lie batting its little arms up and down on its quilt with excitement

179

as the wind made the fish spin. In her imaginings the rest of the family didn't seem to have a place, at least they certainly didn't raise any objections to the addition of numbers. She could take over one of the barn rooms for her work. In her head she could hear Glyn's sensible teacher voice warning her: only disappointment would come of it. 'We've got a huge amount of stuff here.' Madeleine looked at the pile of baby suits and vests and blankets and the pretty wicker Moses basket that they'd assembled by the checkout. She picked up a tiny blue and white fleecy hooded jacket and stroked it thoughtfully as the assistant started ringing up the prices.

'I really am going to have a baby,' she said. 'Till now I've just thought of it as something that made me get bigger and bigger but now it's real. A whole human person.' She didn't look very thrilled, Kitty thought. Perhaps this outing hadn't been such a great idea. The mother who'd brought her up should be doing this, and now Kitty was going to be punished for taking over and trying to push this relationship into a shape that it wasn't ever supposed to have.

'Why don't we collect this lot later and go and have some lunch?' Kitty suggested. Madeleine nodded, her face still sullen, and followed her out of the store into the sharp sunlight. The paved walkway swarmed with people and Madeleine moved gawkily, weaving about to avoid contact with strange bodies. 'It's like they know there's something in me and they're trying to crash into me,' she grumbled. Kitty took her arm and steered her to the edge of the buildings where it was calmer. 'I hate crowds,' Madeleine growled and Kitty was reminded of the sight of her hurling the stone at Lily's cat. Out here she might lash out with a foot, viciously trip up a careless stranger who'd dawdled too close. She didn't know this girl at all. This, on the relevant bits of paper, was her own daughter and there'd only been those few baby days of shared history together.

'Let's go in here and you can cool down a bit.' Kitty led Madeleine round past the post office and into the cathedral.

'Oh God, we're not going to pray are we? Is that your thing?' Madeleine slumped down into a chair on the back row and slipped her shoes off. The nail polish on her toes was now the bright candy pink of old-fashioned seaside rock: Lily's toenails were the same shade. Kitty had heard them giggling and gossiping up in their room and imagined them with their feet up, painting each other's nails and being careless with the liquid. There were often drops of it on Lily's duvet covers, impossible to wash off. When Madeleine had gone (as she surely would) Kitty would think of her when she did the laundry and saw this colour.

'I'm not particularly religious actually,' Kitty volunteered. 'Blind allegiance to one faith or another seems to cause an awful lot of the world's troubles.'

'That's just the formal trappings of religion you're talking about though,' Madeleine said. 'If there's a God he or she can't be held responsible for the stupid dumb superstition rituals we all set up. I just believe in nature. You can *see* nature's for real, stuff growing and that. Glyn must know what I'm talking about, communing with all those vegetables.'

'Tell me about your life.' The words that had been waiting came out before Kitty could stop them. She'd been so careful, not asking, just waiting for little fragments of information to escape from Madeleine. The girl wasn't particularly secretive, just not desperately forthcoming, as if she'd made herself comfortable with a lifetime of quietness. Really she only ever seemed properly relaxed when she was with Lily. Perhaps Lily had found it easy, natural, to

181

say 'Tell me about your life.' and been just as easily and naturally told.

'There's not that much to tell.' Kitty kept very still. 'No really, there isn't,' Madeleine went on as if she'd felt disappointment transmitted on the cool musty cathedral air. A woman at the end of their row was busy, clattering about as she topped up the supply of votive candles and wafted wax-scented air towards them. Kitty wished she'd go and bustle somewhere else – this should be just her and Madeleine. 'I've had an ordinary, quite nice time. I know it's not much to go on – I really can't tell you that being adopted meant I never quite "fitted" or that I was always looking for something else, if that's what you want to hear. I've lived in Brighton most of my life in a house where soft furnishings have far too much importance.' She laughed, the bright sound echoing. An old man a few rows in front of them turned and glared. 'Mum likes squishy beige carpets and everyone had to take their shoes off at the front door. She had, still *has,* a special little rack for visitors' shoes. Like a mosque. Trouble is she also likes sewing, curtains and cushion covers and stuff so there's always pins hidden in the pile. I was always treading on them.'

'Were you . . . this might sound mad,' Kitty hesitated. 'Were you a My Little Pony girl, or a Flower Fairies one or, I suppose you were too old for Cabbage Patch dolls . . . ?'

'I was technical Lego and before that, Tiny Tears. Does that help?'

'Yes it does. It all does. What about school?'

'Glyn asked that. I should have written up a CV for you. I've got nine GCSEs, all good grades, three A levels, English, Art and Media Studies and the degree from Warwick University.' She said it as if ticking off a check-list. She wasn't volunteering whether she was the kind of student who'd sat up all night

182

smoking spliffs or playing poker or if she'd worked diligently and occasionally stopped to sip camomile tea. Maybe later, if there was a later, these things would emerge, make a detailed picture.

'Boyfriends?' Kitty held her breath though the question was light enough, or perhaps would have been if there wasn't the small matter of this pregnancy. There had to come a moment when Madeleine just clammed up and said no more. Each question risked that moment, though this wasn't it. There was too much to know. It was impossible to think of a definitive list of what to ask that could give even the slightest overview of another person's childhood.

'Virginity lost at a friend's house at seventeen. His parents were supposed to be away but they came back and caught us – we were sure it was on purpose. They told my mother I was a slag and Mum . . .' Kitty waited. Madeleine swallowed and looked down at her hands, fiddling with a loose button on the awful cream jacket. 'Mum sort of agreed. She said I'd end up bringing trouble home like . . . well . . .'

'Like me?'

Madeleine laughed again. 'Yeah, like you.' She patted her stomach. 'And now I'm going to, so she wasn't wrong was she?'

'You know, you should tell her about your baby. She'll want to know. I'd want to know if it was Lily.' Sensible though this sounded, it was hard for Kitty to say. Selfishly, greedily, she'd cherished this so-important piece of knowledge that Madeleine's mother just didn't have.

Madeleine shrugged. 'I do phone her sometimes, so she knows I'm OK. Just not lately, that's all. She likes me being independent. She says that's when you know you've got it right as a parent, when your kids don't need you.' Kitty wondered if it had been

183

meant quite as literally as Madeleine seemed to be interpreting.

'Yes but, well she'll have to know, won't she, if you're keeping it.'

'Of course I'm keeping it!' Madeleine stood up and started pacing. 'I'll tell her soon. When I tell her about you.' Kitty didn't push it. She was in no hurry to share Madeleine with anyone – not after twenty-four missed years. It was down to Madeleine now.

As they were leaving Kitty went to the rack of candles, put a pound in the box and thought of her father as she lit the tiny flame. He'd missed out, so had her mother, on this first grandchild. For the first time, she actually felt quite sorry for her parents – in their eyes they'd only been doing their best for her.

George Moorfield was in the cathedral doorway as the two of them were leaving. His shaggy lion-head and broad shoulders were silhouetted against the stark light of the day outside, making him look like a square-shaped door-guarding ogre that had to be sidled past carefully to get out to safety. It reminded Kitty of when she was small, feeling trapped inside the church after the end of every Sunday service, gasping to escape into the fresh air while her father lorded it in the porch, hand-shaking and small-talking with the congregation. 'You can't just rush out ahead of everyone else, we have to wait,' her mother used to tell her, gripping her upper arm tight to pull her back into the front pew when she'd fidgeted to leave the second the final blessing was over. Life and light could be glimpsed outside, inside was only an atmosphere of stale petty sins and a gloomy sense of unforgiveness. They had to be the last to leave and Kitty used to fight waves of panic that a devil-spirit was lurking in the empty church, waiting for her mother to slip through the door ahead of her so that it could trap her, pin down her limbs and lift her up to drown her in the font.

'I've just been in here for a look-see. Great windows,' George said as they came out. 'I saw you sitting there and thought I'd wait for you, see if you fancied lunch.' Kitty looked at Madeleine, trying to read her expression. George's suggestion seemed like a good one, something light and cheering after that life-probing session in the cathedral.

'OK. Can we go to a pub?' Madeleine sounded eager. 'When you're pregnant you spend half your time avoiding the smell of fags and booze and the rest of the time craving it. Today I'm on craving.'

The pub was as perfectly smoky, aromatic and paint-peeled as Madeleine could have wanted. It wasn't a venue for pastel-cardiganed tourists in search of a children's room, chintzy décor or fancy pasta-strewn menu. After they'd ordered ploughman's lunches all round, George and Madeleine made for a corner table next to a guffawing sprawl of men in paint-spattered overalls facing a collection of empty glasses. Kitty followed, pleased that Madeleine was now looking more animated. She was probably hungry, Kitty thought, sliding along the bench seat next to George. Madeleine sipped her lager and stared at the men on the next table as if memorizing them for something later, a piece of writing or a painting maybe. It crossed Kitty's mind, as she was hit by another sign that she didn't really know her, that the girl might just have a weakness for tough-muscled builders.

'So what's it like then, meeting your real mother for the first time?' George asked. Kitty laughed, delighted at his lack of reserve. It seemed such a blessed relief after Glyn's put-out pussyfooting and Rita's fake-witchy know-it-all irritating smiles of conspiracy.

'It's all right.' Madeleine sounded positive rather

than cautious but then added, 'It's, like, well like finding there's one extra person in the world you can take advantage of.'

'And is that what you're doing?' George's eyes were full of amusement. Kitty felt like kicking him under the table, warning him not to take the piss — his glass was still more or less full, but might instantly be more or less emptied onto his head if Madeleine thought there was genuine mockery in him.

Madeleine grinned at him. 'Yeah, course I am. I'm still at the house aren't I, contributing nothing? Kitty's just bought a million lovely things for this baby, all with no guarantees that I'll be anywhere near her when it wears them, and I'm taking up more than my proper share of Lily's room.' Her eyes narrowed and she gave him a hard look. 'I don't expect to read about this in your next steamy-slimy book.'

'I'm a better writer than that.' He leaned forward with his arms on the table, looking intensely into her face. 'If I do use any of this there's no way you'll recognize it.'

'OK, I believe you,' Madeleine conceded. 'And anyway I probably won't buy it.'

The arrival of the food coincided with the departure of the men next to them. The waitress skipped nimbly round the shuffling figures pushing their way out from behind the table. A couple of empty glasses tumbled silently to the carpet and George leaned down to pick them up, getting his hand trodden on by a big boot for his trouble.

'Watch it.' Madeleine pushed the culprit roughly aside with her foot.

'Sorry love, didn't mean to injure your old dad.'

'He's not . . . oh what the hell. You OK George?'

'Sure.' He rubbed his hand. 'Lucky I only type with three fingers.'

'He thought you were my dad. Bloody nerve.'

Kitty pictured Ben-at-eighteen, swiftly followed by Ben-as-now, and wondered if he'd sorted out things with Rose. The bar was now silent, the men had clattered and chattered their way out of the door leaving a heavy peace.

'Yeah. I'm glad I'm not.' George chuckled and grinned at Madeleine. 'Begs the question though, doesn't it?' The two of them looked at each other intently for a few moments then, smiling as if they'd just discovered their own private joke, they both turned and stared at Kitty, questions in their eyes.

'What?' she demanded, a chunky piece of cheese and pickle halfway to her mouth.

'So you're my mother, right . . .' Madeleine said, and George joined in. 'And on the basis that it takes two to foxtrot . . .'

'Exactly. That still leaves me with a father to find, doesn't it?'

Chapter Twelve

'So. Have you got anything to tell me?' Julia Taggart's voice was terrier-fierce as if whatever it was Kitty was due to report she already knew quite well, and was simply looking for an opportunity to be snappy and sarcastic about being the last in the queue for news.

'Give me a clue, Julia. Something to tell you as in. . . ?' Kitty balanced the phone between her ear and her shoulder while she scrubbed potatoes under the sink tap. It amused her that Julia, who lived and worked among the ever-chaotic variations of the busy metropolis, should be expecting to hear of scintillating scandals from the remote tail-end of the country.

'As in the Rose and dead-Antonia's-Tom situation of course! What else would I mean?'

Kitty glanced across at Madeleine sitting at the table with Lily, the two of them being incredibly slow about removing skins from tomatoes. Madeleine seemed to do everything at half-speed, taking hours about getting up in the mornings, unloading the dishwasher plate by careful plate. She only sped up in the company of George, cutting in and finishing his sentences as if her mind worked the same way as his, but faster. He didn't appear to mind, which was surprising considering his entire life was to do with finding the right words.

Madeleine and Lily were solemnly agreeing about the futility of maths, an opinion that Lily didn't need any encouragement about. Madeleine's arrival was another little news bulletin that had yet to be communicated to Julia. Kitty told her, 'But I don't know anything about Rose and Tom, except that Glyn saw her down here in some garden centre doing what she called research and I haven't heard from Ben for at least a week. I assumed he'd got himself sorted out, or that they'd kissed and made up.'

'Huh!' Julia snorted like a small child imitating a pig. It wasn't a pretty sound. Kitty transferred the phone to her other shoulder while Julia continued, 'You only thought that because he's taken to calling me instead of you. He was on for an hour last night, can you believe.' Julia, thriving on other people's confidences, could hardly have minded. Kitty could hear her rustling about, all her briskness diverted for a few seconds into the noisy lighting of a cigarette. '*And* what's more, he kept going on about you and all that "what might have been" stuff. I got terribly bored, I mean he must be on another planet, though he was rather pathetically gooey-eyed over you that night you were up here . . . but there was a decent episode of *The Bill* so I watched that while he rambled.' Kitty could just imagine it, Julia elegantly draped on her pale green sofa with her feet up on the little Victorian stool embroidered with faded foxgloves (shoes off in case of scuff marks), channel-surfing while Ben imagined he was getting her full attention. She laughed, the picture so much resembled the way she too had 'listened' to Ben.

'What's funny?' Julia was still prickly.

'Sorry Julia, nothing's funny really, just the thought of your attention being so neatly divided like that. Quite a skill. You could have just hung up though, pretended your phone gave out.' That was a tease.

Kitty scattered rosemary and garlic over the potatoes in the earthenware dish and put them in the oven. Julia would never hang up a phone while more information might be forthcoming. Ben would have had to repeat himself twelve times before she realized he'd run out of fresh words.

'Anyway,' Kitty was getting a crick in her neck and now needed both hands to prepare the chicken properly, 'Julia, it's not really any of our business is it?'

There was another 'Huh!' followed by a rather crowing, 'Well you might think that now, but wait till he turns up on your doorstep looking for the precious Rose.'

'Is it likely? Why doesn't he just go to where Rose actually is?'

'*Absolutely* it's likely – Rose has been a bit vague about her actual whereabouts and keeps switching her mobile off, telling him she can't get a signal on your side of the Tamar. He said he might try you. Of course that might just be an excuse to see you . . .'

So *that* was why Julia had phoned: to see if he'd arrived. Kitty looked across at Madeleine again and thought about her deceptively throwaway question about finding her father. She blamed George, geeing her up in the pub like that. The question had managed to drift away unanswered, Kitty getting out of it with something vague about it all being so long ago. George had cut in too, reminiscing about long-lost girlfriends from his youth, and his own missed opportunities for being a family man, and neither he nor Madeleine seemed seriously to expect her to come up with an instant father. A scene came to mind: herself, Ben and Madeleine in a row out on the sea wall, arranged in some sort of parody of a family photo. Madeleine had lined up all the skinned tomatoes into a neat triangle as if she was about to start a snooker match with them. Lily flicked at them with her finger and sent them rolling across the table top towards the edge. The two of them giggled and made a clumsy grab for the tomatoes, squashing one flat and sending juice and pips spurting over the floor.

'Lily stop it! Bring them over here,' Kitty hissed at her. Madeleine pulled a face and smirked at Lily.

'Sorry if it's a bad time.' Julia didn't sound at all sorry and then said, 'By the way, did anything ever come of that trip to the adoption people? Any news? Or is that something else I'm not going to hear about?'

'Oh Julia, don't sound so *disgruntled*.' Kitty laughed out loud at her. 'And actually, I was going to ring you about that but . . .' From across the room Madeleine, sensing that she might be the topic, was staring at her with startlingly blue intensity. 'I'll call you tomorrow Julia. Must go now and do things to the supper. Bye.'

'Were you talking about me?' Madeleine stalked across the room looking accusing and reached over to the sink to get a cloth. She waited close to Kitty, the cloth juggled from one of her hands to the other as if she might feel the need to hurl it at someone.

'No. I wasn't. That was one of my oldest friends, talking about another of my oldest friends.'

'I don't have oldest friends,' Madeleine said. 'I don't know if that's because I'm too young and I don't settle or if it's because I'm still waiting to meet the right ones, the ones who'll last.'

'Like Mr Right?' Lily suggested.

'Someone a bit longer-lasting than that.' Madeleine pulled a face.

'Didn't you meet people at university, that you keep in touch with?' Kitty asked.

'Well, yeah I suppose so. One or two. I've been to a couple of their weddings. But then people change when they're half a couple. I've been half that couple, I know.'

191

'Not always for the worst.'

'Maybe not. Not if one of you's old enough not to stifle the other.' Madeleine looked thoughtful. Kitty opened the fridge and pulled out the chicken breasts.

'Is that chicken?' Lily demanded, butting in between them. 'I'll only eat it if it's not those little baby ones, what are they called?'

'Poussins,' Madeleine told her. She went to the table and slowly wiped up the rest of the squished tomato. 'Nobody should eat those, they're too much like they're still at the yellow chick stage. They look even worse when they do that spreading-out thing, spatching or something.'

'Spatchcock,' Kitty cut in.

'That's the one, where they look like tiny torsos of miniature buxom women with spikes through the middle like torture. Gross.'

'Well tonight it's just regular, normal-size chicken, free range, good farmyard scratching around, all that.' Kitty smiled. One good thing about having Madeleine around for meals was that Lily no longer skimped on food. Madeleine, catching her hiding the best part of a pork fillet under mashed potato, had loudly teased her for being picky with her dinner, saying she should have grown out of the eating-like-a-bird stage before she was ten. Lily followed Madeleine round like a puppy, relishing a second opinion on clothes, friends, school and homework and was happy to sit at the table and eat whatever there was going, since Madeleine, in return, seemed willing enough to doze on the sofa as a captive audience, taking a flattering interest in Lily's surfing and listening to endless stories of rips and cutbacks, breaks and barrels.

'I've got spinach.' Glyn came in through the back door waving a huge bunch of leaves like a winner's trophy and bringing a chill waft of early evening air.

'Ugh.' Madeleine shuddered rudely at him. 'Why do you grow that stuff? Nobody really likes it.'

'*I* like it,' Kitty told her.

'Haven't you got anything else out there in your little veggie patch?' Madeleine's tone was dangerously close to antagonistic and Kitty, skinning the chicken, shot her a warning look which was ignored. The relaxed mood in the kitchen had vanished the second Glyn had come in, and Madeleine's petulant scowl was back in place.

'Leeks? Or what about broccoli, do you like that?' Glyn suggested, pulling off his boots.

'Yeah but I can tell you're not going out to get it just for me, are you? You've got your boots off now.'

He grinned at her, refusing to rise. 'Well, you go and get it then. Far side, left-hand bed down at the end. Broccoli is that green crinkly-looking stuff, all right?'

'Yeah, OK, OK I know what it looks like.' Madeleine sounded defiant and stood up, pushing past him to the door. 'Coming Lily?'

'History test on Monday, Lily. You said you'd get down to it tonight,' Glyn reminded her. Lily looked frantic, turning from one to the other, loyalties torn.

'No it's all right, go do the history. I'll go and see what I can find out here in the nearly *dark*, by *myself*, in my con*dition*.' Madeleine opened the door far wider than she needed to and went outside with an exaggerated waddle and her hand to the small of her back like a bad actress doing 'pregnant'.

'Maybe you should . . .' Kitty looked at Glyn.

'No I shouldn't. There's something wrong if she can't even pick a few stalks. Give her something to do. After all, *you* want her to feel at home, she can join in as if it *is* home.'

Everything he said these days seemed to have an edge that could cut, Kitty thought. He hadn't once asked how long Madeleine intended staying with them, but the question hung around like the hint of a bad smell. Kitty didn't want to think about it, in case Madeleine somehow read her mind and came downstairs one morning clutching the scruffy rucksack and asking about train times. Even now, in the warm and hazy moments before she got up, Kitty still dreaded being first into the kitchen in case all that was left of this new daughter was a goodbye note propped up against the jug of primroses on the table, and no clue, apart from possibly home to Brighton, as to where she might have gone. She should have phoned her mother, told her what was happening and where she was, Kitty thought guiltily. She should have argued the case for that more firmly, even at the risk of prompting the very going-away scene she so dreaded — Madeleine might even think she was pushing her that way. They must have a very easy-going relationship, Madeleine and her mother, for nothing had been said to suggest any hostility between them, just this benevolent neglect. If this was Lily, she caught herself thinking again . . .

'Look! I found this as well!' Madeleine hurtled through the back door, one arm crammed with broccoli stalks, the other dragging George whose hair, tossed around by a gathering wind, looked wilder than ever. 'Is there enough food? Can he stay?' Kitty mentally counted potatoes and said, 'Yes, why not. Petroc's gone to see a film with a girl from college so there's plenty of chicken.' George shoved his hands in his pockets and looked mildly embarrassed. 'Really, I don't want to intrude, she just pounced . . .' He sat down at the table, looking as eager to join them as Madeleine was to have him stay. 'Did not!' Madeleine laughed, her face transformed into something quite radiant. Perhaps she'd been feeling a bit bogged-down working her way into this new, intact family, Kitty thought. Perhaps she needed an outside ally just now. George might help her not to want to leave.

'Would you like a drink, George? If you don't want alcohol there's apple juice or Coke or mineral water . . .' Madeleine was peering into the fridge, eager to supply her garden-trophy with a drink. Glyn, coming back into the kitchen, raised his eyebrows at Kitty and gave her a look of amused confusion.

'We've got George for supper,' Kitty told him, juggling boiling water and the broccoli.

'I thought we had chicken,' he said, looking immediately as if he wished he hadn't.

'Oh ha ha!' Madeleine's voice rang out. For once she looked as if she actually found Glyn funny, rather than something to be avoided and ignored. If it took George to be a benevolent catalyst between the two of them, Kitty thought, as she took the chicken out of the oven, then perhaps he should move out from the barn and join them in the house. He certainly looked comfortable enough, moving chairs around and opening a drawer to find more cutlery.

'How's the book going?' Glyn asked George as they started eating.

'Poor George,' Madeleine interrupted before he could answer, 'I bet writers are always being asked which chapter they're on by people who don't intend to read the finished thing.'

'I might well read it. You couldn't possibly know,' Glyn countered.

'It's going quite well actually.' George looked nervous, intuitively getting in before the hostility level went up any further. 'I get a lot done in the night.'

'What, after you've driven Amanda Goodbody all that way home?' Lily quipped.

'And I thought it was a perfectly innocuous question,' Glyn muttered to Kitty. She grinned at him – he was actually trying for once.

'Amanda doesn't need any more help from me with her writing ambitions,' George told Lily. 'She has more than enough personal power to see her through to whatever ends she has in mind.'

'Ouch! Oh God, ouch!' Madeleine's fork clattered to the floor and her hands clutched at her front.

'What is it? Surely it's not the baby . . .' Kitty was out of her seat and close to Madeleine, her arm round her shoulders. Both men, she noted, looked horribly nervous, as if they'd like to adjourn immediately to the pub.

'No. No, it's all right, it just kicked me, really, really hard. I wish it wouldn't do that when I'm eating, there just isn't the room with food and stuff going on as well.'

George actually sighed, a sound of undisguised relief. 'All those limbs inside swimming and swirling, so . . .'

'Hey I haven't got a bloody aquarium in there,' Madeleine was laughing now. 'It's a tight fit. That's why it hurts.'

'Imagine twins,' Lily murmured. 'Eight limbs.'

'Yeah, imagine,' Madeleine agreed, then turned abruptly and said to Kitty, 'I wasn't a twin was I? There weren't two of us that you got rid of separately?'

Kitty felt angry. The girl was just showing off, thinking of the shocking thing to say to impress George. She didn't need to, he was looking concerned enough for her, gently rubbing her back to ease her aches. She leaned against his hand like a stroked cat. If Kitty had done that, she wondered if she'd have shrugged her off. 'No Madeleine, you weren't a twin,' she told her. 'And even if you had been, you wouldn't have been separated.' She felt weary suddenly. She hadn't the energy to counter the 'got rid of' comment. It was such a thoughtless, throwaway phrase that hadn't been given any consideration beyond its capacity to invoke an audience's sympathy. Just suppose this had turned into a game to Madeleine, the being here and the working her way into family life and affection when she really might just disappear without a care, perhaps even deliberately, like some long overdue but well-thought-out punishment. I haven't a hope of really getting to know her, Kitty thought sadly, that would have taken all of those lost twenty-four years.

Glyn didn't usually go to the pub. He didn't particularly want to go now — it was simply preferable to staying in the house. Strangely, no-one had thought it odd that he was popping out into the cold windy dark for something that could hardly be counted as urgent, whereas pre-Madeleine he'd probably have faced a barrage of questions about what for? and why? and can we come? Now the only person whose every coming and going seemed to matter was Madeleine. Lily followed her everywhere, only Petroc seemed to be as self-absorbed as usual. Kitty was forever asking her what she'd like to do, or eat, or if she needed to rest. It seemed to worry Kitty that Madeleine didn't seem to want anything particularly, just to be, as if simply to get from one day to the next was enough. Perhaps it was being pregnant, he thought. With all that going on in her body, and with a birth mother to live with whom she'd never met before, maybe that was more than enough to occupy her mind.

Tonight he'd told Kitty they were out of tonic and that he fancied a bedtime gin later. He wouldn't be missed, they were all still sitting around having coffee and watching what he thought of as The Madeleine Show. As he'd left the room he'd heard her lecturing Lily about becoming a victim of thin-culture, telling her that body strength was as important as mental strength, which, if Lily listened and took in, perhaps wasn't such a bad thing. What he mostly couldn't bear to stay in and see was the rapt attention of Kitty, gazing greedily at Madeleine like a doting, besotted suitor, as if she was trying to reconstruct out of her features a missed near-quarter of a century of change, trying to envisage the girl's life from now to babyhood, going backwards. He could see vast clouds of hurt approaching her, devastation as certain as if she was marching a group of infants across the M25 in the rush hour. He couldn't think of any way to help her avoid it.

The wind was blowing hard against him as he walked towards Rita's house on the way to the pub. The sea was hurling itself loud and angry onto the beach below and would keep Lily awake if it got any worse. He hadn't heard the shipping forecast that night but guessed at force six, and whatever it was he wouldn't want to be out in a boat or even up on the cliffs. Glyn could see only one small light in Rita's kitchen as he got closer to the house. Seeing the light through the waving beech-tree branches gave an impression of flashing, like a signal. She'd been right about Josh going – Kitty had been told all about it in a long lunch-time session on the sea wall with a bottle of wine. She was probably feeling terrible, lonely and hurt.

He pushed the rickety gate open carefully, so that it wouldn't squeak and disturb the goats. So long as they stayed quiet he could change his mind on the path and creep away again. Still unsure, he tapped gently on the front door. All his movements seemed half-hearted, uncertain, as if he was half hoping she wouldn't answer his knock. If she didn't, he could just wander off again and think, oh well, I tried. He was almost turning away to continue on to the pub when she opened the door. She was looking particularly bedraggled, even for Rita, her skirt crumpled and her hair tangled. She looked as haggardly grey and distraught as if Josh had died. She was even wearing a stained old baggy green sweater that he used to wear, as if clinging to the smell and feel of him.

'Sorry, I was dozing with the dog on the sofa. Come in.' She opened the door wide and went inside ahead of him, patting her hair down uselessly as she walked.

'I didn't want to disturb you . . .' he said. The air was dense with the musty scent of warm damp animal. Half-grown cats sat at intervals on the stairs, staring at him coolly as he passed through to the kitchen. 'Take a seat and I'll see if I can find you something to drink.' Rita's voice was dull and lifeless. She started moving dirty plates from the table and putting them with an awful lot more in the sink. The rubbish bin was overflowing with tea bags and newspapers and soup-for-one packets. Used cups were lined up on the arms of the old pink sofa and the edge of the Aga. There were opened tins of dog and cat food littered among a few washed saucepans left draining next to the sink, some with forks sticking out, crusted with dried-on meat.

'It's an awful mess in here,' Rita commented unarguably, collecting up a handful of the cups and rinsing them with no attempt at real thoroughness under the cold tap. 'I seem to be getting into a state of lone-woman sluttishness.' Glyn looked in the fridge, which contained three eggs and some cheese with a generous bloomy growth, pulled out the last two cans of the beer that Josh had favoured and found a couple of dusty glasses in a cupboard. As he shut the door, the handle fell off and Rita burst into tears. 'Everything's falling to bits!' she wailed as Glyn dutifully put his arms round her. Behind her back his hands still clutched a glass and a can. He made some vague soothing noises while Rita sobbed, managing to get the glass onto the edge of table. He felt very much in need of the beer, but it would have taken extremes of cynicism to interrupt the flow of her misery with the frivolous *swoosh* of opening the can.

'He's gone then, has he?' Glyn asked rather pointlessly.

'Oh yes, he's gone,' she said. 'That day when I saw you and I knew, when I could feel the silence, I knew it was more than just the sound of him not working.' She stepped back and reached for a piece of kitchen roll from the draining-board. Glyn unleashed the beer and took a quick restorative swig from the can. 'You just know, don't you? The silence was the space he'd left,' she went on, blowing her nose hard. She slumped down on the sofa, her body leaning forward with her head in her hands and her hair drooping and wispy as if it too had lost all its bounce. Her face was now pink and blotched, with large purple shadows hanging on the loose skin beneath her eyes. Glyn felt enormously sorry for her. Josh had taken all her vitality, all that was left of the illusion of youth, when he'd so casually packed up and gone. He imagined him whistling as he stuffed clothes into his bag, thought of him hauling it out to the gate and perhaps even ambling back into the kitchen to assemble a lumpy sandwich of bread and cheese for the journey.

'I expect he'll come back,' Glyn ventured. 'Perhaps he's just gone for a little visit somewhere.'

Rita's laugh was one of the saddest sounds he'd ever heard. It was exactly what they meant by 'hollow' when applied to mirth. 'What's to come back to?' she said, waving her arm around to include both the squalor of the kitchen and her own sad spiritless self. 'He didn't even leave a sodding note.'

'In time . . .' Glyn ventured, sitting close to her and trying to think of something helpful to say, 'in time maybe you'll think of him as just a stupid, selfish kid. You deserve better.'

Rita gave him a look that was near to contempt. 'In *time*,' she told him, 'in *time* I'll just be older. Nothing else. There *is* nothing else. What's the point of deserving something that you know you're never going to get, never ever, whatever you do? Josh, or something better than Josh, is what someone very much younger than I am gets, whether they deserve it or not. That's life. That's sad bloody reality.' Her eyes were filling up again and Glyn pulled her close to him. Her hair smelled oily, unappealingly dirty. Usually she smelled of thyme or lavender, as if she carried them somewhere on her, like seeds sewn into a hem as he imagined fastidious women of past dead eras had done. With a sense of being polite, neighbourly even, he stroked her arm, moved his hand down and ran it along her thigh. Her skirt was silky and thin and he could feel her muscles stirring beneath it.

'He used to kiss me, like teenagers, you know? Proper snogging, the sort that almost wears your mouth away. Bliss,' Rita murmured, close to his ear. Glyn tried not to hear this as a request. He absolutely didn't want to kiss her, that would be just too intimate. Kissing was too close to the brain, it went with love and emotion and . . . and with Kitty. 'I don't suppose that will ever happen again,' she went on, compounding the hint.

'Of course it will!' Glyn hated himself for sounding so falsely jolly. She might well be right, after all. He started disentangling himself and stood up. 'Just give it time. You're feeling hurt right now, but who knows.'

'I know,' she sniffed.

'Listen, I must go. I'm sorry not to be more use. Er, can I get you anything down at the pub? I'd better pick up the tonics I said I was going out for, so if you like . . .'

'No. No you go, you've got a family to get back to,' Rita said. She hauled herself out of the sofa and went to the sink, clattering about making a trembling start on washing the dishes. 'I'll get on with this lot. Stop me going to bed and brooding.' She laughed suddenly. 'I can't believe I've let myself get into this state at my age! You think it can't happen, you know?'

'Yeah, I know.' Glyn gave her cheek a hasty kiss and left, walking fast down the long dark lane towards the pub. He hadn't coped very well, he felt. When Kitty had been in London and he'd been just the teensiest bit down, certainly by comparison with what he'd just seen, Rita had taken his pain over, soothed it away and shared her body quite easily and selflessly. He hadn't had to do a thing, not even open his eyes. And he wouldn't even kiss her. Walking fast towards the comfort of the pub lights, he was aware that if he persuaded himself he was on moral high ground at all, it was very unstable, volcanic stuff.

Kitty hadn't heard Madeleine follow her into the kitchen. When she turned round from hanging the mugs on the dresser hooks and saw her there, hovering nervously by the door, she felt a mixture of terrified foreboding and delight. This could be confiding-time, something major and secret to be told from that lost childhood. There might be things she felt she wanted to share with Kitty that she hadn't been able to talk about with her mother. It astonished and rather dismayed Kitty that there was a deep need in her to have something of Madeleine that the mother who'd brought her up hadn't had. Surely it was enough that she'd had the experience of her birth?

Madeleine sat at the kitchen table and picked at her thumbnail. 'I want to ask you something, and I don't want you to take it the wrong way. I mean I'm grateful, you've been really kind letting me stay.'

Kitty sat opposite her, reached across and took her hand. 'You're not going? Not yet?'

Madeleine laughed. 'What *now*? In the dark and the wind? No!'

'Do you want to phone home? Is that it? I mean do if you want . . .' Kitty tried to smile and keep panic out of her voice.

'No, well yes sometime soon. It's OK.'

'You really should tell her . . .'

Madeleine scowled and drummed her fingers impatiently on the table. 'Look, just don't bloody *fuss*!' Kitty flinched at the fierce tone. 'She's used to me not being around, or even contactable. I *travel*, I've done Europe, America and Australia, backpacking, you know and Mum never once flapped like you're doing, just 'cos I didn't phone home every ten sodding minutes. It's cool between us and you're interfering.'

Kitty said nothing, waiting to feel inspired with the right words but Madeleine had moved on, eager to say what she wanted. 'It's just, well George and me, we really get on. He's OK.' She shuffled a bit and looked pink. 'And he's asked me, well I'd like to go and stay with him in the barn. You don't mind do you Kitty? He said I could be useful, making his phone calls and fending off his agent and stuff like that. And I'd rather be doing something than not.'

Kitty sighed, relieved but still with some nagging worry. This might be the beginning of moving out, leaving. She'd got a family she spoke of with fondness that might be casual but seemed to be genuine enough, and George himself would be leaving at Easter when the renting season was due to start properly.

'It's not that I don't like being here in the house . . .' Madeleine was twisting the bottom of her sweatshirt in her hands. 'But Glyn doesn't much like me being here and well, I like my own space.'

'Well you'll have plenty of that over in the barn,' Kitty said, trying to be cheerful and hoping her words didn't sound as false as they felt. 'Have you spoken to Lily?'

'Yeah, she was cool. I said I'd watch her surf in the morning. Early she said, so can I borrow an alarm clock?'

There weren't many in the pub. The locals who frequented it tended to be farm-workers with early starts in the morning who got their drinking done soon after opening time. Later in the summer the evening trade would be brisker, with coast-path walkers happy to think they'd found an authentic local that nobody else knew about. Glyn passed a couple of battle-scarred Land Rovers in the car park on his way in, and noticed a gleaming black Porsche alongside like a smart yacht slumming it next to a couple of aged tugs. Early visitors, town sailors checking out the cream of the summer moorings, he assumed, pushing open the door.

'Ah Glyn! Nice timin'! Bloke 'ere looking for your place.' Mick behind the bar was pulling a pint of Tinners ale and indicating with his head a man perched on a bar stool in front of him, sipping orange juice. Glyn's first impression was of a formal, uncomfortable suit among coarse jackets and sweaters, a city-pale face among harsh-weathered complexions. He couldn't be a writer looking for a room on the off chance, Glyn guessed – they always seemed to turn up in scrupulously clean denim – or even a journalist desperate for dirt on George Moorfield.

'Is that right? Were you looking for me? I'm Glyn Harding,' he said. The poor man looked exhausted, as if he'd travelled half Cornwall searching for Treneath.

'Oh! You must be Kitty's husband. I'm Ben Ruthermere — I think you've met my wife, Rose.' A clean plump hand was offered for shaking. Glyn shook it carefully. It felt rather like a latex Pink Panther bendy toy Lily had dragged around when she was little.

'Can I buy you a drink?' Ben looked as if he was about to apologize, though there was no clue as to what for. Perhaps, Glyn thought, he was the type who seemed to be sorry for breathing. He had large greyish eyes that were mildly familiar and brown-grey hair with sweaty curled ends. He looked as if he'd been travelling for years.

'Sure. Gin and tonic would hit the spot.'

'Two large ones, please,' Ben Ruthermere asked Mick, who grinned past him at Glyn, booking an explanation for the next time he was in. 'So,' Glyn ventured when the drinks were poured and Mick had been summoned down the bar to issue refills to the darts players, 'what brings you here, and what can we all do for you?'

'Actually, I'm looking for my wife. I know it sounds pathetic, don't tell me. I thought she might be with you?' Glyn grinned, catching on. Of course, the runaway Rosemary-Jane. So this was the poor sap she lived with, co-custodian of a giant poodle and ex-boyfriend of Kitty. So this, this defeated-looking stranger he was having a comfortable drink with, was Madeleine's father.

Chapter Thirteen

They were really too big for Ben's car. As he lowered
himself carefully into the leather seat and sought
space to arrange his legs, Glyn wondered what kind
of man would buy himself a Porsche when he'd got
to the age and size where getting in and fitting behind
the wheel could only be an effort and an undignified
squeeze. Ben Ruthermere wasn't overweight and
neither was Glyn, but with the extra substance that
accumulates with age they both bulged beyond the
edges of the snappy little sports seats till their
shoulders almost touched and the silly stubby gear
stick was uncomfortably close to their knees. To
choose to drive like this, to fold himself up and puff
himself into place, a man had to be feeling pretty
unsettled about something. Glyn presumed it was the
classic cliché sexual thing, along with an attack of
the middle-age insecurity terrors. He could only sympathize, when he thought about it, but was glad that
his own confidence-boosting indulgence in decent
designer clothes (long-run bargains, as women
usually argued) didn't involve four-figure insurance.

'It's up here on the left, watch the bend though, the
wall sticks out,' Glyn said. They were roaring past
Rita's. There were no lights on now and he hoped she
wasn't lying awake and weeping. Perhaps he should
drop Ben off there, then the two deserted ones could

snuggle up together and soothe away their various miseries. Ben wasn't at all bad-looking, Glyn thought, trying not to chuckle at his idea, Rita would think it was all her birthdays at once. Ben, though, might not.

'Are you sure this is going to be OK?' Ben asked for the third time.

'Absolutely. Kit will be delighted to see you, I'm sure.' Glyn wasn't at all sure but the poor man had driven an awfully long way, straight from a city office by the look of his smart but crumpled suit, and could hardly start searching for a hotel room in Penzance this late in the evening. And besides . . . a terrible demon in him could hardly wait to see Kitty's face. Madeleine would be there. There would be Kitty, Madeleine and Ben – with luck they'd all sit in a row on the bigger of the blue sofas, two of the three not knowing that together they made up a family. A family of sorts anyway.

'I should have phoned,' Ben was saying as they pulled into the yard. Yes you should, Glyn agreed silently, just as Kitty had thought about Rose when she'd turned up weeks ago. 'But the mobile doesn't seem to work here,' Ben continued as they freed themselves rather stiffly from the baby car.

'No, well, this is a primitive outpost of the empire. We tend to rely on carrier pigeons and semaphore.' Ben squinted through the dark, trying to make out what Glyn was talking about.

'For communication?' Glyn said. 'It's OK, it's a joke . . . well nearly.' He headed for the door, realizing Ben was more tired than he'd thought. 'This way, come on in.'

Kitty's face was exactly the gratifying picture of gob-smacked astonishment that Glyn had antici-pated, but disappointingly Madeleine wasn't in sight. He assumed she'd gone up to bed. Even for someone as young as her, being that pregnant must take its toll.

'Ben! How lovely to see you!' Kitty's social graces took over quickly from her surprise. She and Ben kissed politely, like a dinner-party pair. 'Is Rose with you?' she looked behind him as if expecting her to be hovering behind the door. As if, Glyn thought. She was hardly the sort for shy hanging-back.

'I found him in the pub, looking lost,' Glyn said.

Ben laughed. 'Well, you might as well be lost in a pub as anywhere else.'

'Er . . . where's Madeleine? Gone to bed?' Glyn tried to sound casual.

'Actually, she's moved across to the barn. I went across and helped her make up the bed in room six. She and Lily both need the space, Madeleine needs more than a single bed, and George needs a helper, so it seemed a good idea.'

'True. We all need space.' Kitty gave Glyn a hard look. He was looking too pleased with himself, too pent-up with suppressed glee. 'Drink, Ben? There's a bottle of white open in the fridge. I think, well I hope, it's just about good enough to serve to a wine merchant. I'll fetch it.' Glyn left the room, whistling cheerily. Kitty and Ben sat on sofas opposite each other, each waiting for the other to say something. Kitty tried a sort of welcoming how-lovely smile and felt her face collapsing into what must have looked like a uselessly empty grin. What was she supposed to do with him? Ben was leaning forward, his tired hands drooping like big empty gloves in front of him. Any moment, she felt, he might drop to his knees at her feet and plead to be told where his wife was.

'Rose isn't here you know, Ben. Hasn't even called in, or phoned,' she said eventually.

'No. Well I gather that. But you do know where she is and what she's up to.'

'I know she's making her programme near St

Austell, that's the last thing I heard. I can't tell you where she's staying because I haven't a clue.' And I don't give a flying fuck, she added in her head.

'She's with Tom Goodrich. They've been at it for years.' He sounded weary. 'I'll go over there tomorrow and see what it is she wants to do about us. About her and me. As if I didn't know.' Kitty didn't know what to say. Ben looked, just now, more angry than defeated.

'Well if it's a divorce, why not just go for it?' she suggested gently. 'I mean, it's not as if there are children involved.' Put like that it sounded horribly insensitive.

'No. No it isn't,' Ben said, with a wry grin. 'That's some of the problem. She wanted some and couldn't have any. So she started wanting someone else's. Antonia's would do as well as anyone else's, especially when they came with such a plum of a father and a gem of a house.'

'She got used to taking stuff from Antonia round about the age of eleven,' Kitty said. 'Her Conway Stewart pen, her Latin homework. Rose even stole a pair of grotty unwashed gym socks when she'd forgotten her own. It was easy, just a nasty habit.'

'OK, drinks all round,' Glyn interrupted. He looked strangely jolly. He was enjoying himself. Kitty glared at him and stood up, deciding she wasn't up to playing social piggy in the middle for this pair. 'You two finish the bottle. I'll make up the studio sofa bed for you, Ben, and Glyn will show you where everything is, but for now I'm afraid I just have to go and sleep. See you in the morning, we can talk then.'

Petroc had thought there were only a certain number of times you could see reruns of movies you've enjoyed with someone else. The first time he'd seen *Blue Juice* had been about four years before with twelve others skiving a Wednesday-afternoon games session. There were far too many of them, more than a football team's-worth, for their absence to pass without comment and his stomach had been cramped with nerves anticipating his father's wrath. He wouldn't be picked out or made any kind of embarrassing example at school, that hadn't bothered him, but at home there'd be that disappointment thing that parents went in for. Parents like his who went in for Personal Trust specialized in hurt silence and the tight-lipped 'We didn't expect this,' as if that could be even halfway true – if you've got a teenager you get trouble, it's the way life's arranged. What had made *that* particular afternoon blissfully worthwhile had been that, in the scramble for seats, Amanda Goodbody had somehow ended up sitting next to him. Her thigh was squeezed against his in the dark, only an accidental brush of the hand away from being flesh against flesh that back then had only recently started doing serious lusting. He hadn't, now he came to think of it, really entertained the thought of anyone else as a serious object of adoration since then.

This time though, for the rerun of *Blue Juice*, he was in Hayley Mason's bedroom. Propped up on a heap of pillows in Hayley Mason's single bed, watching her video and sharing Ben and Jerry's Cherry Garcia ice-cream straight from the tub. He was contentedly sated from sex with the never-before-considered, all-enveloping Hayley, a girl with warm welcoming flesh that had moved about softly beneath him like feathers in a plump new duvet. If Amanda Goodbody walked in now, all long, hard-muscled thighs and a waist as bony and thin as a violin body, declaring undying love and lust for him, he could honestly say she'd be told to go away and forget it. Hayley had no complications, no complexes, no self-doubts. She was friendly and direct. She had a taste for beach life, detective novels, football, sex and some, but not all, of the bands that he liked. She planned a year off after A levels (no *angst* about failing: you worked, you passed) with a six-month job in London and four months visiting relations in Australia, followed by teacher training. She did not yearn for fame, a life more thrilling, men not attainable, hair that was blonder or a size ten body. Petroc, licking the spoon and passing it over to her, thought that this time it just might be love. Restful, peaceful, blissful love.

'Y'all right?' she asked, plunging the spoon deep into the melting ice-cream. It wasn't a request for reassurance. She just wanted to know. Petroc looked down at her large blue eyes and tangled mass of dark brown hair. Her smile was broad and generous, her teeth even and pretty. There was a tiny smear of pink ice-cream at the edge of her top lip. Petroc leaned across and kissed it away, gently.

''M'all right,' he told her.

Kitty had been waiting over an hour for Glyn to come up the stairs. She didn't want to go to bed, though earlier she'd felt so tired she could have happily curled up on the sofa and spent the night there. Glyn was still downstairs with Ben. She'd heard as she waited the rumble of male voices and every now and then one of them would laugh. There had been the sound of Glyn returning to the kitchen, bottle-opening noises, the clinking sounds of ice and glass, heavy male footsteps, the flush of the downstairs loo, more laughter and more talking. She'd tried to read, lying on the sofa with her feet kept warm under a cushion, staring at the same words on the same page over and over. She'd looked out of the window, stared across at the barn wondering what Madeleine was dreaming about. Girls of twenty-four don't come running up in the morning and say 'Mummy, I had this dream . . . !' She'd missed all that. They didn't share their secrets and hopes either, or tell you what they worried about in the seconds before sleep got them. They didn't tell you if they woke up in the night with a pounding headache. Even Lily didn't do all that any more, and she was only fifteen. Kitty would never know if Madeleine preferred to sleep on her left or right side, or if she flung her arms up above her head like a baby and slept on her back, one leg out to get cool. There was no sign of life in the barn. For all she knew, George and Madeleine and the bulk that was the baby could be awkwardly but contentedly tucked up in bed together. She couldn't know. Nobody needed her to know. All this, and all of Madeleine's life, was none of her business and never had been.

'Oh. You're still up. I thought you'd be asleep ages ago.' Glyn was suddenly in the room, hauling off his sweater, straight from the back the way men always did. For a second, Kitty, who had actually started dozing, had a picture of Ben pulling off a purple ribbed top in exactly the same way in his teenage bedroom, so very long ago. It had lain crumpled on the floor, trodden over and mashed in with the rest of their scattered clothes in their haste to fall into his bed. He'd had an eight-track stereo in his room, one of those technological non-starters that had rushed into oblivion like Betamax video and the Sinclair C5. They'd played David Bowie's *Aladdin Sane* album, she remembered, and burned jasmine-scented joss-sticks. On the wardrobe door had been a poster of Bryan Ferry, strutting in silver, snake-hipped and slick-haired.

'Ben's gone up to the studio. I showed him where everything was. He's knackered, I bet we don't see him before ten tomorrow.' Glyn was taking his time, wandering round the room less aimlessly than it appeared. He always took his watch off as he passed the chest of drawers on the way to their bathroom, always left his shoes just outside his wardrobe and then had to shift them out of the way with his foot in the morning when he needed to open the door and choose clothes.

'What did you two find to talk about till . . . what is it, heavens, nearly one thirty,' Kitty said. She stood up and stretched, wondering what had happened to all those way-back days of clothes-casting and bed-leaping, all too fast and frantic to care about the consequences. The consequence was sleeping just across the yard.

'We didn't talk about you, if that's what you're thinking.' Glyn emerged from the bathroom, tooth-brush in hand. 'There's more to life – there's cricket and wine and the falling pound and slug control . . .'

'Glyn, what are you playing at?'

'Playing?' He went back into the bathroom and she followed him. He slooshed mouthwash and looked in the mirror, tweaking at his hair as he did every night to see if it was more inclined to fall out than it had been the day before.

'Yes, *playing*. You've got this smug "I know a secret" look. I bet you've had it all evening, chit-chatting away with Ben. He probably thinks you're demented.'

He switched off the bathroom light, pushed past her and got into bed. 'Well I *do* know a secret don't I?' he said. 'The question is, is Ben going to be told it too? After all, you could argue that he's entitled. In fact you could hardly argue that he's not.'

'I wish I'd never told *you*.' Kitty was angry. 'It isn't a game and it's nothing to do with you. What Ben didn't know all those years ago he really doesn't need

213

to know now. It wouldn't change anything – well, not for the better anyway – what difference can it make after all this time?'

'Well I don't agree.' Glyn climbed out of bed again and put his bath robe on. It was white waffle cotton, which Kitty always thought looked like judo kit, just now seeming perfectly suited to his combative mood. He strode to the window and stood looking out towards the sea. The wind was getting up. The softly damp new leaves on the old beech tree near Rita's house were rustling urgently, and when Kitty joined Glyn to stare out into the dark she could just make out the awkward jerky twitchings of the great limbs, like a very old man who is determined to have one last go at disco dancing. 'I think you should tell both of them – Madeleine and Ben,' Glyn went on. 'Then everything's out in the open and they can make of the situation whatever they will. They are grown-ups, Kitty.'

'No. I can't do that. Well at least, not without thinking and . . .'

'*Thinking?*' Glyn was shouting now. 'It's a bit late for *thinking*. If you and Ben had done some *thinking* all those years ago, we wouldn't be having this ridiculous conversation.'

'Ssh! You'll wake Lily! And Ben will hear too. He'll think we're arguing about him. He's feeling bad enough about Rose without imagining we're rowing about him being here.'

Glyn sighed. 'Always other people's feelings. You're so sodding saintly, Kitty. Or are you a control-freak? Just tell Madeleine she's got a father. Tell Ben he's got a daughter – that'll give them both something new to think about. You can't keep pulling all their strings for ever. Just let go.' He got back into bed, turned his back on her and switched his lamp off. She felt dismissed, no longer worth listening to or talking to. It was probably something he'd perfected in his teaching days.

Kitty went into the bathroom, shut the door and turned on the shower taps, running the water as hard as it would go. She took all her clothes off, hurled them into the laundry basket and sat on the floor, leaning her back against the ice-cold tiles on the side of the bath. 'Just let go.' The words seethed and spat in her head. How were you supposed to let go of what you'd never had? 'Just let go' was a lot like 'Put it all behind you' and 'Now you can get on with your life' – the cosy phrases that were trotted out when the mistake-babies had been safely signed over to their new parents. The neat clichés were so glib and slick and easy to say – and they took so little thought. Even from Glyn, Kitty thought now as she stepped wearily into the shower, even Glyn.

Lily hated waking in the night. The sleep afterwards was always too light and fidgety. She'd gone to bed early, before ten, as soon as she'd helped Madeleine move her stuff across the yard to the barn. There was nothing to stay up for. Madeleine and George didn't make it obvious that they wanted to be on their own; they included her in what they said, but she kept feeling as if they were waiting for her to leave. She felt she was handing Madeleine over to George and she felt desolate, as if she'd lost her somewhere in the yard between the house and barn. Lily had become Madeleine's special person in the house, and now in the barn it was going to be George. They kept making stupid jokes, finishing each other's sentences and talking in *Fawlty Towers* voices (George being Basil and Polly and Madeleine going between Manuel and Sybil). They didn't do it very well, but they laughed at each other as if they were just the best comedy thing ever.

But worse than feeling that she was only on the edge with them, not right there in the middle, was being sure that after she'd gone they'd stop being TV characters and start taking the piss out of her mum and dad. She wasn't sure why, she was only aware of the sense that that was why they were waiting for her to go. She could just imagine it, too horribly clearly, even if she lay in bed with her hands over her ears; Madeleine acting all crawly and caring like her mum was, copying the way she was with her: 'Madeleine, are you sure you're comfortable? Another cushion?' and 'Yoghourt – what flavours do you really like?' which she said every time she made a shopping list, as if not having a clue about Madeleine's dairy preferences was the one thing she'd really minded missing out on for all those years.

Kitty and Glyn were talking loudly enough for her to hear across the corridor and through two closed doors. Lily had often wondered what it would be like to live in a household of high dramatic tension; to have parents who didn't go in for give and take and careful reasoning but thrashed out the tiniest disagreements at the highest volume, and with door-slamming and plate-smashing and stuff said that should be unforgivable. It was hard work to nurture the soul of a tortured poet in a household of casual consideration and good manners and a sort of easy-going general happiness.

They were close to shouting now, in that way, she could tell, that meant they were only keeping the volume down because they didn't want someone else to hear. She could sense teeth that were gritted and control that was only just there. In the interests of research, Lily slipped out of bed and out of the room and close enough to their door to hear details, but far enough away so that she could bolt back to bed if there was something she needed to pretend she hadn't heard.

Lily hadn't thought about Madeleine having a father – a birth father in the same way that Kitty was her birth mother. She felt, as she shivered outside the room, that she'd had a terrible failure of imagination about that. There were photos that Kitty had kept from when she was young, about Petroc's age, wearing hideous tight skimpy tops with long swirly skirts. She'd had too much long thick hair, a fringe that covered half her nose and was half grown out at the sides, curling round on her cheeks. Lily had looked at those photos and seen someone who was still her mother, but wearing a disguise as someone young, like fancy dress. She'd not been her mother then, she'd been just a young girl like Amanda, or Charlotte or herself, with boyfriends and problems and then a baby and then not a baby. She'd never kept Madeleine a secret, but she hadn't said anything at all about who the father had been. None of them had thought to ask – a name wouldn't have meant anything and besides, Madeleine had always been something, an event, that had happened to Kitty all by herself. Lily, listening so hard she was hardly breathing, now knew Madeleine's father was someone called Ben. Someone with, according to her father, rights.

Lily then heard her father yelling 'Just let go!' He was angry. She heard a light click off and their bathroom door slam and didn't want to leave things there.

'Mum?' She opened the door a few inches. It was dark, silent, as if she'd been dreaming it all.

'Lily? What are you doing up?' Her father's voice was soft, like it used to be when she was little and he was worried that she might be ill or sleep walking.

'I heard you. You were arguing. What's wrong?' He

217

wasn't going to tell her. He'd gone into caring-night-time-parent voice.

'Nothing, Lily. It's OK. Just stuff that will sort itself out in time. Go back to sleep now, it's late and you've got school.'

'No I haven't, it's Saturday tomorrow. Who's Ben?'

'Ben?' Glyn switched on the light and sat up. 'What about Ben?'

'Who is he?' she persisted, leaning against the door-frame.

'He's . . .' Glyn considered for a moment, 'he's the husband of that old friend of your mother's. You know, that Rose who came for a night. He's here, up in the studio, arrived after you'd gone to sleep.' He grinned at her. 'So if you walk into the kitchen tomorrow morning and he's munching toast, you'll know, won't you?'

Lily scowled and chewed her nail. She recognized, just as Kitty had, a schoolmasterly dismissal – a dismissal with only half the truth at that. 'Yeah I'll know,' she snarled, 'sure I'll know.'

She went back to bed. The patch where she'd been sleeping was still warm and Russell had taken the opportunity of sliding under her duvet and curling up by the pillow. She curled her body round him and pulled him close to her. He purred and twitched his whiskers in his sleep. 'Animals don't go through life wondering where their children have got to, do they? Or who their mums and dads are,' she whispered to him. She hoped they didn't. Imagine, she thought, cows pining for every calf. Cats sorrowing after kittens, wondering about the 'Free to a good home' offer and whether it had been checked and certified. All that paw-kneading that cats did when they sat on your lap, she imagined them picturing a big, soft, long-ago mother cat and the remembered taste of her milk.

She snuggled deep down in the bed with the cat,

who miaowed and struggled and then leapt to the floor, protesting at being cuddled so hard. He went to the closed door and started scratching at it, clawing at the paintwork and at the carpet. 'Ssh Russell, come back and let's get to sleep,' Lily called to him but the scrabbling got more frantic. She sighed and swore and climbed out of bed again, opened the door and followed him down the stairs, hungry now from being awake so long that her stomach had started thinking it was time for breakfast. As Russell hurtled out through the cat flap, she padded around the kitchen in the dark, assembling a crust from the end of a big wholemeal loaf, butter and some dense and over-sugared marmalade that Polly at the Spar had made the year before and sold at the playgroup fête.

Lily sat on the worktop with her arms huddled round her knees, munching hard and staring out across the wall at the moonlight on the sea. The wind was fiercer now, moaning through the trees. Silver-edged clouds scudded in the sky, hurtling across the moon. In the morning the sea would be high and the surf would be gnarly and difficult. Madeleine had promised to come out and watch her. She wanted to be impressive, it was important. She slid down off the worktop and went back to the bread bin, cutting another fat slice of bread. Madeleine hadn't liked her picking at food and saying she wasn't hungry all the time. She'd said it was important to keep your body warm inside. You could only do that with food. She'd said you shouldn't let the body starve and fret and crave and then pretend you were doing it to be in control of it. You didn't have the right, she'd said. Your body was there to look after your happiness so you shouldn't be ungrateful to it and refuse to give it what it asked for.

Madeleine wasn't chatty for the sake of it, not like most people which must be why Petroc had given up trying to get her to talk to him and Dad just thought she was moody. It meant though that if she *was* telling you something, it was because she really believed it needed saying and that made Lily feel special. Lily finished the bread and opened the fridge. She took out a carton of milk and drank about half of it, straight from the pack, the fridge door still open. Then she broke off a piece of Cheddar from the big slab on the top shelf. 'You'll have bad dreams,' she could hear her mother warning.

When the kitchen light snapped on, Lily's mouth was bulging with chocolate biscuit.

'Lily! Jeez, what the fuck are you doing?' Petroc stood blinking in the doorway, eyeing the devastation. On the table was the bread, crumbs scattered, the marmalade jar empty and lying on its side. There was a big twiggy skeleton that had once been a bunch of grapes, the chewed bones of a couple of cold chicken legs and a line-up of six cereal packets. Lily was leaning against the sink, her skinny wrist shoved down to the bottom of a tube of Pringles, sour cream and chives flavour.

'I didn't eat the cereal. I just got the packets out.' Lily was defensive and wide-eyed. She slid her arm out of the Pringles tube and pushed it behind her onto the draining-board.

'What for, to read the nutritional values while you scoffed your way through everything else?' Petroc picked up the chicken bones and flung them into the bin. 'What's wrong with you, Lily? You're being scary.'

'Nothing's wrong. Madeleine said I didn't eat enough. No-one else has dared say it, like they didn't care. She does.'

'Oh. *Madeleine* said. Well there you go.' He wiped the crumbs from the top of the table.

'Don't you like her?' Lily looked scared.

'I like her, a bit. I don't know her. She doesn't say anything, not about herself. Surely you've noticed?'

'She says stuff to me. She did when she was in my room anyway. Now she's not. She's gone over to stay in the barn.'

'What, with George?' Petroc grinned.

'Not *with* George. Just with more space, she said.'

Petroc reached into the fridge for a Coke and sat down at the table, tracing his finger through the damp patches the wet cloth had left. 'She might be *with George*, you know. She comes all alive when he's around.'

'She can't be, he's old. Anyway she came here to be with us, with her real mum, not pick up a bloke.' Lily stamped across the kitchen and looked into the fridge again.

'Hey, don't eat any more, please. You'll explode – even precious Madeleine wouldn't expect you to go that far. And sure, he's old, but he's old and rich, old and famous. Perhaps that's what she's into. We don't know. We don't know anything.'

Lily huddled her arms round her body. She was feeling quite sick now, and starting to tremble with cold. There was a gale blowing outside and the wind was whistling under the kitchen door, chilling her feet. 'I know we don't know. But we're *getting* to know, at least I was. I don't want her to leave before I can be sure she won't go away for ever. And imagine Mum if Madeleine just went off and left now . . .'

'She'll go some time, Lily. You can't just keep her in a box like some stray cat that's turned up, hoping it won't remember its way home. Madeleine's got a family somewhere else. Her *real* family.'

'I know, I know. I'm freezing. I must go to bed. Petroc, why are you so late home? Were you with Amanda?'

'Amanda? Who's Amanda?' he grinned at her.

221

Chapter Fourteen

The view from the bedroom window was peculiarly different in the morning. Something had changed in the night that was disorientating, as if the house had secretly shifted angles the tiniest bit. Kitty looked out and tried to work out what had changed. The sky seemed more open, bigger somehow and down the lane Rita's farmhouse was stark against clouds that were still being hurtled along by the wind. Then she realized she couldn't normally see that much of Rita's house.

'Some of the beech tree's gone,' she announced to the dozing heap that was Glyn. 'A *lot* of the beech tree's gone. That whole big branch, the one halfway up on the left.'

The heap heaved itself upwards and joined her to have a look. 'Oh great. And it's fallen right across the lane.'

'So we're stuck?'

'We're stuck.' He laughed. 'And not just us. Now no-one can escape. That should be jolly. We're all trapped in here together like something out of Agatha Christie. I wonder who the first murder victim will be.'

Kitty laughed. 'You could always scramble over the top of the branches and make a desperate bid for freedom.' He might really do that, she thought, anything to get away from conflict.

'I could take Ben with me.'

'You could.' Then she teased, 'But he might not want to go.' Kitty could see Madeleine down on the beach, standing still and facing the sea, her arms stretched straight out crucifix-style as if challenging the keening wind to push her over. She was wearing a hippyish long purple dress of the sort that Kitty had sent to the jumble back at the end of the 1970s. The bottom of it ended in fringing that was tangling round her ankles and her feet were bare. Kitty was entranced, taking in the way the girl's long thick hair rippled backwards, the tension in her spread fingers. She thought she wouldn't look out of place as a magnificent ship's figurehead, strong and fearsome and powerfully beautiful.

'What the hell's she doing out there? She must be bloody freezing.' Glyn was frowning now. Kitty knew she couldn't expect him to look at Madeleine the same way that she did, but she felt mildly disappointed that he couldn't see her, just for one objective moment, as a sight rather wonderful out there alone communing with the churning waves. 'She's supposed to be meeting up with Lily and watch her surf. The sea's horribly fierce though.'

'That won't stop Lily.' Glyn was bustling about now, looking for clothes, picking out sweatshirts from the drawer, unfolding them, having a look, refolding and putting them back as it there was something just very slightly amiss with the first three he tried. She smiled. She was used to this ritual. Eventually he pulled out a Quiksilver fleece, gave it a brief fond hug and laid it on the bed for after his shower. Kitty wondered if Ben had odd little habits like this, and if that was partly why Rose was looking for something less predictable elsewhere. He might be one of those men who always shoves his fist into clean socks to check for holes or dozing moths or splinters – enough to drive anyone to start calculating alimony.

'It might stop Lily,' Kitty said, 'she's not stupid about the sea.'

'She's stupid about Madeleine though, she's desperate to impress her. We'd better have a word when she gets up. The surf's too . . . what's the word she uses?'

'Gnarly; though I guess we old people are still allowed just to call it "rough". You know what she's like if we try to use unsuitably hip words.'

Kitty felt edgy. Breakfast with Ben had to be faced. Glyn would probably hover around giving her significant looks and pushing her to blurt out that by the way, perhaps Ben would like to be introduced to his own daughter? She dressed quickly and went downstairs, praying there would be time for a solitary thought-collecting cup of coffee before he emerged from the studio. The gods weren't listening: there was a rumble of conversation.

'So you wax the top of the board like this for really good grip. The top's called the deck . . .' Kitty heard Lily from outside the kitchen door. Lily was sitting on the table, her surfboard propped against the back of a chair. Ben sat beside her drinking coffee and watching while she rubbed the board with its special wax and a broad loving movement. Her skinny arms emerging from the baggy teeshirt reminded Kitty of the kind of candlestick lamp base that's been given too big a shade. Closer inspection as she worked showed that the narrow little arms had a surprising amount of muscle tone, strength gathered from paddling so hard on the sea. The air smelled sharply of apples from the wax.

'Hello Ben, I see you've met Lily.' He looked a lot more relaxed than he had the night before, in comfortably aged jeans and a beaten-up dark blue sweater with plenty of pulled threads. He looked younger somehow too, as if in the night he'd dreamed away some of his worries or even made a couple of positive decisions.

'I certainly have met Lily. I wandered into the kitchen and the first thing she said to me was "Hi, pass over that block of sex wax."'

Lily giggled. 'Mr Zog's finest sex wax. It's only what it's called. It's just to make you buy it.'

'Well, for those of us ignorant of the arcane culture of surfers I can tell you it came as a shock before nine in the morning.'

Lily was looking pleased with herself. 'Ben said he's one of your old boyfriends,' she said, interested but slightly disbelieving.

'I did have one or two you know, romance isn't something your lot invented,' Kitty told her.

'No, exactly,' Ben agreed, '*our* lot invented it.'

'Don't tell me. Gross.' Lily did an exaggerated shudder.

Kitty made coffee and delved into the freezer, pulling out a bag of the kind of croissants Julia Taggart would certainly scorn to serve to guests. She shoved a trayful of them into the Rayburn and set the timer, knowing she'd completely forget them otherwise and later be faced with a dreadful smell and an oven full of what would then look like a set of earth-brown dog turds.

'You're not actually surfing this morning though, are you Lily? I mean have you seen the state of the sea? And the wind's still howling and gusting.'

Lily looked astounded. 'Of course I am! It's pumping out there! There's an onshore wind on a falling tide, no problem. I promised Madeleine I'd give her a sort of land lesson, show her what I'm doing and explain what it's all about.'

'Who is Madeleine?' Ben asked. Lily looked at Kitty as if asking permission to tell the truth.

Kitty got in first. 'She's staying here, over in the barn with George Moorfield.'

'The writer? Good grief. I thought he'd got a posse of wives already.'

'She's not . . .' Lily cut in. She'd stopped the waxing and was looking at Kitty oddly, wondering, calculating. The oven timer bleeped and Kitty bent to take the croissants out and then assemble butter, knives and all the various jams and marmalades that were in the cupboard. 'Lily's right, Madeleine's definitely not one of George's famous conquests. She's helping him out with phone calls and mail, so he can get on with his book. That's what we're supposed to be selling to writers who come here, the chance to put a good big space between themselves and the day-to-day hassles.'

'Then they give a few chosen people the phone number and the world follows them down the satellite rays or whatever they are. Morning Ben, sleep OK?' Glyn wandered into the kitchen and picked up a croissant on his way to the coffee.

'Fine thanks. Though I did wake up early and wonder why I couldn't hear the thrum of traffic.'

Kitty opened the back door and went outside to the sea wall. The wind was strangely warm as if it had ventured too fast across the sea from a much hotter place and hadn't yet run out of energy. The scudding clouds were parting fast now, showing smeared trails of vibrant blue. Madeleine had gone from the beach, leaving a trail of splayed footprints on the damp sand leading to the water's edge. Closer to the wall the wind had blurred the tracks she'd made in the soft dry sand up above the high-tide mark. Kitty walked down the steps and across the gritty foreshore, kicked off her shoes and planted her feet squarely in a pair of the wet prints. feeling the shape and size of them compared to her own. Madeleine's were bigger, squarer and Kitty's toes fitted so neatly inside the outline that it looked as if someone had drawn a line exactly an inch all round her own feet. She pictured soft plump baby feet with tiny fairy nails, imagined Madeleine's adoptive mother buying her first baby shoes. She wondered if she'd kept them, as she had kept Lily's and Petroc's. The two pairs of blue T-bar Start-Rites, Lily's a couple of sizes smaller than Petroc's, languished carelessly at the back of her underwear drawer. Madeleine's mother might be the type who'd preserved hers in a specially made display case, or, worse, had them cast in bronze, mounted on a plinth and displayed in a glass cabinet. Or she might just have sent them to the Oxfam shop.

'I'll be off in about ten minutes.' Kitty jumped. Ben was suddenly there beside her, the sand having silenced his footsteps. His feet were bare, unexpectedly tough-looking and with a trace of a tan. She'd forgotten that he was a practised sailor and had him firmly categorized as a city-street man, pale-footed and tender-skinned. 'I suppose I'd better go and find Rose and have it out with her. It's what I came for.' He looked terribly young and rather foolish, Kitty thought.

'You don't sound very enthusiastic. Where's all last night's big rush?' she asked. He shrugged, his hands stuffed in his pockets like a boy caught with no good reason for a bit of silly vandalism. 'Evaporated. It's being here maybe? Seeing what playing happy families should be like? Except Rose and I aren't a family and we're not even much of a couple.'

'You mean you've seen the possibility of something else.'

'Yeah. Who knows.' He grinned, looking just as brightly careless as he had at eighteen for a second. 'Maybe I'll sign up with one of those exclusive dating

227

agencies and pull myself a desperate countess with child-bearing hips.' He looked at his watch. 'Gone ten already. I'd better be on my way.'

'Oh. Er . . . that might not be so easy.' There was the small matter of the beech tree. 'A big branch of a tree fell down last night, right across the lane. I could see it from our window this morning.'

Ben looked around quickly as if another route might materialize. He lived in London, too used to alternatives and choices. 'And that's the only way out?'

'The only way out. Sorry.' He grinned at her. 'Don't be. I can use more practice at this winding-down thing.' He touched her shoulder lightly. 'And I'm enjoying seeing you again.'

Lily had pulled her wetsuit on and was ready. From her bedroom window she looked down at the heaving sea and wondered if it was really such a great idea. Petroc was still asleep. If he'd been up and said to her, 'Not today Lily, don't even think about it,' she might have listened. Or she might not. Madeleine wasn't even there. She'd been out there earlier, wandering about and watching the water. Lily had seen her pick up a pebble and fling it at the waves. Perhaps she'd got cold and had gone back into the barn to snuggle up with George, because whatever she or anyone else said, Lily knew that there was going to be snuggling, whether it was now or later when there wasn't the great mound of baby between them. Madeleine had that look when George was around, exactly like the one that Petroc had come in with the night before. Lily had asked who it was who'd made him look like that and he hadn't been able to lie and say 'no-one', even though he'd tried, because he couldn't stop the great goofy smile splitting his face. She'd never have guessed it was

Hayley Mason though. You couldn't get more of an opposite to Amanda Goodbody if you advertised. Big, beamy, curly-haired and dark. Quite like Madeleine, she supposed.

Lily pulled her winter hood over her hair and felt, as she always did, that she looked like a tortoise that lacked a shell, and for the first time she wished she had more curves to soften the wormy black outline of the wetsuit. She pulled on her latex gloves. She was going out there on the surf whether anyone watched her or not.

Kitty thought Madeleine and George looked so very much as if they knew something that no-one else knew. They sauntered along the beach together talking and looking at each other the whole time. Lovers did that, moving in that way people do when they really don't want to look where they are going and don't care if ahead of them there is a mine shaft to be fallen into, just so long as they can keep concentrating on each other's faces.

'We used to look like that. Do you remember?' Ben murmured to Kitty as Madeleine and George approached.

'We did?'

'Course we did. Young love. You can tell.'

Kitty spluttered a laugh. 'George is hardly young!'

'Not the people; the love. When it's new, when it's fresh and perfect.'

Kitty felt uneasy. Sitting on the sea wall with Ben, this didn't seem to be a conversation they should be having. At the same time it made her almost tearfully nostalgic. It seemed a long time since she and Glyn had said anything so emotionally charged. Maybe people simply didn't when they'd been together as long as they had.

'So where is she? The silver surfer?' Madeleine

229

hauled her bulk up the steps and sat on the wall next to Kitty, rudely ignoring Ben.

'She'll be out. Though quite honestly she probably shouldn't be, not in that sea.'

'So tell her not to then.' Madeleine shrugged. Kitty felt an urge to slap her that was very close to parental. The girl was so thoughtless, almost heartless.

'It's you she's showing her skills off to, if you're Madeleine and I take it you are.' Ben leaned across Kitty and put out his hand. 'I'm Ben. Old friend of Kitty's.'

Pouting at his abruptness, and clearly only showing a degree of manners because Kitty was there, Madeleine shook his hand. Kitty expected to feel something poignant, something significantly electric at this first touch between father and daughter, but nothing happened. They were, after all, just two grown-up people who'd never met before.

Lily bounced out onto the beach clutching her board with both hands. 'It's taking off in the wind!' she yelled as she passed them.

'Go for it, babe.' Madeleine smiled at her and went back to chewing off the varnish from her thumbnail. George came and sat close to her and she wriggled along till her thigh was against his. Ben turned to Kitty and raised his eyebrows. 'Sure about her not being a conquest?' he whispered.

Glyn followed the sound of the chain-saw along the lane as far as the tree. Lying there, slammed into what was left of the wall and cruelly ripped away from the main trunk, the huge branch looked like a felled monster, pitiful after slaughter. Rita in her oldest jeans and a pair of stout lime green Doc Martens was astride one of the larger limbs that jutted out across the lane, clutching an implement that leaked the stench of two-stroke. Her hair was tied up in a pink fringed scarf that flapped around her face and was obviously annoying her. She kept spitting frayed ends of it out of her mouth and furiously shoving them back under the knot behind her with quick, stabbing fingers. Mick from the pub was standing surveying the scene, leaning with his arms folded against the bonnet of his old green van and waiting to think of something constructive to say, something cleverly incisive that would express his opinion that cutting up half a tree wasn't a job for anyone born without a penis. Glyn, noting the expression of elated determination on Rita's face, felt like warning him not even to think of it.

'Hi Rita, want any help?' His offer was tentative but genuine. She looked transformed from the cowed misery of the day before, and her face, turned to the wind, was almost manically exhilarated.

'Yeah, let the men get to it! Have it done in 'alf the time!' Mick yelled out, assuming Glyn could be called on as backup if Rita got lippy. 'Sod off Mick!' Rita shouted. 'I can take off these side branches Glyn,' she said, 'and chop them up for the autumn. But there's not much I can do about the main section. I'll need a much bigger saw.' Mick sniggered. 'It's not the size of the tool . . . !' Rita stood on the branch, wielding the saw menacingly. 'Mick, just bog off will you!' Glyn had an instant vision of Annie Oakley, facing a band of outlaws with brass nerve and a shotgun.

'I'n't she lovely when she's angry!' Mick called to Glyn. Obediently though, beaten by a worthier warrior, he climbed into his van, backed it into a gateway and trundled away.

'Nutter!' Rita shouted after him. She sat back down on the branch and started up the saw again. She was, Glyn could see, doing more than cutting up wood. She looked as if she was sawing up the absent Josh's limbs, joyously severing them one by one from his torso. Glyn found a foothold on a bunch of jutting twigs and pulled himself up onto the branch. It was amazing how high up he was. It wasn't even the main trunk that had fallen, just a huge arm, but lying in the road it was easily as big as any full-grown tree. It would take more than himself and Rita to shift it, and he guessed the council highways department would be pretty overstretched from last night's storm. Great fronds of twigs and tangles of smaller branches were crushed onto the lane and spread out for a radius of at least twenty feet. The leaves looked too young and spring-fresh to be coming to such an abrupt and sad end to their lives.

'Isn't it amazing that a tree can go on surviving with such a huge part missing,' he commented to Rita. She'd turned off the howling saw and was pushing the piece she'd cut down towards the ditch. 'What? Oh I see what you mean. Well we get by without bits of us, don't we?' she said. 'Amputated arms and legs, one lung out, no appendix or tonsils, all that. There are even lovers we can do without, given enough time and fury.'

'I suppose so. And the tree can grow a new branch.'

'Not like this.' Rita patted the bark gently. 'This bit was its best piece. It'll never get another with a girth this huge. This is almost a twin to the main trunk. It must be feeling sad.' She leaned down and hugged her arms as far round the giant branch as she could. Glyn felt uncomfortable. He wasn't the kind of man who attributed emotions to vegetation. Once people started doing that, there'd be nothing on the planet that could be eaten. He'd have to apologize to every cabbage for pulling it up and cooking it.

'Lily's surfing, a kind of skills demo for Madeleine. Why don't you come and watch?' he said eventually, wishing she'd just sit up and get back to being her new brisk practical self. He'd help her load logs onto a barrow if she wanted, enjoy sharing the basic physical warmth of gathering fuel.

'No. Not just now. I'll get on with this, it's incredibly therapeutic.' She sat up and retied her headscarf, shoving her rebellious hair roughly under it. The hair had a newly washed spring to it and even her face looked scrubbed of all misery. Perhaps it was the weather, Glyn thought, blasting away the last bits of Josh's power. Perhaps she'd raced out naked into the rain in the early hours and danced in the drops, cackling wildly. She grinned naughtily, showing the glinting gold tooth. 'Perhaps I'll give Mick a call, tell him *I thimply can't* shift the main branch and then enjoy watching him make a macho twat of himself.'

'Good idea. Whatever gets the lane cleared!' Glyn waved and walked back towards home. In spite of its current complications, it suddenly seemed an awfully attractive place to be.

The sun was blazing through whenever the clouds shifted, feeling fierce enough to burn whenever the wind dropped.

'You don't get days like this in London,' George was saying as he stripped off his big hairy sweater, revealing a faded green Rolling Stones teeshirt that was clearly from a very long-ago gig. 'It's either wet or not, hot or not. Here it's everything at once.'

'You get it in Brighton. Coast weather, where we're all on the beach and everyone a hundred yards inland is complaining about how dull it is. But then you get it the other way round, that's the downside.'

Madeleine was fidgety, staring out at Lily who looked frighteningly small paddling alone out on the waves. Kitty could feel how uncomfortable she was, shifting this way and that trying to adjust the baby so that it didn't press on painful nerves.

'Sorry but I can't sit here. I've got to walk.' Madeleine almost fell off the wall. George put a hand out to steady her. Her face looked pained and tight, but she smiled at him before strolling off down the beach to get closer to where she could watch Lily.

'Lily will be pleased. She's got her full attention,' Glyn said. He was standing behind Kitty, kneading the back of her neck gently. He'd brought out a tray of coffee and biscuits for them all, and she wondered if he was regretting his outburst the night before. Contrarily she was beginning to think he'd had a point. For what possible reason should a middle-aged adult be kept in ignorance of the fact that he had fathered a child? Whatever had made her and even her furious parents so adamant that Ben need never know? She could only put it down to some strange quirk of the age: that which is ignored and unmentioned will surely go away.

She relaxed against Glyn's hand but could sense Ben glancing and noting. As far as she knew he hadn't tried calling Rose, unless he'd sneaked out to his car in the night and dialled uselessly. She imagined Rose and Antonia's Tom twined together in an heirloom four-poster, a distant phone ringing and ringing while they made love, passion heightened by certainty that Rose's husband was the caller. Poor dead Antonia. The day she left school she must have been so sure Rose's pilfering days were over.

Lily had intended to give them the show of her lifetime out on the sea. She assumed that it was nerves that made her feel particularly clumsy and unlucky. Every set she went for either petered out into a churning wind-whipped mess or she simply miscalculated and missed. She wanted them to stand on the wall and holler and cheer at her. She wanted Petroc to wake up and applaud from his bedroom window. Her parents should be rethinking any plans they might have secreted away in the backs of their minds and be wondering about sponsorship for the World Surfing circuit. Right then the best one came and she just had to have it. She paddled fast and caught the back of the curve, leaping up fast and dropping in easily to the wave as if water and not land was her natural habitat. It was a long, long, graceful carve, slow and elegant, wet perfection. When she got close to the shore, she baled out smoothly onto the white water and waved. Ben, Kitty and Glyn clapped and George cheered. Madeleine ran down to the water and dashed into the foaming surf, splashing at Lily and laughing.

'Should she be doing that in her condition?' Ben asked Kitty. He looked nervous, as if he'd hardly come into contact with pregnant women before and found them weird and unpredictable.

'Oh she'll be all right. She's got ages to go. Or so she thinks,' Kitty told him.

'The exercise will do her good.' Glyn reverted too easily to caustic, Kitty thought. She glared at him. 'What?' he challenged. 'OK tell me she's done more than just idly waddle about the house since she got here. I'm sure you did lots of breathing practice and strengthening exercises when you were pregnant. She's going to get a hell of a shock.'

'I did do all that, it's true,' Kitty conceded. 'But learning three levels of breathing isn't actually enough to stop the pain being the biggest shock of your life. She's young, as likely as not it'll just drop out.'

She thought of the dowdy Miss Stanhope with the sensible lace-up shoes and beige ankle socks who'd visited the home to instruct the unworthy girls in the workings of the pelvic floor. The air had been choked with suppressed giggles as this elderly spinster had boomed 'Squeeze and *release*; squeeze and *release*'

235

over and over at them, her eyes bulging with effort. Twenty incredulous girls lay panting, more with mirth than with concentration, at the idea of Miss Stanhope in her tightly buttoned hand-knitted navy cardigan and calf-length knife-pleated iron grey skirt ever getting herself in a position where she might need to use her own expertise.

Madeleine was hugging Lily, the waves crashing onto her legs. Her dress was sodden from the spray and the wind made it cling round the contours of the baby.

'I want a go!' Madeleine shrieked, looking back for comment and approval.

'Don't even think about it!' George shouted.

'No, I'm going to! Watch!' Madeleine reached down into the water and pulled at the board, trying to guide it out to sea, but it was still attached to Lily's ankle by its leash.

'Hey stop! You'll fall over!' Lily shouted. She could feel Madeleine's crazy determination, completely reckless idiocy. She struggled with her, knowing you didn't take that kind of chance with the sea. Even she had been pushing it for the sake of showing off. But that was her privilege; it was her skill, no-one else's.

'No come on, show me how. You said you would.' Madeleine wrenched at the board harder, dragging Lily further into the waves. Looking back up the beach she could see George, Glyn and Ben advancing at her. Her face took on a hunted look, and she hauled Lily and the board into the swell, pulling Lily under the foam with her as she tumbled into the water, dragged down by the undertow.

Ben reached them first and hauled Madeleine upright. 'You stupid brat. What the hell are you playing at?' He wrestled with her in the water gripping her wrist hard, both of them soaked, till she quietened. Lily unfastened the leash and retrieved

236

her board, sobbing as she waded out of the sea and up the shore. Kitty ran inside for towels and rushed back out past Lily and down to the sea's edge, where Madeleine was marooned on the wet sand keening a strange sound. She was bent over, clutching her stomach.

'Thanks Mum, I mean just don't think about *me* will you?' Lily yelled after her.

Madeleine had all the attention she could want. Three men and a mother with all those absent years to make up for crowded round her while Lily stormed indoors, alone and bitterly angry, to change. Kitty draped the towels around Madeleine and saw the beginnings of fear in her eyes.

'This *hurts*!' she accused Kitty, almost spitting at her.

'Glyn, I think you'd better phone for an ambulance. This baby's on its way.'

'Ooooow! Oh God, why don't they tell you?' Madeleine rolled on the sand and bunched herself up into a ball.

'They do tell you, but nobody believes it,' Kitty told her. 'Come on, let's get you inside.' Ben and George took an arm each and half carried the drenched and wailing Madeleine back to the house. Kitty followed, suddenly afraid about what would happen next. The ambulance wouldn't get past the fallen tree. She could only hope the driver had done more than simply watch a training video about delivering babies. One with approximately the same lack of hands-on experience as Miss Stanhope would be no use at all.

'Mum!' Madeleine roared as the two men plumped her onto the biggest blue sofa. Kitty pushed past them to get close to her and took her hand. 'I need my mum,' Madeleine whispered to Kitty. 'Will you ring her?'

Chapter Fifteen

Childbirth was a messy, mucky business, awash with blood and gunk and fluids, from what Kitty could recall of it. As soon as she had phoned the hospital, arranged for an ambulance and a midwife, if one able and willing to shin over a horizontal tree was available, she raced upstairs to the airing cupboard to find what there was among the household's older sheets. Madeleine was very welcome to produce her baby on the cream rug on the sitting-room floor. At worst the rug could be thrown out and replaced, but she needed something hygienic to separate her and the child from a surface on which the cat slept and moulted and where so many grubby feet had all been treading.

As she flung her way through the contents of the cupboard, Kitty was extremely thankful that she had swopped the pale blue fitted carpet for the beech flooring the year before, otherwise she might have been callously hustling poor Madeleine in the direction of the hard and comfortless kitchen table. As it was, she could see a case for the wide spreading of newspaper across the beech which had already had its varnish scraped away by the careless moving of chairs. Perhaps that would give George something to do. She'd put Ben on tea-making, that other great traditional home-birth task.

'In the cellar there are stacks of dust-sheets left over from the decorators,' Glyn commented, picking up and refolding a heap of scattered pillowcases that Kitty had discarded in her frantic scrabbling.

'She can't have a baby on something that's covered in paint stains. Besides they'll be dusty and not even close to sterile. The poor little thing would be born with instant asthma or something.' She shoved a pile of clean but threadbare sheets at Glyn. 'Here, can you take these downstairs to her? I still haven't called her mother.'

'No panic there,' he said. 'She can hardly get here in the next hour all the way from Brighton.'

'Madeleine wants her to know.'

'Yes of course. Sorry. Why are they sending an ordinary ambulance? What is the air ambulance for if not for situations like these?'

'There's a bad car crash near Launceston, they've gone to that.'

'Oh right. I don't suppose they'd fancy plonking their machine down in Rita's cabbage field anyway. Hey, aren't we supposed to rush around doing that "Boiling water and plenty of it" thing like they used to do in films?'

Kitty giggled. 'That was just to keep the father out of the way.'

Glyn looked thoroughly excited, the sheets heaped in his arms and his feet still bare and sandy from the beach. He'd trodden sand all up the stairs, something he was always shouting at the children for doing. Kitty reached into the back of the cupboard and pulled out a selection of ancient towels that had been relegated from bathroom to beach use. Thoughts about equipment they might need crowded into her head, informed only by gory scenes from novels and half-remembered passages from the home-birth section of the last baby-care book she'd read, many years before. How much could things have changed? 'Some sort of bowl . . .' she murmured. Glyn, who was about to go down the stairs, stopped and turned. 'What do you need a bowl for?'

'The placenta. Midwives are very keen on inspecting them, don't ask me why. A friend of Julia Taggart's had her baby unexpectedly at home and the placenta ended up in a mixing bowl under the bed. She said the dog had a go at it and the midwife was furious.'

Glyn leaned against the banister rail looking extremely queasy. 'I suppose then you bury it at midnight under a waxing moon?'

'Well not me, exactly,' she teased. 'That's down to the household's most senior male apparently, according to ancient tradition.'

'Oh thanks. Well so long as we don't have to cook it and eat it like on that TV programme.' There was a roar and a wail from Madeleine and Glyn looked as if he was inclined to rush back up the stairs, hurl himself into his room and hide in the bathroom, running their noisy shower at full pelt until it was safe to come out.

'Should we wake Petroc, do you think?' he glanced at the closed door. 'There might be something useful he could do.'

Kitty grimaced. 'I doubt it, I mean he's not exactly . . .' There was another yell of pain from below, a primitive, gut-churning sound. 'I expect Madeleine will wake him soon enough.' She pushed past Glyn. 'We'd better get back to her, after all you and I are the ones who've gone through all this before. George and Ben are probably desperate to get out of the building.'

'They could climb over the tree and go down the pub, do the other traditional male thing.'

'Actually, they could climb over the tree and go and fetch Rita. I mean, she's had three.'

240

'So have you . . .' He hesitated and looked at her, then reached out and stroked her tangled hair away from her eyes. 'But you've got to ring Madeleine's mother,' he said, taking the towels from her and adding them to his heap.

Kitty raced up the attic stairs to the studio. This was a call she didn't want to make where anyone could hear her. She didn't want to risk Madeleine's mother hearing her child yelling in pain down a phone line either. She looked at the name Madeleine had scrawled on the edge of the electricity bill: Paula Murray. An ordinary enough name, nothing in it to frighten or intimidate. She sat on the edge of the sofa bed. It was still made up from Ben sleeping in it. Just for a moment she wondered if he still slept on his front with one arm hanging down towards the floor as he had when he was young. The few times they'd managed to sneak a whole night together she'd woken up and stroked the broad sweep of strong-boned flesh from shoulder to shoulder. Shoulder-blades like axe-heads. She'd even sketched him lying there naked, and her mother had found the drawings, filed away among the portfolio of work she'd been secretly putting together for her longed-for flight to art college.

She tried to conjure up a picture of an archetypal 'Paula Murray' as she dialled, and could only come up with someone quite a lot older than herself, a brisk and fussy woman (the beige carpets and no-shoes rule) with a pale grey head like her father's congregation women and an unflattering maroonish floral dress that bunched and bulged in the middle. Where did the waists of the over-sixties go to?

'Hi! You've reached Paula, Andreas and Marcel's phone. Leave a message after the tone, and we'll get back to you when we get home!' This was a jolly, middle-aged, securely middle-class voice. It belonged to a woman who might well own a velvet hairband and a persuasive role in local politics. Kitty pictured a whizzing character on a bright blue bicycle, confident at a busy roundabout. Paula on the phone sounded husky and overexcited, like an actress who smoked a lot. She sounded far more copper-streaked than grey-permed.

Kitty hung up, almost throwing the phone down, completely off-centred by being answered by a machine, then too fascinated by the lustrous voice to leave a message. The greeting, she noted, hadn't included Madeleine's name, which tied in with what Madeleine had said about her mother being comfortably used to her absence. She should have asked her more about Paula, she realized. Not pushing Madeleine for more detail about her home life was just cowardly selfishness, just not wanting to hear that she'd had a perfectly good mother to bring her up. Contrarily, of course, that was exactly what she'd always wished for for the girl. Wished it every day since she'd handed her over.

As her hand stretched out to redial, the phone rang. She picked it up quickly, annoyed that she would have to talk to someone when she was trying to think how to express sensitively what she had to say. It seemed hardly right for Paula's answering machine to be the method by which she heard that her daughter was about to produce her grandchild.

'Hallo? Did you just call this number? I did 1471.' It was the husky, still breathy voice.

Kitty's heart pounded. 'Are you Paula Murray? Madeleine's mother?' She heard herself being tentative, nervous.

There was a harsh laugh. 'Oh God, what's she done now? Is she pissed again? Or was someone crazy enough to lend her a car?' She didn't sound particularly concerned.

'Er no. Actually . . .'

'And you are . . .?' the voice interrupted.

'Her mother' was the tempting answer, but right now would more than confuse the issue. Kitty thought for a second, then decided on cautious truth. 'I'm Kitty Harding. I used to be Katherine Cochrane.' It would filter through, the name could hardly mean nothing.

'Ah.' There was the sound of slow deliberate breathing and then, 'I thought you'd turn up some time.'

'I didn't turn up, we can't, not till they change the law. But Madeleine did. She's here, with me and my family.'

'Well, it had to happen.' There was another laugh, this time with no hint of mirth in it. 'She's been threatening me with the finding of you ever since she was thirteen and I gave her her original birth certificate. I know they're supposed to be eighteen, but she can nag for the nation. It wears you down. Every time we had a row, every time she was grounded, and that was often I can tell you; heavens, every time I even asked her if please would she mind doing the dishes, she'd say that was it, she was off to find her *real mother*!' She sighed. 'I must say it's a relief, actually, now it's happened. I mean she's surely old enough now to cope. How is she?'

'Extremely well, except, it's just . . . did you know she was pregnant?'

There was no easy way to say it.

'Heavens, that's the last thing I expected. She's always hated the idea of being tied, always likes to be free and to wander, so I suppose she'll want an abortion . . . she should have told me herself, she knows she could, I've always said . . .' Kitty sensed resentment and was sorry, suddenly, to be giving pain to this woman who now sounded so hurt.

Gently, she said, 'It's too late for an abortion. Madeleine's about to give birth on my sitting-room floor and she asked me to ring you. She says can you come? I'm so sorry there's no better way to tell you. And I'm really sorry she didn't tell you herself.'

There was a silence and then another sigh. 'So am I. She hasn't been easy, you know. I did my best. The boys are no trouble.'

The words 'It's not my fault!' shrieked into Kitty's mind. Paula made her feel as if Kitty had sold her faulty goods that she'd been gallantly making the best of and failing. She was not going to accept any blame. If the right thing to do had been to give Madeleine up for adoption, surely no-one but Paula was responsible for what went awry after that? No-one had forced her to take the child, and Kitty bit her lip to stop herself from saying it. 'So can you come?' she asked instead, 'it's almost at the furthest end of Cornwall . . .' Telling Paula that was curiously satisfying.

Lily crouched on the old pink Lloyd Loom chair in the corner of her bedroom, with her fingers in her ears blocking out the sounds of pain from downstairs. Her wetsuit, hanging over the back of the wardrobe door, was dripping cold salt water onto the dark blue carpet and there would be a white-edged stain when it dried. Her mum would be angry, and she'd have to get the Vax spray and give it a scrubbing. She hated cleaning marks off carpet, hated the texture of it, the friction of the rough wool scraping harsh against the soft skin of her palm. Once, she'd rubbed her hand hard against it, deliberately making it itch and burn, seeing how bad it could be so she would get immune to it. The feeling had made her toes tingle, her legs weak. And it had made no difference.

She watched the stain getting bigger and bigger

and sensed the noises down below getting more and more desperate and her heart thudded horribly. It was all her fault. Madeleine had run into the sea to be with her. She should have let her take the surfboard and just get on with it, not fought her off like that. The sea was much too cold for anyone to go more than knee-deep without 5mm of neoprene covering them, and Madeleine would only have paddled a few feet further out and then come giggling back up the beach, shivering. Or would she? The reason Lily had fought her was because you couldn't be sure. Madeleine had a mad streak, something reckless and crazy that Lily really envied but was also afraid of.

Madeleine had told her about hitch-hiking through Italy and stealing food from supplies left on restaurant doorsteps at four in the morning. She said she'd tied her younger brother to one of the Brighton Pier uprights when there was no-one around in winter and gone away and left him, watching from the promenade till the tide went right to the top of his legs. And she'd told her about the Irish wake she'd gone to where the dead man had been dressed in his best suit and propped up in his favourite armchair so that he wouldn't miss the fun – and Madeleine said she'd sat a small boy on the cold lap and told him to tweak the stiff dead nose to wake him up. Lily hoped things like that were made up just for effect, but she was afraid they weren't. She'd only laughed at it all because she didn't want to upset her and make her leave. Madeleine never mentioned friends. She seemed to have done most of her living by herself so far, as if she couldn't be bothered to collect people and have to trail them around with her like baggage. She'd collected George now, though. Or maybe he'd collected her.

Cautiously, Lily took her fingers out of her ears.

There was silence now. Either it was all over or Madeleine had decided shouting and yelling wasn't any use. Or maybe it was worse and she'd died like they always did in Charles Dickens. She crept to the top of the stairs and listened. She wanted to go down and help, but felt scared. Seeing a baby born in real life and not just on the biology-lab video had to be something you didn't miss if you got the chance, but in the bio lab the woman in the film had smiled and grunted a bit and that was all. She hadn't howled like a lost dog.

Her mother rushed past her, making her jump. 'Are you coming down, Lily? Madeleine might like yours to be the hand she hangs onto. After all, you're the one who's got closest to her.'

Lily held onto the banister rail, swinging her foot as if she was still deciding whether to go up or down. 'Apart from George. She'll probably want George now.'

Kitty came back up a few steps and put her arm round her. 'Perhaps, but let's go and see, shall we?'

'Yeah OK. After all it's my niece or nephew.'

George and Ben were sitting out on the sea wall, smoking like a nervous pair of true labour-ward first-timers. Glyn sent them off to the fallen tree in the lane to meet the ambulance and direct the paramedics to the house. He felt an urgent need for order, for someone with a uniform to take charge and sort everything out. Madeleine looked like a strapped-down animal, heaving and writhing on the rug, turning one way and then another, sometimes getting up and squatting, and then rearing herself up onto all fours. Kitty had produced Lily and Petroc with the full assistance of the National Health's pain-relief systems, propped up on the right sort of solid bed with a bank of crisp white pillows and a bustling team of beaming, confident nurses. Fathers were welcome but kept at the head end for brow-mopping and contraction-counting and for holding the Evian spray, dealing with the Brahms tapes (or Eric Clapton or whale sounds) and being a useful wrist to grip when pain went beyond the edge. He looked at his watch. Twenty minutes had gone by since Kitty had phoned for help. It was at least twenty-five minutes from the Penzance hospital, or an awful lot more from Truro. He listened hard but couldn't hear a siren. Then suddenly everyone was there. There was the gritty pounding of men running on shingle and Ben dashed round the corner towards the back door, leading a pair of green-uniformed paramedics, each clutching a bagful of items that Glyn prayed were relevant and useful. George, panting, brought up the rear, followed by Rita looking as eager as if she'd just discovered her true vocation.

'No midwife?' Glyn asked Rita, following her into the house.

'Only at the hospital. I expect they'll take her there.'

But they didn't. 'We don't move women this far gone in labour; against the rules,' Brian, the older of the two said, assessing Madeleine's condition the second he walked through the sitting-room doorway. 'Besides, we'll never get her over that tree in her state.' Madeleine, curled up on her side on the rug, glared at him. The younger one looked panic-stricken. To Kitty's anxious eyes he resembled some sort of hapless youth on day one of work experience. 'Don't worry,' the older one said, catching her glance, 'it's Trev's first time but I've done a couple of dozen, nothing to it. First off, at least half of you lot can disappear. Don't want a crowd. And me and Trev could murder a cup of tea.' He knelt down next to Madeleine. 'OK love, let's see how things are going.'

'I wanted a woman.' Madeleine glared at him, looking as if she might bite if he came too near.

Brian laughed. 'Sorry to be a disappointment. But I'll do my best. I'm good at it. And just think, it could be worse, they could have sent a doctor. Now they're *worse* than useless.' Madeleine's face tightened into agony once more and she moaned and thrashed around, sending Glyn and Ben scuttling for the kitchen where they collided with Lily on her way to join Madeleine.

'I wouldn't go in there, it's too crowded already,' Glyn told her.

'But I want to! She might need me! Mum said!' He gripped hold of her wrist to stop her and she tried to twist herself free but Glyn hung on and the two of them danced awkwardly backwards into the kitchen, crashing against the table.

'Kitty said she'd ask Madeleine if she wanted you. She'll come and get you if you are.'

'No! Let me go!'

'Maybe it would be a good idea if you hung on just a bit longer, just in case it's a bit difficult in there . . .' Ben ventured.

'It's nothing to do with you!' she yelled. 'She's my sister and I want to be with her!'

Glyn let go abruptly and Lily fell back against the fridge. There was a breaking-glass sound from inside it. Lily fled from the kitchen to the sitting-room, flinging open the door and slamming it shut after her.

'So Madeleine is your oldest daughter?' Ben was clearly puzzled. 'I didn't realize. I thought Kitty said she was just someone staying here.'

Glyn opened the fridge and started clearing up the mess that a smashed glass bowl of salad dressing had made. Like Kitty with the egg on the day Madeleine had arrived, he marvelled at how much chaos a small trail of vinaigrette could cause. All the salad vegetables would need to come out, every tomato would have to be washed and it had even splashed over the cartons of milk and apple juice and bottles of water in the door rack. Carefully, he collected up the fragments of glass and started wrapping them in kitchen paper. 'She's Kitty's daughter,' he said at last. He didn't feel the need to volunteer more than that essential basic fact. Anything else was down to Kitty.

'Oh I see.' He didn't look as if he did, Glyn thought. 'From before you?'

'Yes.' He reached into the cupboard under the sink and took out a clean J-cloth, rinsed it out and started very slowly wiping the mess from the shelves. He wanted to be out in the vegetable garden. He could be sowing a rocket bed, hoeing between the land-cress lines.

'So how old is she?' Ben wasn't going to let go. The cogs of his brain could almost be heard grinding gradually faster.

Glyn shrugged. 'Oh er, early twenties, something like that.'

'Surely you know exactly how old? Has she always lived with you?'

'No, no she hasn't.' Would the man never give up?

'So where . . .'

Trev's timid skinny face appeared round the kitchen door. 'Brian says please can you hurry up with that tea. He says it's thirsty work and he wants two sugars.'

'Coming right up. Look Ben, I'm sorry but if you want to know about Madeleine you're going to have to ask Kitty. After all, she was her baby, so the story's all hers, OK?'

Madeleine's baby boy fought his way into the world and landed in Brian's huge pink hands, where he lay and kicked and glared and drew his first gurgling breath. He didn't cry, but frowned as if he already had a grudge.

'Who's first, Mum or Grandma?' Brian asked once he'd checked the child's airway. Kitty choked back tears. George was blowing his nose noisily and Lily and Rita were weeping happily all over each other. Madeleine just grinned and held out her arms for her child, nuzzling him to her and gently sniffing at his hair, like a mother cat with a kitten. It was almost as if Madeleine herself had been reborn, as a soft, loving, start-again creature, folding the baby to her body as if she'd never handled anything so delicately in her life. She looked up at Kitty and smiled. 'What do you know?' she whispered, 'it was a real live baby in there all the time.'

Kitty laughed, the thought so exactly echoed how she'd felt when Madeleine had been born: that strange near-shock, that the lump pushing her stomach skin from concave to massive really was a miraculously fully-formed miniature human being and not some alien fungusy growth. Back then though, Kitty had had no-one to say it to. 'He's beautiful,' she said, inspecting his tiny perfect fingers with their clean rosy nails.

'How come their nails are always just the right length?' Rita asked, marvelling at nature's brilliance. 'I mean if they're a couple of weeks late you'd think they'd be needing a trim, wouldn't you.'

'I think he's early, actually,' Brian said, making notes on his clipboard. 'Wouldn't you say so, love?' he asked Madeleine. She shrugged. 'Sorry, couldn't tell you. He looks OK though. He is, isn't he?'

Brian squeezed her hand. 'Course he is. He's great. What are you going to call him?'

Kitty glanced at Rita and the two of them giggled, sharing an instant understanding that if, as tradition had it, the grateful mother gave him the name of the emergency deliverer, Madeleine was clearly stuck for choice between Trevor and Brian.

'Oliver,' Madeleine announced. 'This is Oliver Cochrane Murray.'

'Who is Oliver?' Petroc stood in the doorway, clad in blue striped boxer shorts, a Surfers Against Sewage teeshirt and a very bemused expression. 'And who is everybody else? Have I missed something?'

Madeleine wouldn't stay in the house. She wanted to go back to the barn with George, who insisted he was more than willing to take care of her. Kitty felt disappointed, still picturing the studio transformed into a nursery. It would only take a day to clear it and paint it, if she really worked and if Petroc and Lily helped. Instead, with Lily she carried across to the barn all the baby items that they'd bought on the trip to Truro. She kept telling herself they would only be across the yard, it wasn't as if she was losing them. And perhaps after a couple of days Madeleine would decide she missed the home comforts of the house. Missed her family.

'When's Madeleine's mother coming?' Glyn asked after the second barn trip.

'Later on today. I suppose she could have room two over in the barn.'

'Well it keeps the family together, I suppose.'

'*We're* family too, aren't we?'

Glyn sighed. 'No Kitty we're not. You're living in a dream world. One day soon Madeleine will be gone. There's more than a fifty-fifty chance you won't see her again. She's found out all she needs. It was information she was after, not a whole new family. Sorry to be brutal, but someone had to say it.'

Kitty felt as if someone had picked her up like old paper and crumpled her. 'You're so wrong, Glyn, you've got no idea. Even her baby's got my name . . . You'd feel different if you were her father . . .'

251

'I might. So maybe you should be talking to the person who *is* Madeleine's father.' He went to put his arms round her but she shook him off roughly. 'Look,' he said, 'I'm only trying to help you not to get hurt. You're like someone inside out at the moment . . .'

Ben was out on the sea wall, trying to get his mobile phone to work and not having any luck. Kitty watched him from the doorway, jabbing his fingers crossly at the instrument. If she was interpreting body language, she'd say this was now a call he was making out of resigned duty rather than real inclination.

'Why don't you use the phone in the house?' she asked.

'Because I'm not so sure any more that I really want to get through,' he replied. 'What's up there, beyond the end of your garden?' He pointed to the cliffs rising beyond the curve of the bay.

'It's the coast path, then round to an old ruined chapel where walkers always stop to have a pee and a look at the view. Do you want to see?'

He slid off the wall and smiled at her. 'If you promise the wind won't blow us off the clifftop and into the ocean.'

'Hey, I thought you were a sailor. You should know this is an onshore wind.'

Together they walked past Glyn's vegetable garden and through the matted bramble bushes on the far side of the gate. The wind was dying down now but still crept up in sharp surprise blasts. Kitty pushed her hands into the sleeves of her fleece to keep them warm as she walked. Ben's hands were crammed into his pockets, and it occurred to Kitty, still thinking of body language, that an observer might say the two of them were pretty determinedly avoiding contact on the narrow path.

252

'Great smell.' Ben stopped and sniffed at the air.

'The gorse is just coming into flower. And even the thrift flowers early up here. Soon it'll be all pink and yellow.' The flowering had crept up on her this year. She hadn't been out as much as usual, not roaming across the cliffs and the rocky heathland up there like she usually did. Away in the far bay, St Michael's Mount was bright and stark against the pale spring sky, looking close enough to touch, like an old-fashioned toy fort. She should get a dog, she thought, like absolutely every other person who lived in the country. She could roam for miles along out-of-season empty beaches with maybe one of those giant poodles like Ben's, or a mad spaniel.

'It's breeding weather,' Ben said. 'Glyn must have a constant battle with rabbits.'

'He does. But he won't shoot them, he just can't bring himself to. Locals think he's a soft townie, even though we've been here for nearly twenty years.'

Ben stopped abruptly on the path in front of her, too quickly so that her body stopped only an inch away from his. She could smell the wind-damped wool of his jumper. 'Tell me about Madeleine,' he demanded. 'Who is her father? I know she's your daughter but I also know she isn't Glyn's.'

She could just tell him it was nothing to do with him, to go away and sort out things with Rose, who was, in turn, nothing to do with her. 'Come up the path a bit further. Let's get as far as the chapel and we can sit down out of the wind,' she said, playing for time.

The chapel smelled of urine and dogs and the floor was littered with cigarette packets, crushed drinks cans and a couple of condoms. 'Amazing you can buy them in any old petrol station now,' Ben commented as they looked inside and then retreated to sit outside

253

against the back wall, sheltered from the wind but facing the searing sun.

'Yes. Pity you couldn't back in the old days,' she said.

'Back in our days you mean, when everything like that was whispered and under the counter. Tell me about Madeleine.'

'OK.' Kitty took a deep breath, for a run at it all at once, 'I had her when I was eighteen. She was adopted, babies still sometimes were then.' She went on quickly, feeling that she'd choke if she didn't, 'You know what my family was like. If you're going to ask why I didn't just have an abortion, well it wasn't so easy, especially when you've got a dinosaur for a GP who also happens to be your father's church-warden. Everyone seemed to agree that adoption was the best thing all round. For everyone.'

Ben was silent for a moment and then said, 'And was it?'

'How can I know?' Kitty was angry. 'How can any-one know the might-have-beens? They don't exist, so there's no best or worst. All I know is that whatever they said at the time, you don't give a baby away like it's a kitten or a toy. You don't forget about it, you don't have others as replacements. I love Petroc and Lily enormously, but they weren't some form of com-pensation.'

'Then why didn't you keep her?'

'Because I had neither the nerve, the practicality or the support. When you're a single parent now there's a vast amount of information about benefits and housing possibilities. They could have told us quite a bit then but no-one wanted you to know about it — they made sure you didn't. There's a huge difference between the Single Parents of now and the Un-married Mothers of then.'

A group of overdressed hikers, cagouled, booted,

hatted and with maps dangling in waterproof folders round their necks, panted round the edge of the cliff and passed them on the path. Each of them nodded with curt politeness, not breaking their determined stride. Ben stood up and started pacing restlessly up and down in the patch of sun in front of the chapel. Kitty felt vaguely faint, realizing she hadn't had lunch.

'You still haven't told me. I'll put it this way,' Ben sounded like a lawyer. 'Have I got any right to ask who her father is?'

'Yes. Yes, Ben you absolutely have. But I can tell you don't really need to.'

Chapter Sixteen

The rise-and-fall whine of Mick's chain-saw keened like a pained gull way above the deep pounding of the waves below the cliffs. The huge piece of tree would soon be reduced to a meticulous log pile stacked against Rita's barn wall. During the summer, parties of passing walkers would look at it and note its elegant symmetry with approval, reassured that they could just about trust those who inhabited the depths of the country to carry on doing things the way they liked to see them done.

Kitty leaned back against the sun-warmed chapel wall, pulled ragged golden stalks of grass from the earth beside her and plaited them round her fingers, waiting for Ben to ask the inevitable next question. He was still pacing, scowling and angry. Then he turned abruptly and came and slumped down next to her, too close so their legs touched.

'Why did you never tell me?' he asked at last.

'Because there wasn't any point in you knowing. At least, that's what I thought at the time. After all, there wasn't anything you could do about it.'

'Well there might have been, we could have . . .'

'What? Got married? Ben, we were just kids and anyway, we'd already decided to split. We were a summer thing. It was great and then it was over.'

'Not necessarily married, but something, maybe

something useful. At least I'd have been there for you. A baby would have changed things.'

Kitty felt weary. She wished suddenly that she'd simply invented a fling with someone else, not even thought of letting Ben in on the truth. But there was Madeleine with her own questions, and if she was owed the answers there was no avoiding Ben knowing too. She plucked some more grass to play with and tried to be patient and calm.

'It did change things. But only for me, and even then it was supposed to be just a simple thing. I couldn't know then that for ever after I'd think about her, wonder what had happened, if she was all right. Everyone said it would be OK, that you just put it behind you and get on with your life and I believed them because it didn't occur to me that they didn't really know. So for a while you do just what they say and you try to look forward, not back.' Kitty could feel her voice getting faster and less controlled, 'But then her first birthday comes, and then her second and you can't even give her a present. You think about her learning to walk and talk but you don't know what her voice is like, or even if English is her first language, and later you start thinking, surely she must be starting school now, and much further on things like GCSE results come out and you wonder how she's done. And then every time there's a plane crash and you don't even know what name to look for, and when you read about child abuse in children's homes and you think, suppose it didn't work out and she went into care . . . ?' Kitty was crying now, her words too fast and close to incoherent.

'I'm sorry.' Ben's arms were round her and she was pressed tight against him. His face was blotting away her tears and she could smell the soft homey scent of fabric conditioner on his sweater.

'So that's what you missed, Ben. It's all negative

isn't it? There's none of that you'd have chosen to share.'

She felt him sighing into her neck.

'I can't tell, I suppose if Rose and I had had children I'd have said no, I wouldn't have wanted to know. It's just that we didn't. And now I know that all the time there was Madeleine.'

Kitty pulled back and looked at him. He still didn't get it. 'But that's the point,' she said. 'There *wasn't* Madeleine. Don't you see? For you there wasn't Madeleine. Or for me. She came to find me out of curiosity, to fit together the complete version of her history for herself and her own baby, not to find a "real" mother. She's already got one of those — that was who she asked for the moment she went into labour. I think that's when I realized that I can't ever expect to have any real part in her life, even though I feel I've been existing alongside her, like being just the other side of a wall, ever since I handed her over. I'll only ever know what she lets me know and we start from the day she turned up — those twenty-four years will stay lost.'

'But it was you she had her baby with.'

Kitty sighed. 'Nice thought, and I hope that'll be some kind of bond for later, but I can't kid myself that was her choice. You should have seen her face when she asked me to phone her mother. There was fear and need. She thought she'd got longer to go before it was born — plenty of time to get home. It's where she should have been.'

Later Kitty decided that Ben only kissed her because he couldn't think what to do next. Everything had been said. There they were, curled together on the hard dry earth, squashed against the chapel wall out of the wind. The last time Ben had kissed her, so very many years before, his Mark Bolan curls had flopped against her face. He'd smelled of

258

patchouli and tasted of the joint they'd just shared, sensations entirely of their time, and, Kitty realized, there was no lingering back-burner passion between them just waiting to be fired up. Crushed between his body and the grit-sharp chapel wall, Kitty wondered if he was wishing she was Rose as much as she would have preferred him to be Glyn. 'Sorry,' he said eventually. 'It just seemed . . .'

'Appropriate?' she smiled. She disentangled herself in a tactfully leisurely way and stood up. There wasn't anything else to be said and it was time he went off to find Rose. Far below in the vegetable garden she could see Glyn earthing up the earliest of the potatoes, and she very much wanted to be down there with him.

Glyn's back hurt again. As he straightened and stretched his spine he looked up towards the cliff path and saw Ben and Kitty coming down to the house. From that distance they looked lithe and very young. Kitty still had a coltish long-legged stride, sure-footed on the familiar steep rutted path, and Ben was moving fast to keep up with her, fuelled, Glyn assumed, by a dollop of male ego.

'Is he staying long, that bloke?' Petroc shambled up the path looking perplexed. 'I mean, who *is* he?'

'Good question. There's more than one answer, but the one we'll settle for is that he's that Rosemary-Jane woman's husband.' Petroc shrugged, his attention already diverted. Along the newly cleared road, rattling and revving, came a battered old Land Rover. Glyn looked at his son's face, recognizing the dopy doggy grin of infatuation.

'And who is *that*?' he asked, watching the car zooming in too fast through the yard gates and narrowly missing the wall. But Petroc, rushed on by the thrill of new lust, was already on the far side of the garden gate, opening the Land Rover's rusty door and scooping out a large but lively chestnut-haired girl. Turning away just in time to avoid having to watch a fervent teenage clinch, Glyn looked over the wall and up towards Rita's house. The chain-saw had stopped some time before but Mick's van was still parked in the lane. He flexed his back again and wondered if Mick was even now getting *his* massaged. Tricky work, cutting up a tree, you could do a lot of damage. Next time he was in Truro he would buy a book on aromatherapy. He had a feeling Kitty would like it.

'You will tell me if I'm in the way.' Lily must have said it at least three times. She felt welded to her chair watching Oliver sleeping. There was a yeasty waft of the pizza George had got warming in the Rayburn oven and the sharp tang of onion that he had cut up to put in a salad. She wondered if baby Oliver could smell them and if he instinctively associated the scents with food or hunger. She didn't know anything about babies, hadn't a clue (did anyone?) what knowledge he was born with, or if every sense was a kind of blank until one by one experiences got thrown to him to do his learning from. She thought of parents at Guy Fawkes night parties, taking hold of toddlers' hands, leading them safely away from bonfires and saying 'No, *hot*'. She would have thought that if the Great Designer had got it right, a child ought to be programmed with at least enough information to keep it safe and fed.

Madeleine was lying on the barn kitchen sofa, her bare sandy feet comfortably up on a cushion and her baby snuffling softly against her body. 'Stay here if you want, it's fine,' she told Lily. She didn't look up though, but kept her eyes on the tiny head, stroking his little pink ear and feeling his small firm body moving beneath her hand as he breathed.

'Amazing,' she kept saying.

'Yeah,' Lily agreed. It was amazing. It was amazing that for all the morning there'd been shouting and pain and swearing; probably more physical agony than Madeleine would ever feel again and yet now, just a few hours later, she looked as if she'd got the most happiness she was ever going to get in her whole life, right there on the sofa. Being in labour just had to be the most ultimate out-of-control feeling that your body could throw at you, something Lily would have described as her absolute worst nightmare – putting up with periods didn't even come close. And yet it was obviously worth it. Anyone looking at Madeleine could see that.

'I wish my mother would hurry up and get here. I can't wait for her to see him.' Lily felt thrown for a moment.

'Oh right. You mean your Brighton one.'

'My real mum,' Madeleine corrected her. 'Yours gave me away. No real mum could do that.'

Lily felt her face sparkling with instant anger. She wanted very much to hit Madeleine but just couldn't move. Any kind of violence, even the thought of it, wasn't possible in the presence of this tiny newborn child. It was like having a baby saint in the room.

'You shouldn't have said that. You've got no right or reason to. My mother only did what she thought was the best thing at the time.' Lily kept her voice as calm as she could, hardly daring to risk souring the air with bad feeling. 'She didn't really get any choice. And I know she's regretted it ever since. That's why she's never kept you a secret. She always made sure we've known you were out there somewhere. She used to cry on your birthday.'

Madeleine shrugged. 'Maybe. Maybe not. It doesn't matter now, does it? I just know that I couldn't do it.'

Lily stood up, overwhelmed by longing to be back

in her own kitchen, close to her own family. 'You might think you know *now* that you couldn't do it, but that's because you don't have to. You don't know that with other conditions and other kinds of family and upbringing you wouldn't have done exactly the same. You know, Madeleine, you really should try using your imagination more.'

'You've told him then.' Glyn went on with the stir-frying, fussing away at the vegetables more than he needed to because he didn't particularly want to look at Kitty's face. It might be treacherously rapturous from whatever she and Ben had been doing up there on the cliffs by the chapel, or it might be tearful and full of regrets. They could have had poignant, old-times'-sake kind of sex up there. From the state of the chapel, he'd guess practically everyone else in the county had. She might have come back brim-full of twenty-five years of wishing that she had stayed with Ben and made a family with him, starting with Madeleine. He'd seen Ben looking at Kitty in that doleful puppy-like way and he didn't blame him. A life with Rose must be tough and restless to say the least. And of course if he tended to look at Rose like that, well it probably just drove her nuts, provoked her to behave even worse than she meant to.

'Yeah I told him.' She sounded weary and he heard her slump heavily into a chair. 'It was you who thought I should, remember.'

He turned and looked at her, puzzled. 'You mean you want me to share the responsibility for him knowing?'

She covered her face with her hands for a moment. 'No of course not. Glyn, please let's not make this a battle. There really isn't one to fight. And there's certainly nothing to win. I expect I just said that to remind you you're supposed to be pleased that I did what you thought was right.'

'OK, sorry. Listen, go and call everyone. For those who want it there's plenty of food.'

Hayley looked a bit like Madeleine, it occurred to Kitty as Hayley and Petroc sat at the table and edged their chairs closer together. She had the same kind of wild corkscrew hair and the same confidence in a large body. Ben said a brief hallo to her and to Petroc but nothing more, perhaps dreading more bizarre secrets from the past being dragged out for him to deal with. He kept looking at the door as if he half expected Rose to wander in. It wasn't beyond possibility. It would be just like her, Kitty thought, to amble in, hand in hand with Tom Goodrich, and expect them all to be thrilled to see her.

Glyn had cooked a vast dish of chicken and stir-fried vegetables, more than enough for the whole family.

'There's loads here. Shall I go and ask George and Madeleine if they want to come?' Petroc volunteered.

'No!' Lily and Kitty said together. They looked at each other, each surprised by the other's vehemence.

'She shouldn't move about too much yet,' Kitty said.

'And George has defrosted a pizza and made a salad,' Lily added.

'I've already had lunch,' Hayley said, spooning a generous portion of food onto her plate, 'but I can't resist this.'

Thank goodness, Kitty thought, another big girl who isn't the slightest bit twitchy about her weight. Lily, as if she'd never heard of pickiness, took an amount that, a few weeks ago, would have made her feel queasy at the thought of eating.

'Mum's a grandma. Since this morning,' Petroc told Hayley, casually.

'Oh cool. Congratulations. Boy or girl?'

'A boy. Oliver,' Kitty told her. From her seat she could see Petroc's leg and Hayley's twined together. Only another year or two and he too would be gone to university or college or travelling. She could feel tears threatening again and was glad to escape when the phone rang. She made a dash for the sitting-room rather than using the kitchen extension.

'Kitty it's me, Julia.' Julia Taggart had her usual voice of urgent importance as if what she was about to say could at least bring down the Government or threaten the monarchy. 'I've got Rose with me and she's gone mad.'

Kitty laughed. '*She's* mad. You should be here!'

'Why? Oh never mind that, let me just tell you while she's in the loo. She says Ben has left her. He's put the dog in kennels, taken clothes and stuff and gone so she got into a taxi and arrived here because she thought she'd catch him at it with *me*!'

'Why with you? You haven't . . .' It was quite a thought, the Labrador-puppyish Ben and terrier-like Julia. She'd nip him to shreds.

Julia snorted a laugh. 'No, I absolutely haven't! No, what happened was she had a good look at the item-ized phone bill and found all these calls to my number. And more than a few to yours as well, as we both know. Anyway I was a lot nearer than you geo-graphically so she came storming in accusing.' Kitty could just imagine her, shoving her way past Julia the second she opened the door, rampaging round and barely stopping short of peering into wardrobes and under the bed.

'She's got more than a bit of nerve, considering.'

'Oh what, the Tom thing? That's all over, including the shouting apparently. And now she wants Ben back in the nest. Any ideas?' Kitty reached out and closed the door then told her, 'Yes. He's here. He

264

came down to find her, all ready to go over to Tom's place and drag her home screaming. Don't tell Rose, I'll just tell him she's with you and he can decide whether he wants to call her or not.'

It seemed typical of Rosemary-Jane, Kitty thought sadly as she went back to the kitchen. All the things she'd taken from Antonia – the pen, the Zippo lighter, the leather jacket that she'd stolen from her at the school disco and managed to tear before she let Antonia 'find' it again – she hadn't really wanted them, she'd just wanted to know she *could* have them. And now her husband. Unless he'd had enough of her. That possibility was quite cheering. Rose hadn't faced a lot of comeuppance in her life, perhaps she was due some.

'She's such a silly girl,' was Ben's odd reaction when Kitty told him, on the beach later that afternoon, that Rose thought he had left her for either herself or Julia. He sounded almost fatherly-fond, smiling indulgently and looking soppily pleased.

'Ben, does this sort of thing happen a lot? You seem to have a bizarrely unsettled sort of marriage for one that's been going so long.' She and Glyn seemed practically welded into a boring dotage by comparison.

'Mmm. I suppose it does,' he agreed, then added, with a sly glance, 'Actually, to be honest, it isn't always Rose who makes trouble. Till now, we'd almost thrived on it. I suppose this time I was scared it might just be the real thing for her. It keeps us rocking along, you know?'

'Whatever it takes,' she agreed, grinning. 'Though I bet your poor poodle would prefer a more quiet life.'

Ben brightened, taking her too seriously. 'That's a very good point. We should get another. We'll get him a mate, he'd like that.'

It was time for Ben to meet Madeleine. If they left it much longer, Paula Murray would be arriving and there'd be more confusion and explaining to be got through. Kitty was beginning to feel as if she was in one of those plays where the doors are always opening and closing on characters who really need to meet but constantly manage to miss each other. She was glad of a few minutes walking along the beach before taking him over to the barn, just to collect her thoughts between home and where Madeleine now was, and to think a bit about how to say what there was to say. The wind had dropped to almost nothing, though the few small high clouds were still streaking fast across the sky as if they had somewhere urgent to get to. Further along the beach, Petroc and Hayley sat on a rock, wrapped up close together and gazing out to sea.

'Sometimes we get seals out there, just where the surf line is,' Kitty told Ben. 'When you think you've spotted one, you can sit here for hours trying to see it again.'

Ben squinted towards the horizon. She could tell he was looking way too far out. 'The more you look, the more you think you can see something,' he said. 'Every wave could have a cute black head bobbing about on it. We could get a white one this time.'

'Huh? Oh the dog.' She laughed. 'Come on, let's go and tell Madeleine that she was spawned by a poodle-fancier.'

'Ugh, sounds obscene.'

Madeleine was still on the sofa but dressed now in her black leggings and big purple sweatshirt, and with her hair shining and still damp from the shower. She smelled faintly of vanilla essence. 'Hello!' she called softly as Ben and Kitty came into the room. Oliver was in his Moses basket beside Madeleine and Kitty recognized the blue and white striped sleepsuit she had bought in Truro. Madeleine had had to fold back the cuffs and probably, enviably Kitty thought, hadn't a clue how dreadfully fast he would grow both into and out of it. He was sleeping, his raspberry mouth making dreamy sucking shapes, and his small pale fists were curled into a soft punch.

'The midwife's been and she says he's perfect,' Madeleine told them. 'That's because he is,' George, making tea, interrupted. 'This baby's going to ruin my career – I now know there is such a thing as the state of human sinlessness.' Kitty looked at him with suspicion, searching out signs of irony, but didn't find any. George, arch-cynic and exploiter, writing-wise, of all who could be corrupt, was actually looking quite worried. 'Without being too Words-worthian about it, I mean,' he went on. 'A day-old baby. Someone who's never ever had a dodgy thought or had a go at anything devious. I've never met any-one like that before. You just have to pray life throws him all its best bones.'

Madeleine, Kitty suddenly realized, was having a very intense stare at Ben, as if slowly working out what he might be doing there. Kitty looked from one to the other. There were similarities. They had the same blue-grey eyes, wide open with well-curled lashes, giving them both a look of slightly infantile wonder. She hadn't really noticed that about Madeleine before, probably because the girl, pre-Oliver, had mostly tried to keep up a defensive scowl.

'So. Who are you exactly?' she asked Ben, direct and challenging.

'I'm . . . er . . .' Ben licked dry lips and looked at Kitty.

'Ben is, was, your father,' she said simply.

Madeleine grinned. 'Ah. Less a father, more a sperm donor.' Kitty could sense Ben wincing.

Madeleine was undeniably right though, Ben's input had really been no more than that.

'I'm sorry, it's the only way I can think of you.' Madeleine sounded apologetic. 'Because Kitty told me you didn't know I existed. I suppose she must have told you today or yesterday.' She turned to Kitty. 'Did you get him to come, specially? I mean if you did, that's really, well . . .'

'Good or bad?' George sat on the arm of the sofa and played with her hair. 'Just say it, Mads.'

'I don't know. It's like if you did get him to come, then maybe you thought I'd be pleased, like he was a present or something. But,' she smiled and reached out, stroking her baby's arm, 'really it's too late now. I don't care any more who I was, or whose. This is the only person who feels real to me now. I'm going to get it right for him, whatever cock-ups you lot managed in the making of me, and then handing me out.'

Later, after Ben and his Porsche had gone (and wouldn't he need something bigger to drive two giant poodles around in?) Kitty wondered how much Madeleine would have wanted or not wanted to find *her* if she'd already given birth to Oliver. 'She may not have been over-interested in Ben, but surely mothers are different, aren't they Glyn?' she said as she leaned on the greenhouse staging and watched him pricking out the baby tomato plants. 'Surely she'd still have wanted to find *me*, maybe even more than before.'

Glyn scooped compost into five pots at once, a dextrous knack that made him feel he was on his way to being a real gardener. 'Don't pick at it Kitty, there's no point in speculating what she'd have done. Surely it's enough that she actually did find you.' He grinned. 'You can't have expected her to be more impressed with Ben, after all she hasn't mentioned her own baby's father apart from that once. I expect she sees *all* men as simple sperm donors, with as much use or personality as pond life.'

'Apart from George. I just hope she stays in touch. Once her mother comes and takes her home . . .'

'Is that what you think will happen?' Glyn put the pots down and grinned at her. 'You haven't been paying attention really, have you Kit?'

Lily felt better after she'd cleaned the salt marks off the carpet. The house was just about normal again, now that Ben had gone and Madeleine and the baby had gone across to the barn. All that was left to show things were different was the big patch of blank wood floor in the sitting-room where the cream rug had been. The rug was wrapped in bin bags and destined for the local tip, and Glyn had said something about getting one specially made by a local weaver.

Lily was hungry again and the feeling was no longer a threat to be fought off. She'd got it all wrong before. Being so intent on being in control of her body, she knew she'd let the fight with food take control of her mind. No wonder Fergus on the bus had worried about her. In his clumsy, blokey adolescent way he'd just been telling her, with that taunt about her tits, that he was scared of her getting so thin, perhaps even scared she'd end up like that furry girl who nearly died. He'd be quite good-looking when he got a bit taller. She'd give him six months, see what he looked like then.

Paula Murray did not have vivid copper hair or a body toned from determined Slimnastics. A grubby purple Rover pulled up in the yard just before dark and Kitty, her insides churning with nerves, found herself greeting a small cube-shaped woman with striped grey and white hair that reminded her of mattress ticking.

'Thanks for taking care of her,' Paula said. 'I mean it can't be easy for you . . .' Her husky voice was trembly and she avoided looking straight at Kitty.

'No it's fine. Really — and the baby's lovely. Come and see him.' It was what Paula was there for, Kitty told herself, to meet her grandson and to take her daughter home. Madeleine was more than grown-up now, this really wasn't a second giving-away of her child. There were choices involved.

'Mum! You got here fast!' Madeleine's hug swamped Paula. Kitty stood back by the door with George and waited to feel sure of what she should do. Good manners would decree she should leave them alone together, simple instinctive curiosity and a feeling that she should hang onto all these moments told her to stay where she was.

'So let me see this baby then. What have you called him?'

'Oliver.' Madeleine picked up the dozing bundle from the Moses basket and handed him to Paula.

'Oliver. After your father.' She sniffed, and Kitty could see a teary smile. 'He'd be so happy.'

'We're keeping him, Mum,' Madeleine said quietly.

'What? Oh of course we are darling.' She rocked the baby gently and smiled at Kitty. 'It'll be dark soon, so I thought if we just make a move right now, we can stop off for something to eat on the way back and then get home.'

'You could stay the night, or a few days . . .' Kitty felt panicked, she knew Madeleine would be going, but surely there had to be a few more hours for her to get used to the idea. It was, she suddenly realized, *exactly* like giving her away all over again. She wanted to bolt the doors, keep them all there, kill Paula if she had to.

'You have to let them go, Kitty.' Glyn, arriving silently behind her, put his arm round her, holding down her terror. 'After all, it doesn't have to be for ever this time.'

'That's right,' Paula said comfortably. 'And it's a special bond, isn't it, being with someone when they give birth.'

'Madeleine was with *me* when I gave birth, I still lost her.' Kitty felt fierce. She hugged her arms round her and leaned hard against Glyn.

Madeleine frowned. 'Look, do you two mind not fighting over me? I mean it's a bit late now. And right now I'm not going anywhere, not till George does anyway.' She reached out and took Paula's hand, then said more quietly, 'No offence Mum, but me and Oliver are going to live with George in London. I've been a daughter for long enough and if I'm going to see what it's like to be a mother, then I have to do it my own way.'

'You're going to live with . . . him?' Paula looked at George, confused. 'So is he . . . ?'

Madeleine laughed. 'No he's not the father.'

'He's old enough to be yours,' Paula said tartly.

'Oh Mum, so what? This is what I want.'

'Twenty-four years just went like a flash. You don't get to hang onto your children for long, do you?' Paula said as she climbed back into her car after breakfast the next morning. Kitty thought it was possibly the most staggeringly tactless thing Paula could have said to her, but let it pass. She understood what she meant. If she'd learned nothing else since Madeleine had turned up, she now understood how irrelevant was the idea of 'possession' when it came to children. They weren't anyone's really, just small, young, people aiming at independence. Having them grow up and stand on their own feet and then go off and leave you was what you got for being a good parent. Maybe it felt just as bad, worse, to have to hand over your child after twenty-four years as it did after only a few days. She wouldn't know till it was Lily and Petroc's turn to go. But that wouldn't be for a while yet.

THE END